Advance Praise for *The Beautiful Pretender*

"When it comes to happily-ever-afters, Melanie Dickerson is the undisputed queen of fairy-tale romance, and all I can say is—long live the queen! From start to finish *The Beautiful Pretender* is yet another brilliant gem in her crown, spinning a medieval love story that will steal you away—heart, soul, and sleep!"

—Julie Lessman, award-winning author of The Daughters of Boston, Winds of Change, and Heart of San Francisco series

"I couldn't stop reading! Melanie has done what so many other historical novelists have tried and failed: she's created a heroine that is at once both smart and self-assured without seeming modern. A woman so fixed in her time and place that she is able to speak to ours as well."

—Siri Mitchell, author of *Flirtation Walk* and *Chateau of Echoes*

Praise for Melanie Dickerson

"Readers will find themselves supporting the romance between the sweet yet determined Odette and the insecure but hardworking Jorgen from the beginning. Dickerson spins a retelling of Robin Hood with emotionally compelling characters, offering hope that love may indeed conquer all as they unite in a shared desire to serve both the Lord and those in need."

—RT Book Reviews, 4 1/2 stars, on *The Huntress of Thornbeck Forest*

"I'm always amazed at the way Melanie Dickerson creates a world. Her writing is as fresh and unique as anyone I know, and I am always pulled into the story and taken far away on a wonderful, romantic, and action-packed journey."

—Mary Connealy, author of *Now and Forever*, book two of the Wild at Heart series, on *The Huntress of Thornbeck Forest*

"Melanie Dickerson does it again! Full of danger, intrigue, and romance, this beautifully crafted story will transport you to another place and time."

—Sarah E. Ladd, author of *The Curiosity Keeper* and The Whispers on the Moors series, on *The Huntress of Thornbeck Forest*

"Melanie Dickerson's *The Huntress of Thornbeck Forest* is a lovely, romantic read set during one of the most fascinating time periods. Featuring a feisty, big-hearted heroine and a hero to root for, this sweet medieval tale is wrapped in a beautiful journey of faith that had me flipping pages well after my bedtime. Delightful!"

—TAMARA LEIGH, *USA Today* BESTSELLING AUTHOR OF *Baron of Godsmere*

"Melanie Dickerson weaves a tantalizing Robin Hood plot in a medieval setting in *The Huntress of Thornbeck Forest*. She pits a brave heroine with unique talents against a strong, gentle hero whose occupation makes it dangerous to know him. Add the moral dilemma, and this tale makes a compelling read for any age."

—RUTH AXTELL, AUTHOR OF *She Shall Be Praised* AND *The Rogue's Redemption*

"*The Huntress of Thornbeck Forest* is a wonderful romantic tale filled with love, betrayal, and forgiveness. I loved this book and highly recommend it for readers of all ages."

—CARA LYNN JAMES, AUTHOR OF *A Path toward Love*

"*The Huntress of Thornbeck Forest* reminds me of why adults should read fairy tales. Author Melanie Dickerson shoots straight to the heart with a cast of compelling characters, an enchanting story world, and romance and suspense in spades. Reaching The End was regrettable—but oh, what an ending!"

—LAURA FRANTZ, AUTHOR OF *The Mistress of Tall Acre*

"For stories laden with relatable heroines, romantically adventurous plots, once-upon-a-time settings, and engaging writing, Melanie Dickerson is your go-to author. Her books are on my never-to-be-missed list."

—KIM VOGEL SAWYER, AUTHOR OF *When Mercy Rains*, ON *The Huntress of Thornbeck Forest*

"Ms. Dickerson deftly captures the flavor of life in medieval Germany in a sweet tale filled with interesting characters that will surely capture readers' hearts."

—KATHLEEN MORGAN, AUTHOR OF THESE HIGHLAND HILLS SERIES, *Embrace the Dawn*, AND *Consuming Fire*, ON *The Huntress of Thornbeck Forest*

The
BEAUTIFUL
PRETENDER

The
BEAUTIFUL
PRETENDER

A Medieval Fairy Tale

MELANIE DICKERSON

THOMAS NELSON
Since 1798

Published in Nashville, Tennessee, by Thomas Nelson. Thomas Nelson is a registered trademark of HarperCollins Christian Publishing, Inc.

Thomas Nelson titles may be purchased in bulk for educational, business, fundraising, or sales promotional use. For information, please e-mail SpecialMarkets@ ThomasNelson.com.

Publisher's Note: This novel is a work of fiction. Names, characters, places, and incidents are either products of the author's imagination or used fictitiously. All characters are fictional, and any similarity to people living or dead is purely coincidental.

Library of Congress Cataloging-in-Publication Data

Names: Dickerson, Melanie.
Title: The beautiful pretender / Melanie Dickerson.
Description: Nashville, Tennessee: Thomas Nelson, [2016] | Series: A medieval fairy tale; [2] | Summary: "The Margrave of Thornbeck has two weeks to find a noble bride. What will happen when he learns he has fallen for Avelina, a lovely servant girl in disguise? But something else is afoot in the castle. Something sinister that could have far worse—far deadlier--consequences. Will Avelina and Lord Thornbeck be able to stop the evil plot?"—Provided by publisher.
Identifiers: LCCN 2015045318 | ISBN 9780718026288 (paperback)
Subjects: | CYAC: Nobility--Fiction. | Love--Fiction. |
    Impersonation--Fiction. | Identity--Fiction. | Middle Ages—Fiction. |
    Christian life—Fiction.
Classification: LCC PZ7.D5575 Be 2016 | DDC [Fic]--dc23 LC record available at http://lccn.loc.gov/2015045318

Printed in the United States of America
16 17 18 19 20 RRD 6 5 4 3 2 1

1

The year 1363, Thornbeck Forest, The Holy Roman Empire

REINHART STOLTEN, MARGRAVE of Thornbeck, spotted the pack of wolves devouring their fresh kill at the bottom of the ravine. He nudged his horse in their direction as he let go of the reins and readied his bow and arrow. He was still too far away for a good shot, but he urged him closer, until his horse brought him into range of the bloodthirsty killers.

Reinhart took aim and let the arrow fly, striking one of the wolves in the neck. It let out a shriek, causing the other animals to look up. Two of them kept their teeth in their meal even as they snarled and searched for the source of the danger.

Reinhart quickly nocked another arrow and shot, striking another wolf in the shoulder instead of the intended kill shot to the head.

The wolves had spotted him and started to run. Only one of them was more interested in his food than in the danger pursuing him. He kept hold of the carcass as he ran away with the others. Reinhart aimed and shot at the one lagging behind, dragging the dead animal, but the arrow missed him.

The wolf let go of his kill and ran harder.

Reinhart urged his horse after them. The wolf with the arrow in his shoulder ran along with the other six wolves.

Reinhart and his horse chased them up the ravine, through the heavily wooded hills of Thornbeck Forest, and eventually the injured wolf grew tired and fell behind. Reinhart was able to finish it off, but there was no use going after the others. They were too far ahead now.

He put his longbow away and turned his horse back in the direction of Thornbeck Castle. The sun was just coming up, sending a glow through the trees as he neared the castle mount.

His castle mount. He was in charge of Thornbeck—the town, the region, and the castle. He was responsible for all of it, and he did not want this pack of wolves roaming the forest, which would lead to tragedy when they ended up attacking and killing someone.

He arrived in front of the stable and dismounted, holding on to the saddle with one hand while he waited for the stable boy to retrieve his walking stick.

Where was that boy? Reinhart growled at having to wait, at the humiliation of needing a cane to walk.

Finally, the boy came around the horse with his cane. Reinhart took it and limped toward the castle.

He had been a powerful knight who could sword fight, joust, and anything any other soldier could do, and better. Now he had to depend on a cane, walking with a limp, with even the servants staring at him in pity.

He held on to the railing with one hand and his cane with the other as he very slowly made his way up the steps to the castle door. The pain in his ankle and lower leg was as bad as ever, and his scowl became a growl.

No one could pity him if he was growling at them.

"Lord Thornbeck." Jorgen Hartman, his young chancellor, met him at the door.

"What is it, Jorgen?"

"My lord, a letter from the king has just arrived. His courier awaits your reply."

"Well, where is this letter?"

"It's in your library, my lord."

Reinhart made it to the top of the steps and stumped down the long passageway that led to several rooms on the lowest floor of the castle.

"My lord," Jorgen said, walking beside him, "were you out hunting wolves this morning? Alone?"

"I was."

"Should you not take someone with you? A pack of wolves can pull a grown man off his horse."

"Are you suggesting that because I'm now a cripple, I am unable to hunt alone?"

"No, my lord." Jorgen did not look intimidated by Reinhart's angry tone and scowl. "Any man would be in danger against a wolf pack. I also mention it because I think Odette—who you know is an excellent shot with a bow—misses hunting, and she and I could help you kill twice as many."

Reinhart frowned at him. "I am surprised you are so quick to allude to your new wife's lawbreaking activities."

"She would not be breaking any laws by accompanying you on your wolf hunts, my lord."

Reinhart grunted.

Finally, with his slow, halting limp, they arrived at his desk in the library. There lay the missive from the king, wax seal, ribbon, and all.

Reinhart broke it open and read it. He threw it down on his

desk and walked a few steps. He leaned his shoulder against the wall, staring out the window.

"What does it say, my lord, if I may ask?"

"Read it for yourself."

There was a rustle of parchment behind him, then Jorgen said, "My lord, the king is asking you to marry."

Reinhart's new role as margrave certainly came with a price.

"Do you know any of these ladies he's suggesting you marry?"

"No."

"Do you have one in mind you would like to ask?"

When he was the captain of the guard for the Duke of Pomerania, he could take all the time he wanted to choose a wife. But everything was different now.

"I do not believe I shall choose anyone . . . for now."

"But, my lord." Jorgen came to stand beside him and held out his hand to him, palm up. "You cannot ignore a command from the king."

"I would not call it a command. It's more of a . . . suggestion."

"A suggestion from most people is a suggestion, but a suggestion from the king is a command. No, my lord, I believe you must choose a wife, and you must choose one from among the noble ladies in his letter. He particularly mentions the daughters of the Duke of Geitbart and the Earl of Plimmwald."

He was expected to choose a wife based on who her father was, and the king had suggested the ladies whose fathers had feuded the most with the margraves of Thornbeck before him—his brother and father. The king wanted peace and unity among his noblemen, and there had been more contention than peace in the last thirty or forty years.

The Duke of Geitbart had once controlled both Thornbeck and Plimmwald, but when Geitbart's father defied the king's wishes and married a woman the king did not approve, the king had taken Thornbeck away from him and given it to the Margrave of Thornbeck, Reinhart's father, and he gave Plimmwald to the present Earl of Plimmwald. And now Geitbart wanted them back.

Reinhart would be expected to purchase peace and unity for the people of his country by marrying a lady without ever seeing her or knowing anything of her character or temperament. This wife would be thrust upon him, for as long as they both lived, for his personal good or for ill.

"You should choose a wife as soon as possible," Jorgen said.

"And how do you propose I do that?"

"Perhaps . . ." He turned to pace in a short path from the window to the middle of the floor and back. "So you could meet these ladies and choose which of them you deem worthiest, we could arrange to have them all come to Thornbeck Castle. It could be a ball, or better yet, a party lasting many days. Odette could help plan it. We could invite every lady on the king's list and even put them through a series of tests, based on what you want in a wife."

Jorgen stopped his pacing and turned to him, his brows raised. "What do you think of this plan, my lord?"

"I think . . . I hate it."

"But is it not better than choosing without knowing anything about them?"

Of course it was better. But how did he know how to choose a wife? He knew nothing of women. His own parents' marriage had been arranged for them, and they had hated each other. They rarely spoke more than two words to each other, and both of them had lovers. Reinhart certainly had no desire for *that* kind of marriage. But neither did he believe that husbands and wives "fell in love" before they married.

Believing there was one woman among many with whom he could fall in love was a naive concept invented by traveling minstrels and addled youths. And yet, Jorgen and his wife had chosen each other. Though neither of them had anything of material value to gain from the marriage, they had chosen each other solely because of a fondness for each other. And even Reinhart had to admit, they seemed very content.

Perhaps he should trust Jorgen's judgment. But at the same time . . .

"I shall feel a fool, holding a party to choose my own wife."

"You shall not feel a fool, my lord, and the ladies will feel very flattered that you invited them. Odette and I can arrange it so the ladies do not know you are putting them through tests. And Odette, as a woman, can give you her thoughts and can help you discern—that is, if you wish it. The ladies will enjoy the party, and you can observe them and see who would make the most ideal wife."

But would they consider him an ideal husband? A man who couldn't even walk without a cane? Reinhart stared down at the floor, at his maimed ankle. His blood went cold at the thought of appearing pitiable to the woman he would marry, of her scorning his weakness. But he had little choice but to try and choose wisely from among the ten.

"When should we plan it? Next summer?"

"Oh no, my lord. That's nearly a year away. I believe the king will expect you to marry much sooner than that."

"There is no knowing what the king expects. But even though I have more important things I should be doing with my time . . . you may begin the process now. I am leaving it in your hands." Reinhart turned away from the window.

"Of course, my lord."

Two weeks later, Plimmwald Castle, The Holy Roman Empire

Avelina stood behind Lady Dorothea, brushing her long golden hair.

What were Jacob and Brigitta doing today? Had they found the breakfast of bread and pea porridge she'd left for them? Would they remember to tend the vegetable garden and milk the goat? She would have to ask them if they had washed—

"Ow! What are you doing?" Dorothea spun around and snatched the brush out of Avelina's hand. "Are you trying to tear out my hair?"

"No, of course not." Avelina knew from experience that it was better not to cower but to look Dorothea in the eye when she was in a passion.

Dorothea frowned and handed her back the brush. "My ride this afternoon has my hair in a snarl. See that you don't tear it out of my head."

Dorothea turned back around on her stool, and Avelina continued brushing her thick, honey-colored hair, Dorothea's fairest feature.

A knock sounded at the door, and Hildegard, one of the older maidservants, entered the room carrying a tray. "Lady Dorothea, Cook sent this up for you." She smiled, flashing all her teeth. "She made it from the last of the cherries. A perfect tart for my lady."

The last of the cherries. Avelina tried to keep her eyes off the tart, but the smell of warm fruit made her take a deep breath through her nose. Her mouth watered. She could almost taste it.

"It does look good." Dorothea picked it up and took a bite.

She waved her hand. Did she want Hildegard to leave? Avelina continued brushing.

Dorothea turned and snatched the brush out of her hand again, glaring at her while her mouth was full. Hildegard glared at her too.

Avelina shrugged, smiling apologetically.

Another knock sounded on the door. Dorothea swallowed the bite of cherry tart and called, "Enter."

One of her father's guards opened the door and bowed. "The earl wishes to speak with you."

Dorothea's face turned pale. She put the tart back on the tray, brushed her hands off with a cloth, then preceded the guard out the door.

Was Dorothea worried her father had found out about her trysts with his knight Sir Dietric? The earl never punished her, so why did she look so afraid?

Hildegard followed her out, leaving Avelina alone.

Cherries were Avelina's favorite fruit. The tart drew her closer. It was rather small, but if she took a tiny bite, no one would notice.

She leaned over it. Did she dare? Another whiff of the warm, tangy cherries filled her head. She reached down and pinched off a small piece, making sure to cradle a whole cherry on the bit of pastry crust. She placed it in her mouth and closed her eyes.

Tart and sweet melded together and spread over her tongue.

Hildegard burst back into the bedchamber. Narrowing her eyes at Avelina, as if she knew she was contemplating eating the rest of the tart in two bites, Hildegard snatched the tray up and carried it back out, her leather shoes making shushing sounds on the flagstones.

Avelina swallowed, sighed, and went to work putting away Dorothea's sewing materials that she had been searching through, as well as the hair ribbons she had strewn everywhere before finding the one she wanted. Avelina put away the tightly fitted bliaud

Dorothea had discarded in favor of a looser cotehardie, and finding nothing else to do, sat on the cushioned bench by the tall, narrow window clutching her gray mantle around her shoulders, staring out at the foggy night.

The light of the moon cast a pale glow on the fog that was rolling up to the castle walls. She hoped Brigitta would be able to heat the frumenty she had left for them without burning herself, and Jacob would be able to keep the fire going. Father's back always pained him more on foggy and rainy days.

Footsteps sounded on the stone floor in the corridor. Avelina turned her head just as Dorothea rushed into the room—and burst into tears. She bent forward at the waist, her hands covering her face.

Avelina stood and waited for her mistress's orders. Should she go to her and try to comfort her? Dorothea rarely welcomed any sort of affection from Avelina, though she had been her maid-servant and confidant for the last eight years—since Dorothea was ten and Avelina was twelve.

"Whatever is the matter?" Avelina asked.

Dorothea continued to cry, but the sobbing sounded more angry than sad. She suddenly straightened and glared. "My father is sending me to Thornbeck Castle. He wants me to marry the mar-grave. But precisely what do you think the Margrave of Thornbeck will say if he were to suspect . . . ?" A defiant look came over her face. "I won't go. I won't." She raised a fist, tossing her head and sending her blonde hair over her shoulders and cascading down her back, the ends dancing at her waist.

Avelina almost said, "But if you don't go, they will suspect something is amiss." She bit her lip and refrained, not wanting to risk a tongue-lashing. Dorothea's green eyes were ablaze, even as they swam with tears.

"What did your father say?"

"He says I must go, that I can simply wear looser clothing." She scrunched her nose and curled her lip. "Father says I can give the child to someone far away and forget about it after it's born." She folded her arms across her chest and stomped her foot. "But I want to marry Dietric."

Avelina's breath stilled. Would she defy her father?

"Get my things packed into some traveling bags." Dorothea smeared the tears over her face with her fingers and hurried to one of her trunks. She started throwing clothing on the bed. "Pack these."

"Will you leave right away? Should you not wait until morning, at the least?"

"I must go now. My father plans to send me to Thornbeck in the morning." She set her jaw, closing her eyes for a moment. "If Dietric refuses to take me away, I'll kill myself."

She said those last words so calmly, a chill went through Avelina.

"Make haste, Ava! Don't just stand there."

Avelina ran and grabbed a traveling bag from another trunk and began rolling her mistress's clothing into tight bundles to keep them from wrinkling, then stuffing them into the leather bag. But her heart was in her throat. If she helped Dorothea run away with Sir Dietric, what would the earl do to her? But if she didn't help Dorothea, she might do violence to herself.

Avelina continued stuffing clothing into the bag until it was full and she had to retrieve another bag.

"Put that down for a moment," Dorothea said suddenly, striding to the trunk against the far wall and opening it. "I need you to open a lock for me." She bent and drew out two ornate ivory boxes that contained all of the family jewelry. Her father said he would give her the key when she got married. But Dorothea could never accept being locked out of anything. Consequently she had forced Avelina to learn a new skill.

Avelina retrieved her metal tool out of her woolen bag. She picked up the first box and went to work with the hooked end of the long, slim piece of metal she had gotten from the castle blacksmith. In a few moments she had opened the box, and a few moments after that, the second box lay open.

Dorothea barely gave the boxes a glance. "Put some into each bag so all of my jewels are not in one place."

Avelina wrapped the bejeweled necklaces, bracelets, and rings inside various pieces of clothing. Soon she had nearly filled a second bag.

A noise came from outside. Dorothea ran to the narrow window and flung it open, letting in the cold, late-autumn air. She stuck her head out. "Dietric!" She gasped the name, then flung her arm out, obviously throwing something down, possibly a note. Then she stood still, her hand covering her mouth as she watched.

Avelina turned back to her task, lest Dorothea scold her, but she listened for signs of what was happening behind her at the window. After a few more moments Dorothea let out a cry of joy. "Make haste and give me the bags."

Avelina tossed her a bag, and Dorothea pushed it through the small window and dropped it, then turned and held out her hands for the second bag and tossed it down as well.

Avelina approached the window as the end of a rope came sailing through. Dorothea caught it and tied it to the post of the solid oak bed.

She wanted to ask Dorothea if she was certain she was doing the correct thing but instead caught hold of her arm.

Dorothea's cloudy green eyes barely met hers. "You should not try to stop me, Ava. I will not yield nor give Dietric up. Not for anyone. I don't care what Father says."

"I will not try to stop you." She thought of hugging Dorothea, of telling her to be careful. But it wasn't the sort of thing her mistress would stay still for.

Dorothea grabbed the rope. Avelina helped her up to a sitting position inside the window as Dorothea said, "Don't go and marry some peasant farmer who can't give you pretty things."

Without another word or even a smile or glance, Dorothea quickly lowered herself out the window, hand over hand on the rope. Avelina hung her head out the window to see Sir Dietric standing below with outstretched arms. Dorothea made it to the bottom without losing her grip and was enveloped in her lover's waiting arms. He helped her onto her horse, then mounted his own, and they disappeared into the dark night and thick fog.

"Fare well, Dorothea," Avelina whispered. "You were sometimes cross and vindictive, but we were companions for many years, and I will miss you."

What would her life be like without Dorothea? And what would happen to Avelina now that her mistress was gone?

If Avelina went and told the earl that his only daughter had run away with one of his knights, he might be able to send some men to intercept them and bring them back. But what if Sir Dietric was killed in the struggle or Dorothea's father had him executed? Dorothea would never forgive her. Besides, if she was able to get away, Dorothea would obtain the one thing that Avelina had dreamed of, written stories about, and imagined in many a long hour—true romantic love—about which the troubadours sang, the subject of epic poems and tales.

No, out of loyalty to Dorothea and a hope that she would be happy and live a life of romance and adventure and love, Avelina would not tell Lord Plimmwald that his daughter had run off with Sir Dietric.

At least not until he realized his daughter was missing and sent for her maidservant to tell him where she had gone.

Avelina could not run away, as she must think of her two young siblings. Jacob was twelve and Brigitta was only six. Her father needed her to help care for them. Besides, she had never ridden a horse in her life, and there was no knight waiting below to carry her away to adventure and love.

Avelina was left to await the consequences of Dorothea's actions alone.

2

AVELINA WAS AWAKENED by a shaft of sunlight across her face, pouring through the window where the shutter was slightly ajar. She jumped out of bed, nearly falling headfirst on the floor.

Why was she on Dorothea's tall bed instead of her own narrow cot in the next room? Then it all flooded back to her—Dorothea's flight, Avelina's inability to sleep, how she had wandered into her mistress's room and lay down on her soft feather bed. She'd been dreaming about being trapped in a gloomy, dark, half-ruined castle where there lived a beastly lord so hideous and animal-like that no one would go near him. The mood of the dream still enveloped her like a fog.

She fell back across the bed. For once in her life, there was nothing to do—no Dorothea to wait on, no hair to braid, no clothing to mend, no shoes to clean, no games to play to amuse her young mistress. So she lay thinking about her unsettling dream.

She could still see the castle, but its lord was a dark figure obscured by shadows. "He's a beast," a maidservant had whispered in her ear. Her skin tingled as she tried to get a better look at him. He suddenly growled at her and she jumped. That was when she woke up.

Avelina should be thinking about what she would say to

Lord Plimmwald when he discovered that Dorothea was missing. Would he know where she went? What would he do with Avelina? She needed this position as a maidservant to take care of her family. Her father could no longer work, and her younger brother and sister would starve without her pay.

A knock came at the door. That would be Dorothea's breakfast. "Come in."

Hildegard entered with a tray of food. "Where is Lady Dorothea?"

"Uh . . . she, uh—"

Hildegard glanced up at the ceiling and frowned. "Never mind. Let her know her food is here so she can eat before it gets cold." She slammed the door behind her.

That was easy. She didn't even have to tell a lie.

Avelina ate Dorothea's breakfast—or a small portion of it—before her stomach began to feel sick. What would the earl do when he found out his daughter had run away with a knight?

Avelina finally decided to work on a story she had been writing to amuse Dorothea. It was about the daughter of an earl who fell in love with a knight. Dorothea chose the premise of the story, but Avelina enjoyed making up all the details, of how the two fell in love against their parents' wishes and were cast out of the kingdom, forced to run for their lives from various dangers and disasters. But always they were saved by the sacrifices they made for each other.

It was nearly noon and Avelina had been writing for hours when a sudden loud pounding came at the door. Avelina dropped her quill pen on the floor and jumped to her feet.

The door swung wide and one of Lord Plimmwald's knights stood in the doorway. His eyes were cold as he looked at Avelina.

"The earl wishes to speak to Lady Dorothea's maidservant."

She preceded the knight out the door, then he led the way down the corridor to the Great Hall.

Though it was time for the midday meal, he was not eating. Instead the earl was sitting at his place on the dais with his head in his hands and his elbows on the trestle table. He must have heard the knight approaching, his sword clanging against his mail tunic, but Lord Plimmwald did not look up.

"I have retrieved the lady's maidservant, my lord." The knight spoke formally in an even tone, and Avelina sensed his cold disapproval.

She curtsied to her lord, although he still had not looked up at her. Would he order her punished and send her to the pillory to be humiliated, standing with her hands and head inserted in the wooden boards in the town square? She'd always had a horror of the indignity of the pillory. Perhaps if she pleaded with her lord he would punish her in some other less publicly humiliating way.

Lord Plimmwald finally lifted his head and caught sight of his knight standing beside Avelina. He waved him away with a languid flick of his wrist. The knight bowed and left the banqueting hall.

Avelina focused her eyes on the floor, but she couldn't help taking furtive peeks at her lord. Dark bags sagged under his eyes, which were faintly shot through with blood.

"Avelina." He finally looked at her, his bushy white eyebrows hanging low over his eyes. "As you know, the Duke of Geitbart is threatening to claim Plimmwald Castle for his own, since Plimmwald belonged to his ancestors, and I have no son or heir. Our allies have turned a blind eye to his aggression, and he has threatened to come and besiege our quiet, peaceful town and take Plimmwald Castle by force."

He sighed and shook his head. "I had thought to seek the help of the Margrave of Thornbeck, and even hoped I might betroth

Dorothea to him. But he has decided to hold a two-week party and choose a bride from the guests—all the eligible daughters of the noblemen of the northern regions of the Holy Roman Empire."

He leaned forward, piercing her with his gray-green eyes. "Now my daughter has run off with my best knight, Sir Dietric. My hopes are dashed. All appears to be doomed for me and for the people of Plimmwald."

He fixed her with a stern look. "You are my daughter's closest servant and confidant. You must have known my daughter was sneaking away to go on secret trysts with Sir Dietric. But you did not warn me." He slapped his hand down on the table. "And now she is with child. I would be justified in having you banished from Plimmwald."

Avelina's heart pounded sickeningly against her chest. It was true. She had known all along what was transpiring.

His eyes narrowed as he stared at her, his face a craggy stone and just as cold. "You knew what it would cost my daughter, and yet you never told me."

"Please forgive me, my lord." Avelina's voice shook. None of her reasons would sound good enough to Lord Plimmwald. They seemed rather foolish now, even to her.

"The deed has been done, my daughter is gone, and there must have been many others who knew what was happening. I, the lord of the land, was the last to know." Bitterness and anger infused his voice. He stared at the wall, then pressed the heels of his hands into his eyes.

"Now, I have a task for you," he said, finally looking at her again, "that is far beyond being a lady's maidservant for my spoiled daughter. I only hope you will be able to succeed in it as well as you kept my daughter's secrets."

What could he mean?

"We need the favor of Lord Thornbeck. We need the margrave's help to defend us from Geitbart. I have little hope of finding Dorothea and bringing her back, and the Margrave of Thornbeck has asked that she come to Thornbeck Castle for two weeks. You must take her place."

Avelina stared into his wrinkled face. "Take her place? Do you mean, pretend to be Lady Dorothea?"

"Precisely. You are the only woman I know who is fair enough. My daughter was a renowned beauty, but with fine clothes and someone calling you 'my lady' and treating you like a noble-born woman, anyone might consider you as beautiful as my wayward daughter."

Her thoughts spun around and she couldn't quite catch hold of one. The earl was speaking again.

"You must not ever let Thornbeck realize that you are not Dorothea. He must never suspect. He must also not choose to marry you, but you must not offend him in any way. He is by far our most important ally and our best hope of defeating Geitbart. It is rumored that Thornbeck killed his own brother to become margrave." He shook his finger at her face. "What do you think he would do if he realized he had been duped by us, that I had sent him a servant instead of an earl's daughter?"

The blood drained from Avelina's face, and she swayed on her feet. *I must listen.* No matter how dizzy his words made her.

"You must understand that you will be saving us all. Every person at the castle and in the town will be in danger. Geitbart will certainly kill at least some of the people when he takes control of Plimmwald. And though Dorothea has gone away with Sir Dietric to no-one-knows-where, the margrave must never know that." The corners of the earl's mouth dipped in a grim frown.

How would Avelina, the daughter of a crippled former stable

master and a lady's maidservant, ever fool the Margrave of Thornbeck and all his guests into believing she was an earl's daughter?

"Cannot you simply write to the margrave and tell him that your daughter is sick?"

"No, I cannot, impertinent girl. I wrote a letter to the king complaining about Geitbart sending his men to scout out our land, and also advising the king about the rumors surrounding Thornbeck's brother's death. The king apparently told them both about the letter, and now I am certain Geitbart intends to attack us. Thornbeck will not be inclined to help since I accused him of murdering his brother. That is why you must go and try to make peace with the Margrave of Thornbeck."

The earl sounded nothing like he did when he was speaking to Dorothea, the way he often pleaded with her to behave more like a lady. Instead he growled the words at Avelina.

"When he attacks, Geitbart will kill innocent people simply to prove that he is master and frighten the rest into submission. Your own family could be killed."

The earl spoke in a cold, quiet tone.

"And now you must take the rest of Dorothea's clothes and jewelry and prepare for the journey to Thornbeck. You will leave in two hours."

He was not asking her if she would do it; he was ordering her to.

She must think. She must be wise and ask something for herself. "If I do this, I will be deceiving one of the most powerful men in the Holy Roman Empire. I am risking my life."

Unmoved, Lord Plimmwald stared back at her.

"If I succeed, you must give me a sum of money . . . enough to constitute a dowry so I can marry. And—and a goose and a side of pork every month for my family."

"Very well. It shall be as you have asked."

He agreed so quickly. She should have asked for more.

"But I warn you, if you should in any way destroy what little alliance I have with the margrave by being found out to be a servant instead of the Earl of Plimmwald's daughter, I will not spare either you or your family. I will banish you all. And you will have failed every person in Plimmwald."

Avelina's throat tightened at the cruelty in the earl's voice, cruelty that would hurt her father as well as her little sister and brother. She swallowed past the constriction.

"Do you understand?"

"Yes, my lord." She would not fail. She could not.

Somehow she had to convince a powerful margrave that she was the Earl of Plimmwald's daughter, and she must not allow herself to be chosen to be his bride.

The latter task would no doubt be easier than the former.

3

"LORD THORNBECK, SOME guests have arrived."

Reinhart did not look up from the report he was reading. The servant cleared his throat. Finally, he lifted his head as two ladies swept into the room—his own personal library where he kept his important documents and letters, his private sanctuary.

"The Lady Fronicka, daughter of the Duke of Geitbart," the servant announced, "and the Lady Applonia, daughter of the Earl of Hindenberg."

Reinhart glared at the servant. Was it not clear that ladies were not to be ushered into his presence when they arrived? Bad enough that he had to make conversation with them at mealtimes in the Great Hall.

The two young ladies probably expected him to stand and bow politely. Instead, he grunted.

Lady Fronicka stepped forward. "My lord, you are so gracious to invite us to Thornbeck Castle for the next weeks' festivities. I am very—"

"Lady Fronicka, I did not invite you to be gracious. I simply am following the king's wishes that I marry a nobleman's daughter, an alliance that will strengthen the Holy Roman Empire and the king's authority in it. And now you and Lady Applonia may feel free to rest in your rooms after your long journey. I have work to do. The servants will see to your needs."

Lady Fronicka raised her brows. Lady Applonia stared with her mouth slightly open.

Finally, Lady Fronicka smiled. "We shall look forward to seeing you, Lord Thornbeck, in the Great Hall."

He nodded and they left. "Come here," he ordered the manservant who was still skulking by the door.

"Yes, Lord Thornbeck?" The man eagerly strode forward.

"Your job is to make sure I am not disturbed unless something of vital importance occurs. You are not to show any ladies into this study. If it happens again, you shall be sent to feed the pigs. Is that understood?"

"Yes, my lord. Forgive me." The man's face turned red.

"Now go."

⁓

Avelina made her way to her family's home just beyond the castle courtyard, picking her way around the manure piles in the dirt streets.

Before she reached the door, a high-pitched voice called out, "Avelina!"

She turned to see the two little faces she loved more than any others in the world. "What are you both doing?"

"We were playing with Frau Clara's new puppies," Brigitta cried.

"We haven't been gone very long, and we helped Father before we left," Jacob said.

"Did you bring us sweets?"

"Come inside with me. No, Brigitta, I don't have sweets. I have some news for you."

Very little light entered the wattle-and-daub structure, as there were few windows and it was a cloudy, gray day. Avelina was able to make out her father's still form sitting in his chair, which his friend, a carpenter, had made for him.

"Avelina." Her father squinted up at her. "Why aren't you at the castle?" Long pieces of hemp lay in his lap. He had obviously been braiding them into rope. Good. He was at least finding something to do. He was much less morose when his hands were busy.

Avelina knelt in front of him on the dirt floor, and he placed his massive hand on her head.

"Father, I have to go away for two weeks, perhaps three, but then I will return. Do you think you and Jacob and Brigitta will be able to manage while I'm gone?"

"Why are you going away?" Brigitta asked in a shrill voice. The little girl threw herself between Avelina and their father.

Father was staring hard at her, waiting for her to answer Brigitta's question.

"The earl has asked me to go to Thornbeck Castle. Lady Dorothea has been invited there to meet Lord Thornbeck, who is trying to choose a wife from among the noble ladies of this part of the Holy Roman Empire. There has been some feuding, as you know, between the regions and their noblemen, and Lord Plimmwald explained to me that the king thinks if Lord Thornbeck marries the daughter of one of them, it will help restore peace and build alliances between the regions."

"We shall pray he chooses Lady Dorothea, then," her father said. "Lord Plimmwald has long been afraid of the Duke of Geitbart attacking and taking over."

Her father would remember that from when he had been the earl's stable master.

"There will be other noble ladies there," Avelina said quickly, trying not to think about the fact that she was deceiving them, letting them believe she was only accompanying Lady Dorothea. "Lord Thornbeck might choose any of them. Nevertheless, I shall return before you start missing me very much, I should think." She smiled into Brigitta's upturned face.

"You shall not go away like Mother did, will you?" Brigitta's lips were parted and fear darkened her six-year-old eyes.

"No, of course not." Avelina's smile fled. "Mother did not want to go away, darling. And we shall see her again in heaven."

"Are you going to heaven?"

"Of course not, you daft girl." Jacob frowned. "She's only going to Thornbeck."

"There's no need to call her daft, Jacob." Avelina gave him a warning look, then softened it with a half smile. "I expect you to be kind and watch after your sister while I'm gone."

Father said very little on any given day, and today was no exception. He nodded to her. "God give you safe travels, Daughter."

"Thank you, Father."

Avelina hugged her little sister, then kissed her cheek. "You obey your father, yes?"

"I will. Bring me something pretty—a ribbon! Or a sweet!"

"If I am able." Avelina turned and hugged her little brother. "Don't mistreat your sister. Listen to Father."

Jacob squirmed. "You treat me like a little boy."

"Twelve years old is not too old to obey your older sister and your father."

Jacob rolled his eyes, but he gave her a half smile. She smiled back. He was at the age of wanting to pull away and be like the other boys, but he had a good heart, and he'd fight to keep his little sister safe.

As Avelina turned to leave, she had the distinct feeling that her journey would be longer than she had anticipated.

~~~

Hardly two hours later, with help, Avelina mounted one of the earl's gentlest mares. Two guards accompanied her as they started away from Plimmwald Castle and proceeded north. The day was gray and dreary, but even as the sky did not shed much light, it also held back the rain.

Irma, who was being sent as Avelina's maidservant, rode on the horse beside her. She was a plump kitchen servant with red, curly hair, a few years older than Avelina's twenty.

"I have always wanted to go on a long trip." Irma spoke not so much to Avelina as to herself. "And now I am a lady's maidservant! I am sure to see the margrave, and so many ladies. Perhaps even dukes and duchesses." Irma's wide gray eyes and smile gave Avelina the sudden urge to laugh. But she managed to control her hysteria.

Regardless of how flippantly Irma viewed this situation, Avelina could only think of the dangers, and she was thankful to have the company of any familiar face.

She glanced over her shoulder at the traveling bag that had been secured to the back of her saddle. Avelina, who was nearly the same size as Lady Dorothea, had brought the clothing her mistress had left behind, not owning any clothing of her own that was suitable enough. The earl had also told her to take Dorothea's jewelry, to help her look the part of the earl's daughter, but Avelina had to inform him that Dorothea had taken the jewelry with her, along with many of her best dresses.

After her visit to her family, Avelina finished packing up the rest of Lady Dorothea's dresses. The earl had also given her some of his dead wife's cotehardies, which smelled stale from lying in a trunk for the last few years since her death. Several of them were made of silk. One in particular was a becoming shade of violet. The countess had been slightly plumper than Avelina and shorter, but the gown was made in an overly long style meant to be gathered and tucked into the belt around her waist. Avelina could simply wear it untucked.

The earl had also given her one of the countess's necklaces— the only piece of her jewelry that had not been given to Dorothea. It was lovely, though a bit bulky, with dark-emerald stones surrounded by gold filigree. Lord Plimmwald told her, when they reached Thornbeck Castle in two or three days, she should put it on for the balls.

Irma held on to the reins and the pommel with both hands, and Avelina did the same. Neither of them was used to riding a horse, and riding sidesaddle required her to use muscles Avelina did not know she had in order to stay in the saddle. It was a long way to the ground, and she did not wish to fall and break a leg— although the thought of a broken leg was almost appealing. She would have a good excuse to go back home, but what if it did not grow back straight?

She only had to stay quiet—Lord Plimmwald had warned her not to talk much—and not to attract attention to herself. In two weeks the margrave would choose someone to be his wife, she could come home, and the earl would be happy with her and not punish her. And with the rewards the earl would give her, she would be free from the life of a servant—a life even more uncertain now that Lady Dorothea had gone away. Avelina might have had to work in the kitchen, a job more difficult than catering to Dorothea's whims.

Gradually Avelina grew more comfortable with the steady

pace of the horse and with holding herself in the saddle, and she sat tapping her chin with her finger, wondering what the two-week party would hold for her. Would she be able to fool them all into thinking she was an earl's daughter?

"The earl did not give you very much time to get ready, did he?" Irma asked in a quiet voice, presumably so the guards would not hear, as the men rode in front of and behind them.

"No."

"And he did not tell me exactly what he has asked of you. He only said you were going to Thornbeck and that I was to be your servant. He also said he would cut out my tongue and feed it to his falcon if I breathed a word to anyone that you are not Lady Dorothea." But even with this dire pronouncement, her eyes did not lose their excited gleam.

"I must pretend to be Lady Dorothea, and I must not offend the margrave in any way. If he suspects that I am not Dorothea, bad things will happen."

"*Ach, ja,* I suspected that was it. Your hair is more brown and not as light as Lady Dorothea's, and your eyes are blue while hers are green, but with some pretty silk cotehardies and our departed lady's necklace, you shall be just as beautiful. You should not look so worried. Besides, would it not be wonderful if the margrave should pick you to be his bride?"

Avelina turned wide eyes on Irma. "I cannot marry the margrave. You must not wish such a thing on me. But he surely would never pick me. He is looking for someone who can behave as a nobleman's daughter would, a margrave's wife, and I, of course, have no idea how to behave as a nobleman's daughter." Avelina muttered the last several words to herself. If her way of speaking did not give her away, her ignorance of the dances would.

She must try to speak and behave as Dorothea would. After

all, she had been Dorothea's servant for so many years, it should not be difficult. But she did not relish the thought of being rude and demanding.

~⌐

The evening of the second day of their journey, Avelina felt bruised and sore beyond anything she had ever experienced before. The guards stopped to rest the horses and to inform them that they could reach Thornbeck Castle before midnight if they pressed on. Since the moon was full, there were no clouds to obscure the light, and they did not expect to see any bandits this close to Thornbeck, they would press on.

After stretching their legs, Irma and Avelina got back on their horses for the last few hours of the journey.

Avelina had slept little the night before, as they had been unable to find shelter and had lain on the ground on blankets. And even though she'd had two blankets to cover herself, her feet had felt like two blocks of ice long before morning came, and they had not thawed all day.

She had awakened several times, dreaming either of brigands attacking their horses or of wolves and wild boar snarling at them. She had overheard the guards, when they thought she was not listening, saying that there were wolves in Thornbeck Forest.

Darkness kept her from seeing very far ahead. Irma kept up an almost-constant chatter.

"What do you suppose they eat at the margrave's table? Goose and suckling pig, no doubt. He probably never eats barley bread or porridge."

Avelina wondered if Thornbeck still had cherries.

As the night wore on, she could barely force her eyes to stay open. When they stopped again to rest, she curled into a ball on the ground and fell asleep.

She awoke to someone shaking her shoulder.

"Get up, my lady." Someone shook her again. "Lady Dorothea."

Avelina startled, jerking away from her, then remembered. It was Irma, and she was only practicing calling Avelina "my lady" and "Lady Dorothea" before they reached Thornbeck Castle.

"How much farther?" Avelina asked as the guard helped her mount her horse. He boosted her up, and she had to cling to the horse's mane to keep from falling off, as if exhaustion was making her so heavy it was pulling her back down to the ground.

"Another hour or two."

They continued on their way. Irma had all but ceased talking, and when she did speak, it was usually to say something such as, "I can't remember when I've ever been so tired. I may fall off this horse yet."

When Avelina's head bobbed forward, forcing her to jerk herself back upright, she started pinching her arms and then her cheeks to stay awake.

"I see something," Irma said, the old excitement back in her voice. "Is it the castle? No, I think it's the town."

A walled town lay below them in a slight valley. They skirted around it, following the wall to the east of the town, then came around the south side. They started moving up a winding road, and that's when Avelina saw the castle.

Thornbeck Castle stood high on a ridge that rose out of the forest. A single road led up to it, with tree-lined ravines all around. Several towers of varying sizes, some with pointed roofs and others flat and ringed with crenellations, stood out against the moonlit sky. She could see no other details in the dark, except that the terrain around it seemed steep and heavily forested. The castle itself stretched out along the ridge behind it, giving it a somewhat narrow facade, but it appeared much larger than Plimmwald Castle.

A bend in the road blocked Thornbeck Castle from view. The air had been getting steadily colder since they'd left Plimmwald, and now a gust stirred the loose strands of hair around her face. She shivered. Finally, this exhausting journey would end. She had been dreading the moment she would reach the castle, but now she was all too thankful at the prospect of getting off this horse and out of the cold.

They drew close to the front of the castle. A guard and a stable boy came toward them, and Lord Plimmwald's guards caught the harnesses and brought their horses to a halt.

I must remember I am not a servant. I must behave as Dorothea would . . . as the daughter of an earl.

She did not wait for someone to help her down. She slid off the saddle and handed the reins to the approaching stable boy. Her backside and thighs were so sore, it hurt to move, and exhaustion made her weave and list to one side as she walked.

She should be pretending perfect grace.

The guard announced her as Lady Dorothea, the Earl of Plimmwald's daughter. Irma allowed her, as the daughter of an earl, to go first. She put one foot in front of the other up the stone steps to the front door.

A white-haired middle-aged woman greeted her in the entrance hall. "I am Frau Schwitzer. Follow me and I shall take you and your maidservant to your room."

Avelina followed her, with Irma just behind. They made their way down a long corridor, lit by wall sconces, and then up an enormous staircase, and finally arrived at a door. The servant opened it and motioned them inside.

"There is water in the pitcher. I shall bring a small repast from the kitchen. Is there anything in particular you require, Lady Dorothea?"

Avelina stared and blinked. "No, but thank you very much."

She probably should not have thanked the servant. Dorothea certainly would not have thanked her.

The woman eyed her for a moment, then nodded and closed the door behind her.

Both Avelina and Irma moved to the fire and stretched their hands toward it.

"I can't even feel my feet." Irma took off her shoes, pulled down her hose, and held one naked foot out toward the flames.

Avelina ought to tell Irma that a lady's maid should ask her mistress what she could do for her. She should not be tending to her own needs. But Avelina was not a lady, and she couldn't bring herself to pretend to be one to poor Irma, who was as cold and tired as she was.

The servant soon returned, placing the tray of food on a small table. She gave Avelina a pointed look. "Is something wrong? Is the food not to your liking?"

Avelina should not be standing back. She should be sitting down to the food and dismissing the servant.

"Oh no." She searched her memory for what Dorothea would have said. "It looks very . . . adequate. We shall ring the bell if we need anything else."

The servant curtsied, then slipped out, closing the door soundlessly behind her.

The food was more than adequate. It looked like a feast. Avelina sat down, and Irma quickly joined her and took a bite of the fruit tart. The tart apples and plums tasted like summer sunshine, and the delicate pastry melted in her mouth. Her brother, whose favorite fruits were apples and plums, would have loved it. Even though it wasn't cherry, it was still delicious.

Feeling indulgent as she sampled all the foods on the tray—there was even cheese!—a pang of uneasiness flowed through her.

What would the days ahead bring? She would be a guest in this castle for at least fourteen days. She would play a part, pretending to be something and someone she was not. Would she shame the Earl of Plimmwald and the name of his daughter, Dorothea? If she failed to fool everyone into thinking she was an earl's daughter, she and her family would be punished, banished from Plimmwald.

The tart suddenly didn't taste very good.

4

THE SUN PENETRATED Avelina's consciousness.

She looked around, but nothing was familiar. The bed was big and soft and surrounded by dark-red curtains with gold fringe.

She turned onto her side—and groaned at the pain. Then she remembered. She was at Thornbeck Castle, pretending to be Dorothea.

The bed felt so good and smelled so clean, Avelina closed her eyes and stretched. And groaned again.

"Are you sore too?" Irma stood from the little table where the servant had apparently set her breakfast. "I've never been so beat up in my life. I don't know if I could get back on a horse today if my life depended on it. I thank the saints above I don't have to." She rubbed her lower back, then poured herself a cup of whatever was in the pitcher and drank a long gulp.

Avelina looked down at the floor from the edge of the bed. She was so high, she got dizzy. She lay on her stomach and let her feet hang over the side until her toes touched the floor. Then she poured herself some water.

"Do you know what I'm supposed to do today?" Avelina eyed Irma over the top of her goblet.

"Frau Schwitzer said you and the other guests would be taking the midday meal with the margrave in the Great Hall. And the margrave will want to speak privately with you, as he is taking time to ask all the eligible maidens questions about themselves." Irma's eager smile grew even wider. "You'll meet the Margrave of Thornbeck."

Avelina stared at the short young woman. "Do you honestly think I am excited about the prospect of meeting the Margrave of Thornbeck?" She lowered her voice to little more than a whisper. If having to fool the margrave was not enough to terrify her, making sure she did not anger him by her unrefined manners surely was.

Irma waved her hand dismissively. "I do not know why you're so worried. Lord Plimmwald told you he does not think anyone here has met his daughter, and the margrave has no reason to think you are not Dorothea. And as for making sure the margrave does not fall in love with you . . ." She made a hissing sound through her lips. "With all the other lovely noble maidens, I do not think you have anything to worry about."

"Thank you for the compliment." Avelina looked at the breakfast tray, hoping for a cherry tart. There were plum pastries and stewed spiced apples with sweet cream instead.

"Oh, you are pretty enough, Avelina—"

"Please don't call me that, Irma. You know we cannot risk it."

"I am sorry, *Lady Dorothea*." She frowned and raised an eyebrow. "As I was saying . . . you don't know how to be flirtatious, how to make a man fall in love with you. I've seen you. You are very blundering around men you think are handsome, and you were naively oblivious when that stable boy, Hans, showed interest in you."

Avelina tried to think of a retort. Irma had already stated that she need not worry that Lord Thornbeck would want to marry her, since he could not possibly want her.

These noble ladies might be better at flirting, but could any of them take care of a little brother and sister and a father who was lame in both legs, cook for her family, then go and work all day at the castle, fetching for and cleaning up after a spoiled earl's daughter?

"Perhaps you will find a husband here, from one of the noblemen, a brother accompanying his sister. You are beautiful, after all."

"I don't think any of them would consider me a possible bride." Avelina shook her head.

"They would if they thought you were the Earl of Plimmwald's daughter."

"Irma, I cannot deceive someone into marrying me. If I married someone under a false name, he would have the marriage annulled, especially when he found out I am only a maidservant."

She kept eating the delicious fruit pastry. Perhaps if she gained some weight she would look more attractive to a tradesman, and when she returned to Plimmwald with her dowry, she might marry a butcher or miller or someone else who could improve her brother and sister's situation in life.

But . . . the fruit pastry could hardly give her courage for meeting the margrave in a few hours.

Avelina went down the long staircase toward the ground floor of Thornbeck Castle wearing the deceased Lady Plimmwald's silk dress. The looking glass in her bedchamber told her that the jewel-like plum color was actually very becoming, as it brightened her brown hair and pale complexion.

But when she entered the Great Hall and saw the clothing of the noble ladies already gathered there, she realized her style of dress was somewhat old compared to theirs. Still, she held her head high. *I am the daughter of an earl. I am of noble birth. I am Lady Dorothea of Plimmwald.* She only had to pretend to believe it for two weeks.

A servant announced her as "the Lady Dorothea Seippach of Plimmwald" while she strode forward. Those standing around talking among themselves turned to stare.

Please don't let me trip.

She stopped when she came within a few feet of the nearest group of ladies. A few men stood around as well, fathers and brothers who had accompanied them.

Out of the corner of her eye, she caught a group of three young ladies giving her furtive glances and whispering. Her cheeks burned. Were they talking about her old-fashioned clothing? How long must she stand here, conspicuously alone, while no one spoke to her?

Finally, the servant announced, "The most honorable, the Margrave of Thornbeck."

Everyone faced in the direction of the margrave and curtsied or bowed.

Avelina was almost too afraid to look. When she dared raise her eyes, Lord Thornbeck was staring right at her with a most severe expression. Her heart stopped.

He glanced away and her heart started beating again. Saints above, but he was handsome. His dark eyes pierced her, then moved on to delve into everything else they alighted on. His skin was dark, his chin square and strong, his chest broad and thick, and his cheekbones high. The contrast to his look of power and intensity was his slight limp as he walked with a cane.

She hoped no one could see her hands shaking as the margrave walked to the head of the enormous trestle table and sat down.

The other guests gravitated to the long benches, obviously trying to get seats closest to the margrave.

Trying to sit in the least likely place to draw attention, she ended up at the farthest end from the margrave, sitting beside a young maiden wearing a pale-pink gown.

As a squire filled their goblets, the maiden said, "I am Magdalen of Mallin."

To the friendly tone of Magdalen's voice, Avelina replied, "I am Dorothea, from Plimmwald." Even though she had said the correct name, she probably should not have stated it that way. She was not *from* Plimmwald. She and her father *were* Plimmwald. Or so everyone was supposed to think.

"That is, I am Lady Dorothea." Now she sounded proud and presumptuous, since Magdalen had not called herself *Lady* Magdalen.

"I myself have never been outside Mallin. You shall have to tell me what to do as I am completely inexperienced with parties and balls."

"I am sure you must know more than I." Truly, it would be the blind leading the blind if she looked for guidance from Avelina. "I do not even know how to dance. You shall look quite refined and noble beside me, I assure you."

"If I cannot marry the margrave, my mother is determined to marry me off to the wealthiest person she can find who would want a poverty-stricken baron's daughter. I was betrothed to an earl's son, but when they found out I had no inheritance and no dowry, his father had our betrothal annulled."

"Oh, I'm sorry."

"No, it is perfectly well. I had heard he was given to violent tirades and had impregnated two of his house servants. I do not wish to marry someone like that."

Avelina shook her head and shuddered inwardly.

Another squire came to serve a large pheasant to their section of the table. Truly, Avelina would be eating better than she ever had before, if she was not too nervous to swallow.

"Did you bring anyone with you?" Avelina asked quietly. "I have only my maidservant."

"I have only my servant as well. I have a younger brother and younger sisters, but they are too young to accompany me."

"I do not have any brothers or sisters."

"Oh yes. You shall have a large inheritance. I should think a lot of noblemen would want to marry you."

"I do not think so. Am I the last guest to arrive?"

Magdalen nodded. "Most of us have been here for a day or more. I can tell you everyone's names, if you wish."

"Oh yes, thank you."

"The girl next to me is Applonia of Hindenberg, and she's talking to Otilia of Steenbeke. Across from them is Beatrix of Darghun, and next to her, Gertrudt of Wolfberg, a tiny but very wealthy duchy on the north coast, at the Baltic Sea."

Avelina tapped her chin with her finger. How would she ever remember all these names?

Magdalen named three more young women, all of them clad in silk and embroidered fine linen, their hair immaculate and swept up in sophisticated styles, which Avelina had been able to achieve with Dorothea but was unable to implement on her own hair. Irma, she had discovered, had no skill with dressing hair. So Avelina's was simply braided down her back and fastened with ribbon.

"Last but not least," Magdalen said with a slight twist of her lips. "See that girl sitting at the margrave's right side? That's Fronicka. Her father is the Duke of Geitbart." Magdalen leaned over to whisper in Avelina's ear, "She is determined to marry the margrave and she's given every other girl here notice that if they try to flirt with him, they will find something horrible in their bed the next night."

Avelina leaned forward to get a better look at Fronicka. She was smiling at the margrave, looking quite demure and sweet. "Perhaps she was in jest."

Magdalen raised her brows. "Perhaps."

The other ladies sitting around the table were also smiling at Lord Thornbeck. All Avelina had to do was stay out of the way and let the other ladies flirt with him.

However, if Fronicka managed to marry Lord Thornbeck, it would mean certain destruction for the Earl of Plimmwald. The margrave would likely help his wife's father, Geitbart, take over Plimmwald rather than stopping him and defending Plimmwald. The earl would be killed or imprisoned. All the people of Plimmwald, including her father and siblings, would be at Geitbart's mercy.

She whispered under her breath, "God, be merciful and do not let the margrave choose her."

As Avelina and Magdalen ate, Magdalen spoke of her younger sisters and brother with warmth and affection. "I wish they could have come with me, but the invitation was only for myself." She talked about her mother and siblings a bit more, then spoke of how poor the villagers of Mallin were. "The copper mines have been Mallin's main source of wealth. But about ten years ago the copper suddenly ran out. My father died soon after." She sighed. "Our land does not grow much food, as the soil is very rocky. It would be good for raising sheep and other livestock, but the people don't have money for buying livestock. It is why my mother wants to marry me to a wealthy nobleman, hoping he will help our people."

Avelina nodded. "Plimmwald is not very wealthy either. Most of our people are farmers or woodcutters . . . peasants." That was what Lady Dorothea called all the people of Plimmwald.

"My father always emphasized to me that as the noble family of Mallin, we were ultimately responsible for our people. I feel guilty sometimes living in a house made of stone, with silk dresses and plenty of food, when so many in our villages are going hungry."

Avelina knew that guilty feeling too, but it was because she often slept and ate at Plimmwald Castle, while her little sister and brother had to fend for themselves in their little dirt-floor, wattle-and-daub hovel they shared with their father, who was dependent on the neighbors to help him get from his chair to his bed.

"But what can we do to help them?" Avelina wondered aloud.

"There is only one thing a woman might do, and that is to marry someone wealthy—and generous."

Avelina started tapping her chin, then stopped herself as she realized it did not look very regal or ladylike.

"My maidservant said the margrave would want to ask me some questions. Did he already talk with you?"

Magdalen nodded, her mouth full of pheasant.

"What did he ask you? Will I be too frightened to even be able to speak?" She asked the latter question more to herself than to Magdalen.

"It was not frightening, although I do think the margrave himself is a little gruff and frightening. His questions were not what I might have expected, but they were respectful and nothing was difficult to answer. Do not worry. You will answer him well."

"It hardly matters. I do not wish to marry the margrave in any case," she confided.

"Do you not?"

Avelina shook her head.

"Is there someone else you wish to marry?"

"No, not at all." She should not have said that. How would she explain? "As you said, he is a little frightening, that severe look on his face, as if he is always angry. I should like to marry someone with more of a gentle, romantic expression, a man of poetry and learning." That was true, at least, however unlikely it was.

"How do you know Lord Thornbeck is not a man of poetry and learning?"

"He used to be a knight." Avelina shrugged, trying to think what Dorothea might say. "Most knights I know are rough and like to fight."

Magdalen smiled. "I might feel the same, except I know my mother is hoping the margrave will choose me. It would solve so many problems for my people and ensure them the protection they need."

Avelina decided immediately: If the margrave seemed to be a good person, she would try to turn his attention toward Magdalen and convince him to choose her. Magdalen was a deserving person, and it would make her happy to be able to help her people. And anyone he married who was not Fronicka would benefit Avelina. Yes, the margrave should marry Magdalen.

As soon as the midday meal was over, the beautiful blonde wife of the margrave's chancellor approached Avelina.

"Lord Thornbeck is ready to speak with you now, Lady Dorothea."

Avelina nodded. Somehow, after deciding to champion Magdalen, she felt much less afraid of the margrave. She had a plan.

She followed the servant through the Great Hall—accompanied by the stares of the other guests. Fronicka was smirking at her.

Avelina smiled back at her and winked. Perhaps it was not a wise thing to do, but she was looking forward to the margrave choosing Lady Magdalen and erasing the annoying smirk off Fronicka's face.

5

Reinhart waited in his library for the last of the ten ladies to come so he might ask her questions.

Odette's quiet steps alerted him to their arrival only a moment before his chancellor's wife appeared in the doorway, followed closely by the last of the noble maidens who had come to his party.

"Lord Thornbeck." Odette Hartman curtsied. "Lady Dorothea, daughter of the Earl of Plimmwald."

Reinhart nodded to her.

Odette sat near Jorgen and smiled at the young lady.

He forced himself to say politely, "Lady Dorothea, it is my pleasure to welcome you to Thornbeck Castle. Frau Hartman, who brought you here, will stay in the room so you might feel more comfortable, while my chancellor, Jorgen Hartman, will record our conversation. You may sit."

He hated formality and pretense. People should say what they wanted instead of hiding behind hypocrisy. He had allowed Jorgen and his wife to teach him a few of the niceties that others of the aristocracy would expect of him. But the woman he married must realize that he could not abide insincerity, and he would always be forthright himself.

He might as well get these questions over with. At least she was the last one. "Lady Dorothea, in your opinion, what is a lady's most important task?"

The lady, quite pretty, with brown hair and blue eyes, looked as though she might faint as the blood drained from her face.

"Lady Dorothea? Are you well?"

She nodded, visibly swallowing.

She did not have to say anything brilliant. He came up with the questions as a way to discover a bit about them, to get an idea about their temperaments and character, since he was not so interested in his wife having strong opinions. A simple maiden who was not too opinionated would suit him.

But he was not so sure this one could even speak.

⁓

Avelina's breath traitorously left her. She tried to think what she might be expected to say. She did not want to impress the margrave, but she didn't want him to suspect that she knew nothing at all about being a lady either. She should say whatever Lady Dorothea would have said. But Lady Dorothea probably would have said something about looking beautiful so as to bring her husband the most praise, and Avelina could not bring herself to say that.

"Lady Dorothea?" The margrave was looking at her as if he was afraid she had gone deaf. The chancellor's fair wife who had led her into the room was also staring at her, along with her young, handsome husband, who sat with his quill pen poised to write.

With so many thoughts swirling in her head, she was too confused to think of anything other than the truth. "In my opinion, a lady should take care of her people, first and foremost. They are dependent upon her and upon their lord for their well-being, and therefore a lady should consider them in everything she does and every decision she makes." *Something the real Lady Dorothea had utterly failed to do.*

She studied Lord Thornbeck's expression, but he was unreadable. Frau Hartman, however, widened her eyes and glanced at her husband, who was too busy writing to return her gaze. Was her answer surprising? She must be more careful.

The margrave folded his arms across his chest as he sat behind his desk. His cane leaned against it in easy reach. "And how does a lady take care of her people? Can you give an example?"

She closed her eyes for a moment, balancing on the edge of the deep hole that she had just dug for herself. She might as well tell the truth. She had never been good at lies.

"A lady takes care of her people by making sure they have what they need—food, clothing, and shelter—to the best of her ability. She should discover what her people need and keep the lord of the land informed of these needs. One such lady is Lady Magdalen, whom I was speaking with during the midday meal. Her people are having difficulty since their mines were exhausted of their copper supply, and she is very concerned for them. She is willing to do whatever is necessary to help them. That is a perfect example."

Thank You, God, for helping me think of that! She only hoped she had not put him off by making it obvious that Magdalen's region needed the margrave's wealth to help it survive. Frau Hartman had raised her brows. Avelina went on.

"Furthermore, a margrave's wife should have lots of ideas—and should share those ideas with her husband and other prominent men of the region. She should tell the margrave how to solve the problems of the region and not just share what those problems are. Do you not agree, Lord Thornbeck?"

He fixed her with such an intense scowl that she could hardly breathe. How could he look severe and frightening and yet overwhelmingly handsome at the same time? His brown eyes, masculine forehead and jawline, broad shoulders, and well-formed mouth all combined to make him the most handsome man she had ever seen. She quickly looked away from him, her cheeks burning, embarrassed that she found the man so attractive. She hoped he could not read her thoughts.

"You are saying a lady should tell her husband what the region's problems are and how to solve them?"

Had she gone too far? *God in heaven, I am only a maidservant! What am I saying?* "Um . . . I . . . that is . . . perhaps. I mean, yes, my lord." Could she be any more blundering and unpolished? He quirked one brow at her.

At least she didn't have to worry that she was impressing him too much.

He cleared his throat as he looked down at the piece of paper in his hand. "What kinds of things do you like to do, Lady Dorothea? Sewing? Riding? Hawking?"

What should she say? She didn't know how to do most things a lady would do. She hated sewing and had never gone riding until the trip here, which had not exactly been enjoyable, and she knew nothing about using birds of prey to hunt. She was good at dressing Lady Dorothea's hair, but her mind wandered too much to play games of skill like chess or Nine Men's Morris.

But there was one thing she knew how to do that most servants did not: she knew how to read. She had convinced Lady Dorothea to teach her years ago and then to allow her to join the lessons with her tutor.

"I like to read and make up stories."

This time both his brows quirked up. "Stories?"

"Tales. I write tales of adventure, quests of courage and love. Romances."

The muscles around his mouth went slack.

Was it bad for a lady to make up tales? The chancellor's wife was staring at her with round blue eyes and a half smile.

After a few moments he said, "I should like to read one of your tales."

"Oh," Avelina spoke through her sigh of relief, "I'm afraid I did not bring any with me." She smiled, trying to look apologetic.

Was that a disapproving look on his face? Though the margrave's chancellor and his wife looked very pleasant, the margrave was definitely scowling. "And what kind of things do you like to read?"

"I don't actually—" She was about to say, "I don't actually have any books of my own." Her heart skipped a few beats. An earl's daughter would never say that. "That is . . . my father does not approve of my reading romances, so I must read them in secret. I also read the Bible." *When I can sneak the German-translated version out of Lord Plimmwald's library.*

"Do you like to hunt? We will form a hunting party at least once while you are here."

"Oh no, I cannot abide hunting." Truly, she had never been hunting before, but the prospect filled her with horror. "I shall stay at the castle during any hunting parties." That should annoy him sufficiently.

"Do you enjoy dancing? We shall have two balls."

"I am not a good dancer." She had never learned to dance. She was too busy working at the castle to dance in the streets during festivals with the other villagers, and she had never learned the courtly dances Lady Dorothea knew, the ones the margrave's guests would no doubt be dancing at the ball. "I shall watch all the other ladies dance during the ball."

His brows low and drawn together, he did not look pleased.

With her strident answers, he'd never guess she was a lowly servant. And voicing such strong opinions made her hold her head a
little higher.

"I see. And what are your thoughts about marriage?"

"My thoughts about marriage?"

He nodded.

The question made her heart speed up and her breath grow
shallow.

Her feelings about marriage were . . . fanciful and unrealistic.
The other servants laughed at them, and Lady Dorothea rolled her
eyes and called her "daft." Noblemen and women saw marriage
as a contract, a means to an end, and most of all, a duty. But why
change her tactics now? She would tell him the truth.

"I have always thought one should marry, if at all possible, not
because the person you marry can give you the most position or
wealth, but out of love. After all, if there is no love, if you have
no romantic thoughts about each other, then you are much more
likely to treat each other badly. And all the position and wealth in
the world will not make a person happy if they feel unloved."

The margrave opened his mouth as if to answer but said nothing. She couldn't resist going on. She had given this a great deal of
thought, after all.

"A woman wishes to be swept up by a man's fervent feelings for
her, by love and longing and depth of feeling. She does not wish to
be married for her father's coin or her noble birth or because she is
a sensible choice. She wants to be wooed, even after she is married,
to be cherished and loved for her very self, not just because she has
a beautiful face, long after she has passed the age of freshness and
youth."

She had said too much. She sensed it by the way no one spoke
or even seemed to breathe—besides she herself, who was breathing

rather fast. The chancellor was still writing furiously. The slight scraping of his quill was the only sound.

Her face burned and she suddenly was quite smothered in the closed-up room. "That is, if one does not have to marry for duty. For, as I already said, a lady must think of her people first and foremost . . . not about love or feelings or any of those . . . things."

What a clumsy, unrefined person she must seem to the sophisticated margrave, the chancellor, and the chancellor's beautiful, polished wife. *Ach*. She must have frightened him away from ever wanting to marry her, at least.

She pulled at her sleeves, wishing it were permissible to push them up past her elbows. Was it hot in this room? Sweat was starting to trickle down the center of her back.

While the silence stretched on, she examined her fingernails, which were rather more chipped and stained than any lady's nails should be. She curled her fingernails inside her palms. When would this be over?

Had she made a complete fool of herself? She shouldn't even be here, talking to the Margrave of Thornbeck as if her opinion mattered.

The margrave cleared his throat again. He seemed amused. He wasn't exactly smiling, so it could be her imagination. My, but he was appealing, in a large, rugged sort of way. She imagined him as he was before he became the margrave, when he was a knight and the captain of the guard. He must have looked even more formidable than he did now. Power was etched in every line of his face, in the proportions of his shoulders and chest and stature. Even his voice was deep and powerful.

"My last question is, what do you hope to gain from your stay here at Thornbeck Castle?"

"Oh." *A dowry, and a goose, and a side of pork every month for my family.* "I hope to meet some new people—I do not have opportunities to meet other ladies very often—and . . ." Should she admit to wanting to see what books he had in his library that she might read? She shrugged. "To enjoy your hospitality, my lord."

The scowl was back on his face. "Thank you, Lady Dorothea, for answering my questions so honestly and openly."

Ach. She had said too much. *Honestly and openly.* She must have sounded like the furthest thing from a dignified, self-possessed daughter of an earl.

"And thank you for coming to Thornbeck."

That seemed to be Frau Hartman's cue to escort her back, because she stood and walked over to Avelina.

Avelina curtsied to Lord Thornbeck. He bowed, leaning on his cane, and she hurried out of the room. This must have been how Daniel felt when he was drawn out of the den of lions.

———

Reinhart listened until Lady Dorothea's footsteps could no longer be heard, then walked to Jorgen's desk. "May I?"

Jorgen handed him the paper he had been writing on.

He read Lady Dorothea's answers. He had not quite believed his own ears, but here it was from Jorgen's pen. Her very answers as he had heard them.

She did not like to dance. She did not—and would not—hunt. She liked to write tales—romances. And . . . here it was. "A margrave's wife should have lots of ideas—and should share those ideas with her husband and other prominent men of the region. She should tell the margrave how to solve the problems of her region."

Odette swept into the room, her eyes wide open, looking like she was bursting to speak.

"What did you think of her, Frau Hartman?" He might as well hear her opinion.

She smiled. "She certainly did not make all the usual replies, did she?"

"I am sure you liked her comments about helping the poor among her people."

"Yes, my lord." Odette's smile grew wider. "And then she held up Lady Magdalen as the example." She shook her head, a disbelieving look on her face.

This whole business of choosing a wife had made him uncomfortable, including the way he had ultimately decided to go about it. He had been looking at each lady in a rational way, basing his opinion of each of them on facts, weighing each word they had spoken to decide whether they would make him a compatible wife. But with Lady Dorothea . . . Several of the ladies had been fair of face and form. None of that had swayed his intellectual approach. Lady Dorothea's opinionated answers had been exactly what he did not like, and yet . . . he had felt his usual rationality slipping from his grasp. He had felt drawn to her in a most irrational way.

Odette was still smiling. "I liked what she said about love too. Something about a woman wishing to be loved and wooed for herself and not her wealth. That was beautiful. And so true."

Yes, that was the part Reinhart had wanted to read again, to show himself how unreasonable and foolish it had been. *Swept up by a man's fervent feelings for her.* Irrational. *Doesn't wish to be married for her money or alliances or her noble birth or because she is a sensible choice.* Nonsensical. So why did he feel his breath quicken, remembering it? *She wants to be wooed, even after she is married, to be cherished and loved for her very self.* His heart thumped hard against his chest at the honest sentiments. What did she think of him? Did she scorn his limp as much as he hated it himself?

"I admire that she feels so strongly about love, and that she was brave enough to say it." Odette and Jorgen were gazing at each other.

"Yes," Jorgen replied, "she has spirit and an air of innocence and honesty. And she was not as stiff and formal as the other ladies, although she did seem nervous."

"True." Odette turned to Reinhart. "What did you think of her, my lord, if I may ask?"

"I cannot say she has passed the first test." After all, he had wanted someone who knew her place as a woman and a wife, who would not be opinionated.

"Are you saying you did not like her?" Jorgen looked surprised.

He grunted. "This is not meant to be a sentimental process."

After a pause Odette said, "I have not yet given Lady Dorothea a tour of Thornbeck Castle. Will you come with us? Say polite things, ask her about herself, maybe offer her a book from your library since she likes to read?"

"Of course, my lord. I think it is a very good idea," Jorgen said, a bit too eagerly.

"And don't snarl at her if she asks you about your injury, the way you did to poor Lady Beatrix."

Reinhart glared at Odette and resisted the urge to growl.

Had his chancellor and his wife become enchanted by Lady Dorothea? He was not enchanted. He only wanted to delve deeper into her temperament. In truth, she was the only lady whose answers had piqued his curiosity. But she was not at all what he had thought he wanted—a docile, quiet, simple maiden.

Besides, he only had two weeks to mine the jewels—or rocks, as the case might be—of each woman's character; two weeks to choose who he would take as his wife; two weeks to find the woman he would spend the rest of his life with.

6

"Oh, Irma, it was terrible." Avelina covered her eyes with her hands. "I babbled on and sounded ridiculous. I don't even remember half of what I said, but what I do remember . . . it didn't sound anything like what Lady Dorothea would have said."

Irma sighed as she reclined on her sleeping couch, eating pastries from a plate she was balancing with one hand. "What does it matter?" She took another bite, then spoke through the crumbs that blew from her lips. "No one here knows Lady Dorothea, and after we leave, no one will be the wiser."

"I still have to get through the next two weeks. I feel so out of place. I don't know what to do or what to say or how to behave. I was never taught to be an earl's daughter. I feel every moment as if someone is going to accuse me of being an imposter—which I am."

Never before had she been treated like her opinion mattered. If only she could enjoy it without feeling like someone was going to brand her a fraud and order her to leave at once.

But in her heart she truly believed she was a better lady than Lady Dorothea ever was. Was it wrong to think she was nobler in her heart than the true nobleman's daughter? If only *she* had been born the daughter of an earl instead of Dorothea. If only she had not been born to a poor man who himself was only a servant.

A pang of guilt smote her breast at the envious, disloyal thoughts. Her own father might not know how to read or write or control his own fate, and he might never tell her he loved her or appreciated all she did for her little brother and sister, but he was still her father, and he had never tried to marry her off to the first person who asked for her, or betroth her to some rich and powerful nobleman she had never even met, as a titled father would do.

A knock at the door made Avelina jump. "That will be Frau Hartman to take me on a tour of the castle. I think you are supposed to come with me so you can learn where everything is."

Irma jumped up. She set down the plate of cake and hastily brushed the crumbs off her chest.

"At least Lord Thornbeck won't be along." Avelina glanced in the mirror. "It should only be you, me, and Frau Hartman."

Irma was still brushing herself, muttering, "Very well."

Avelina took a step toward the door, then remembered she was supposed to be an earl's daughter. "Irma, you have to get the door."

"Oh yes." Irma scurried to the door and opened it.

Frau Hartman entered. "Is Lady Dorothea ready?" Her gaze fell on Avelina. "Shall we take a look around the castle?"

"Of course." Avelina came forward. "This is my maidservant, Irma."

Irma curtsied.

"Lord Thornbeck is also coming with us. Shall we go?"

Avelina's throat suddenly went dry and she swallowed. Why was Lord Thornbeck coming with them? She distinctly remembered Magdalen saying he had not accompanied the other ladies on their tours around the castle. *Oh dear.* He looked just as severe as she remembered.

Irma actually started back at seeing him behind Frau Hartman.

Avelina faked a smile and placed her hand at Irma's back, trying to be discreet as she pushed her forward.

They followed Frau Hartman, and Lord Thornbeck dropped back and walked beside Avelina. Her heart trembled instead of beating. What did the margrave mean, coming with them? Who was she that he would want to accompany her on her tour?

"This corridor is where most of the second-floor bedchambers are located," Frau Hartman said. "All the ladies are staying either here or on the third floor."

They passed several closed doors, then came to the stairs. "This way to the main floor."

Avelina was painfully aware of Lord Thornbeck walking beside her, silent and scowling, his walking stick thumping on the floor as he limped. Since the stairs were wide enough for all of them, they walked down the elegant staircase with Lord Thornbeck on the side with the handrail. His expression was tense as he made his way slowly down the steps.

"Are you in pain, Lord Thornbeck?"

The margrave growled deep in his throat.

Odette gave him a look over her shoulder, almost as if to scold him.

He cleared his throat. "I have some pain. In my ankle. From the accident. When my brother died."

"Oh. I'm very sorry." Stupid that she should have asked him such a question, reminding him of the fire when his brother was killed—the accident that many believed was no accident at all, but the margrave's deliberate murder of his brother. Her heart began to pound.

He cleared his throat again and said gruffly, "Is your room comfortable?"

"Yes, my lord. Very comfortable, I thank you."

"The staircase," Frau Hartman said, "is part of the newer section of the castle, along with the ballroom here at the bottom where Lord Thornbeck hosted a masquerade ball some weeks ago. Did you attend that ball, Lady Dorothea?"

"I regret that I did not." Though not altogether truthful, it was the polite thing to say.

They walked across the beautiful, gleaming floor as Odette went on. "This part of the castle was begun by Lord Thornbeck's father and finished two years ago by his brother. The floor is made from marble that was quarried nearby." They made their way across it, heading toward a doorway.

"And this is the gallery where the previous margraves' portraits are displayed, along with the large painting depicting the battle scene of Prussian invaders being driven back from the nearby border. At the end of the gallery is a balcony. Would you like to see the view?"

"Yes."

They walked slowly across the narrow room. "Lord Thornbeck, will you supply the names of the portrait subjects?" Odette asked.

He rattled off the names of his father and brother, not offering any other information about his family.

They reached the end of the gallery and Lord Thornbeck stepped forward and opened the wooden door wide, then held it for both Avelina and Frau Hartman with one hand, his cane with the other.

"It is getting colder," Lord Thornbeck said. "We can stay inside if it is too cold for you."

"No, it is not too cold for me, my lord." Avelina stepped out onto the broad balcony and walked to the railing. Below was a densely forested ravine, the leaves mostly gone from the trees, as the limbs stretched, like spindly skeletons, toward the overcast sky. There was a wild beauty about the rugged, steep terrain. Somewhere beyond the trees was the town of Thornbeck.

The air was crisp and cold. Would it be even colder when she and Irma had to make the long trip back to Plimmwald? But she would not mind so much as long as Plimmwald and its people were kept safe by the margrave. Which gave her an idea.

She spun on her heel and faced Lord Thornbeck. "What are your duties to the king, my lord? I know you are charged with keeping the border safe and defended from invaders, but what about preventing attacks on other castles in nearby regions? If you don't mind my asking." She bowed her head to soften her pointed questions.

When she glanced up, he was staring into her eyes in a way that made her heart stutter and stammer. He seemed to have no idea how good he looked, which made him even more attractive.

"I am a knight. Even if I were not the Margrave of Thornbeck, I would come to the aid of any ally who was being wrongfully attacked."

Any ally, he said. She hoped he considered the Earl of Plimmwald an ally.

"I am pleased to hear that."

"Why do you ask such a question?"

"Oh, well, I . . . I was thinking of . . . of my father, the Earl of Plimmwald. I'm afraid he has reason to fear that someone might try to take over Plimmwald and its castle."

"And who might this someone be?"

Her heart skipped another beat, but this time at the severe look on his face. "The Duke of Geitbart, my lord."

A moment went by, then he gave her an almost imperceptible nod. He took a deep breath as he moved closer, staring out over the wooden railing at the wild ravine below. "The Duke of Geitbart's daughter, Lady Fronicka, is my guest here, and the duke will be arriving before the final ball."

Her stomach sank. Was he trying to tell her he considered Geitbart a closer ally than Plimmwald?

"Therefore, Plimmwald is safe for two weeks at least." He looked at her out of the corner of his eye, one brow quirking up. "I do not approve of anyone wrongfully trying to take Plimmwald. However, your father sent a letter to the king accusing me of murdering my brother. Is there some reason I should not look the other way when the Duke of Geitbart decides to seize Plimmwald?"

Her heart jumped into her throat. She swallowed hard. "I do not know—that is, I'm sure my father did not accuse you. Perhaps he merely mentioned the rumors . . ."

"Yes," he said slowly. "Perhaps."

How could she convince him not to hate the Earl of Plimmwald? To consider him an ally worthy of helping, should Geitbart attack?

"You are shivering." His brows lowered in that severe way of his. "Let us go inside."

She hadn't even noticed how cold she was. They made their way back through the gallery and into the ballroom, with its high ceilings and decorative banners and frescos on the walls.

As they were walking across the ballroom, Lady Fronicka appeared at the top of the stairs. The duke's daughter narrowed her eyes at them.

They soon passed out of sight of Lady Fronicka, and Odette led them around the rest of the main floor, including Lord Thornbeck's library, where he and his chancellor conducted business, Odette explained. The margrave allowed Odette to do all of the talking, to the point of awkwardness. He stayed silent as she explained that his business included writing letters and documents and keeping all sorts of records and ledgers.

Odette gave Lord Thornbeck a pointed look, and he cleared his throat.

"Do you enjoy corresponding, Lady Dorothea?" he asked.

"Oh . . . yes . . . when I have someone pleasant to correspond with." It was the first thing that came into her mind and seemed like something Dorothea might say. Avelina wrote stories, not letters. She had no family but her father and younger brother and sister. She also had few friends, and none that knew how to read or write.

Lord Thornbeck was moving toward the bookshelves. "I have a few books you might be interested in reading. You are welcome to take whatever you fancy and read them while you're here."

"Oh, that is very generous of you." And thoughtful. Her heart stirred strangely inside her as she looked up into his warm brown eyes. What would it be like to be married to this man?

No. She absolutely could *not* let her thoughts turn in that direction. But she couldn't seem to stop her heart from fluttering as her eyes were still locked on his.

You are only a servant. He would never look at you with interest in his eyes if he knew that. It was enough to make her turn away from him, her hand shaking as she reached out for a book on the shelf. Besides, she did not like gruff men.

But at least for now she would have access to all these books. There were so many, her eyes hungrily took in all the leatherbound spines. She ached to read them all.

Out of the corner of her eye, she caught Odette inclining her head in Avelina's direction.

Lord Thornbeck reached past her shoulder. "Here is a favorite book of mine. *The Song of Roland.*" He took a book off the shelf and showed her the cover. "It's an epic poem about a battle during the time of Charlemagne."

"Oh yes. I have heard of it. I always wanted to read it." Avelina reached for it, then drew her hand back.

"You may take it." He held it out to her. "It's long, but I think you will like it."

She took it from him, not allowing her fingers to touch his. "Thank you, my lord."

Staring down at the heavy book in her hands, she wasn't sure what she was supposed to do next. Should she open it and start to read? Should she keep looking at the other books on the shelf? Or stare up stupidly into Lord Thornbeck's eyes, as she was doing?

The margrave called Irma over. "Take this book and place it in Lady Dorothea's chamber. Then you may come back and join us."

Avelina could just imagine Irma's consternation over having to go back up to the second floor, then come back down all those steps again. But Irma took the book, curtsied to Lord Thornbeck, and hurried off.

"Let us continue. Shall we?" The margrave held out his arm to her.

Was that a smile and nod of approval from Odette? It was so slight, Avelina may have imagined it.

She placed her hand lightly on his arm, and they moved from the library through the corridor. "The chapel is worth seeing, I believe," Lord Thornbeck said. "The fortifications, the guards' rooms, and the defense towers are on the other side, as well as the west wing." His mouth pursed tighter, his jaw hardening when he mentioned the west wing. "But I don't think you would be interested in any of that."

They moved through a narrow corridor and through a wooden door to a chapel with stained-glass windows that illuminated the room with brilliant colors.

Thornbeck Castle's chapel was twice as large as the one at

Plimmwald Castle, which had no windows at all and was dark and soot covered, lighted only by torches. This chapel featured an ornate altar with a rood screen that was covered in wood and ivory carvings, along with many lighted candles and an altar cross made of gold.

But the enormous stained-glass windows surrounding the chancel were what took her breath away. They were twice as tall as she was and brighter and more colorful than any rainbow. Truly, whoever built this chapel was quite wealthy. Perhaps they wished to pay penance by lavishing so much expense on the chapel. But those riches might have been put to better use helping the people in Plimmwald who barely had enough food to keep themselves alive.

A pang shot through her stomach. Judging other people's piety and the amount of money they spent on a holy chapel was surely a grave sin. Wishing to have their money for another purpose was perhaps even worse.

"You may come here any time you wish to pray." Inside the sanctuary, Lord Thornbeck's voice was hushed and even deeper. His suppressed tone sent a tremor through her. "The priest is available to you any time you might wish to speak to him, and he performs all the services of a cathedral priest. On Sundays everyone is expected to attend."

"Of course."

As they were turning to leave, Irma arrived at the door, a few wisps of hair hanging out of her wimple and her face red.

"Odette," Lord Thornbeck said, "I shall escort Lady Dorothea back to her chamber if you will show her servant around the kitchen and lower rooms."

Odette curtsied and left with Irma just behind her.

Avelina placed her hand once again on Lord Thornbeck's arm. Being in such proximity, and suddenly alone with him, her stomach fluttered. He walked slowly, his walking stick making regular thumping noises on the floor.

She should probably say something. His face was set in its usual serious expression, as if he'd forgotten about her as he looked straight ahead.

She only had to keep from revealing that she was Lady Dorothea's servant. But something made her want to talk to him, to discover his thoughts. It was a peculiar curiosity, borne of knowing she would never have the opportunity to talk to this handsome, intriguing young margrave again when these two weeks were over.

"There you are." Lady Fronicka came down the corridor toward them. "And this must be Lady Dorothea of Plimmwald." Fronicka barely glanced at Avelina before directing her smile toward Lord Thornbeck. "How kind you are to show her about the castle, Lord Thornbeck, especially since she was so late to arrive."

Fronicka fell into step beside them—on Lord Thornbeck's side. "When will we go on our hunt? I am very accomplished with a crossbow. At home I once shot three deer and a wild boar in one day."

Avelina nodded, smiling, but her insides were churning, remembering what Magdalen had said about Fronicka's determination to marry Lord Thornbeck. As long as she didn't see Avelina as a threat, she had nothing to worry about. But the fact that Lord Thornbeck had chosen to accompany her on this tour would certainly displease Fronicka.

"Did you see Thornbeck's beautiful chapel?" Fronicka seemed to address Avelina but did not give her time to respond, and she kept her eyes on Lord Thornbeck. "I have always thought you could tell how much piety a man has by the place where he worships. Geitbart Cathedral has a crucifix made of ivory and an altar of gold. I could never worship at a wooden altar. Can you imagine?"

Fronicka chattered on, not requiring any reply.

What did it matter if one worshipped at a gold altar or a wooden one, so long as one's heart and mind were focused on God? She recalled their own modest church in Plimmwald. The chapel where Avelina sometimes prayed was certainly less ornate than Thornbeck's.

"Are you intending to say," Avelina interrupted Fronicka, "that poor people are less pious than the wealthy because they worship at a wooden altar and not a gold-and-ivory one?"

Fronicka stared at her with her mouth hanging open.

"I'm just curious. Do you think a God who sent His Son to be born in a lowly stable to poor people, announced to shepherds in a field, could care about gold and ivory and jewels? Perhaps God cares about our hearts, not our wealth." Avelina smiled very innocently.

Lord Thornbeck's lips were slightly parted as he stared at her.

Fronicka fixed her cold black eyes on Avelina. There was a long pause, then Fronicka, ignoring what Avelina had said, started talking again about hunting and how good she was at killing things.

Avelina certainly had not endeared herself to Lady Fronicka, but it was worth it to momentarily erase the scowl from Lord Thornbeck's face. She liked the idea that her opinions surprised him.

⌒

Reinhart stood leaning on his walking stick as he faced Jorgen and Odette.

Jorgen cleared his throat. "Do you feel you are discovering what you need to know about the . . . young ladies?"

No doubt his chancellor was also wondering what to call them.

Candidates? Choices? Contenders? Perhaps the most polite term was "prospective brides."

Before they arrived Reinhart had thought of them as young maidens who would line up and try to hide their imperfections during their stay at Thornbeck Castle in order to catch a margrave. But once they arrived and he acquainted himself with each of them, he was faced with the fact that they would have opinions about marrying him.

And after he met Dorothea and heard her irrational ideas about love, she reminded him that these women were all different, and likely their motives for being here were very different. If the woman he chose should turn out like his mother, bitter and hostile . . . He simply could not allow that to happen. His father had been cold and withdrawn from her. They slept in opposite wings of the castle, and Reinhart wondered how two children, himself and his brother, had come out of such cold avoidance and open hostility.

"My lord?" Jorgen looked at him with raised brows, and Odette was also giving him a look of expectation.

He had not answered the question. "I have discovered some things."

Lady Fronicka was easy to talk to. He did not like to talk very much, and she was more than willing to fill the gaps. But there was something he could not put into words, except to call it a hard edge that he sensed about her. Most of the others were timid, silly, and self-centered. They'd lived comfortable lives of indulgence and ease. Lady Magdalen had a sweetness and intelligence about her that most of the others lacked. But Lady Magdalen was so young, he felt uncomfortable thinking of her as a wife. The only one who drew him, who made him want to get to know her better, was Lady Dorothea.

"You have said you want to know if they are kind or mean-spirited"—Jorgen looked down at his notes—"and you wanted to know their attitude toward the poor. We have a plan in place to find out those things tomorrow when we take them all on a tour of the town. Is there anything else you would like to know about them?"

His chest tightened. He wanted to be certain the woman he married would be conscientious in doing her part to be a good wife. Consequently he would go about this in a very logical, reasonable way. The fact that he was attracted to Lady Dorothea was not important—and very strange, since he did not like opinionated women and did not think they made good wives. But emotion should play no part in his decision.

"I should like the woman I choose to be very honest, generous, and to have a sincere faith in God, rather than mindlessly following rules." Those seemed the ideal qualities of a wife. He had admired various skills and characteristics of his fellow knights, but he had spent very little time in the presence of women.

Jorgen and his wife, who had their heads together and were talking quietly, looked down at what Jorgen had just written. No doubt they were trying to figure out a test to determine if each girl met his criteria.

"When we take the tour of the town tomorrow," Jorgen said, "you only need to be on hand to observe. We shall take care of the rest."

Until a month or two ago, it had never occurred to him to make a list of character traits he would like in a wife. But it seemed the wise and logical thing to do. Emotion made things uncomfortable. Being forced to marry a stranger was uncomfortable. But his reason would help him make the best choice.

Avelina ran, trying to get to Jacob and Brigitta. Plimmwald was burning, the entire village as well as Plimmwald Castle, and it was all her fault. Geitbart had attacked. People were screaming all around her. Geitbart's soldiers were galloping about with swords drawn, striking down everyone they saw. And Avelina couldn't find her siblings. She screamed their names.

Suddenly she was surrounded by the villagers, her fellow servants from the castle, and even Lord Plimmwald. They were all glaring at her with rage-filled eyes and smoke-stained faces.

"Forgive me. Please forgive me," she kept saying. "I did my best. Help me find Jacob and Brigitta!"

But they pointed at her. Some spit at her. Others turned away in disgust.

Avelina sat up. The curtains were open, letting in the light from the fire in the fireplace.

Thornbeck. She was at the margrave's castle, pretending to be Lady Dorothea. She sank back onto her pillow and squeezed her eyes closed, trying to shut out the awful dream.

"It was just a dream," she whispered. Plimmwald was not burning. It was not being attacked. Her brother and sister were not in danger. No one blamed her for Geitbart attacking their town.

But it could happen. Perhaps the dream was a specter of the future. What was it the old women used to say? If you dreamed something three times it was bound to come true. *Oh, Father God, please don't let me dream it again.*

⁓

Avelina and the other nine ladies bundled up in their warmest cloaks and various head coverings, left their maidservants behind, and went to the patch of ground in front of the stables where they were supposed to mount their horses and make their way down the castle mount to the walled town of Thornbeck, a short ride to the west.

As she walked beside Lady Magdalen, Avelina asked her if she was well.

"Very well. But will you laugh at me if I admit I miss my sisters and brother, and even my mother?"

"Of course not. If I had a mother, I should miss her, and I miss—" Avelina was about to say she missed her brother and sister too! Her face burned. Then she remembered—Lady Dorothea's mother was also dead.

"Are you well?" Magdalen studied her.

"Oh yes." Avelina laughed nervously. "I am very well."

"Is there anyone you shall miss," Lady Magdalen lowered her voice to a whisper, "should Lord Thornbeck choose to wed you?"

"I do not think he would ever choose me. But if I must wed someone far away, I suppose I would miss all the familiar faces of home." She tried to think as Lady Dorothea would. "But I don't suppose there is anyone I would miss enough to make me sad, as long as I was content with my husband."

Magdalen looked thoughtful. "Lady Gertrudt has an older

brother, the Duke of Wolfberg, who is unmarried and not betrothed to anyone."

"Is he well looking?"

"We met once as children. I am looking forward to seeing him again at the first ball. He is coming so the ladies will have enough partners."

As the stable boys were helping the other young ladies find their horses, Magdalen said, "May I tell you a secret? You must promise not to tell."

"I will not tell."

"Mother says if I don't marry Lord Thornbeck, she may try to betroth me to the Duke of Wolfberg. His father died a few years ago and he is the only son. Although it is quite unlikely he would accept me, since I have no real fortune to bring to the marriage."

Avelina did not have a chance to discuss the young man any further, because the stable boys approached with their two horses. The other young ladies were already mounted, and Lady Fronicka was talking to Lord Thornbeck. The margrave, who rode a large black horse, gave orders to four of his men, who were apparently accompanying them.

By the time Avelina and Magdalen had mounted their horses, most of the rest of the group had already started on the winding road that led down through the forest to the town.

Avelina's horse suddenly began snorting and sidestepping.

"Is everything all right?" Magdalen asked.

"I don't know what's wrong with her." Avelina hung on to the reins and tried not to lose her balance. "I rode her all the way here from Plimmwald. She was very gentle."

Wasn't anyone noticing what was happening? The two guards who were supposed to bring up the rear were talking to each other and laughing. Should she call for help? Should she pull back on the reins or give the horse slack? What was wrong with her un-cooperative horse?

Her horse screamed and raised her front legs in the air. Avelina clutched the mare's mane, trying desperately not to fall off.

"Someone help!" Magdalen called. "Help us!"

Two stable boys ran toward them and tried to grab the reins, but Avelina's horse pawed the air with her powerful hooves. The boys could not get close enough to reach the reins.

Avelina was losing her balance. Her grip on the horse was slipping, even as she was slipping from the saddle.

Suddenly Lord Thornbeck rode straight up beside her and grabbed the reins. "Hold on to me!"

While Lord Thornbeck forcefully pulled back on the reins and leaned on the horse's neck, Avelina clutched Lord Thornbeck's shoulders. His arm encircled her waist as he lifted her out of the saddle. He held her tight against his side until the stable workers were able to take the reins. Then he lowered her.

Her feet touched the ground and her knees crumpled.

8

MAGDALEN DISMOUNTED AND hurried to Avelina's side. "Are you hurt?"

Avelina leaned on her arm. "No, I am well." She was breathing hard and shaking.

"Hans," Lord Thornbeck ordered, "check this horse. Check the bit and the bridle, then check the saddle. You"—he pointed to the second stable boy—"saddle the brown mare with the one white leg for Lady Dorothea."

The margrave turned toward her. Their eyes met. His expression softened. But she was very fanciful, her father often told her. She was probably imagining it.

"My lord, here is the problem." The stable boy, Hans, held up two large shards of pottery with sharp edges and points. "They were under the saddle."

"How did those get there?" Lord Thornbeck's expression was thunderous.

"I don't know, my lord."

"Someone knows. Who saddled this horse?" The margrave shouted, glaring at any stable boy who was foolish enough to meet his eye. "I demand to know who saddled this horse. When I find out who put these sharp pieces of pottery under this saddle, I shall have him beaten and placed in the pillory in the town square."

An older man, possibly the stable master, came toward them.

"See that you find out who is responsible." Lord Thornbeck held out his hand and the boy gave him the shards. "I will not tolerate such shoddy supervision. If I find you have been negligent, you shall be punished and sent away."

The stable master looked quite ashamed as he bowed his head before Lord Thornbeck. "Forgive me, my lord. I shall do my best to discover who did this."

Lord Thornbeck did not give the poor man another glance but placed the pottery shards in his leather saddlebag.

Avelina's stomach felt sick, her heart beating hard and fast.

Meanwhile the other horse was saddled and a stable boy helped Avelina mount. She was still shaking after nearly being thrown from her horse. She closed her eyes for a moment and it flooded back to her—how Lord Thornbeck had rushed to save her, how he had pulled her off the horse with one arm, her body pressed against his as he carefully lowered her to the ground.

Instead of dwelling on that, she should be thinking about who might have placed those shards of pottery under her horse's saddle. But why would anyone want to harm her?

Magdalen and Avelina set off, accompanied by Lord Thornbeck and the two guards.

Lord Thornbeck said, "Go on. I must speak with my guards, but I shall keep my eye on you."

He slowed his horse and fell behind them. She heard his voice behind her.

"One of my guests was in danger," he growled, "and you did not even look her way, talking and laughing as if you were at a wine festival. What do you have to say for your disgraceful behavior?"

The men mumbled something, then Lord Thornbeck warned them, "We shall speak of this later, and I shall expect a full explanation of what you were doing while someone was sabotaging a young lady's horse with intent to do her harm."

She imagined that angry scowl on his face as he rebuked his guards further, accusing them of nearly allowing an earl's daughter's death. The rumor that he had murdered his own brother darted through her thoughts.

They made their way down the castle mount on the road that led them through the thick forest. The trees were similar to the ones around Plimmwald, with oak, fir, and spruce, but this forest had more beech trees. It was late fall and a few of the trees still had their leaves, which were bright spots of color in the otherwise cloudy day.

After a quarter of an hour of riding, they came to the town gate.

When Avelina had passed by the gate on the way to the castle, it had been dark and she'd been too tired to even notice it. She stared up at it now. High and impressive, it was built into the brick-and-stone wall that surrounded the town. Two men stood guard, but they looked rather sleepy and dull—until they caught sight of Lord Thornbeck and his large party of about fifteen well-dressed guests riding toward them. They stood up straight and their eyes were suddenly alert.

Lord Thornbeck stopped to speak to them while the rest of the party moved through the gate and down the street.

Their guides were Chancellor Jorgen and his wife, Odette, who began telling the ladies the history of the town and of the margravate of Thornbeck. Fronicka and two others ignored her and talked among themselves, but the rest of the ladies seemed to be listening.

As it was not a market day, the streets were not very crowded or noisy, and there was no wind, so they could hear her quite well.

"This street is known as the Jewish section of town."

One of Fronicka's friends whispered rather loudly, "Jews? Did she say Jews live here?" She, Fronicka, and her friends wrinkled their noses and said, "*Ach*," and "Let's go faster."

Being Jewish was a lot like being a servant. No one outside your work status, or in their case, outside their ethnicity, wanted to have anything to do with you. But there was one difference: From the looks of the four-story, half-timber houses, many of the Jews were quite wealthy.

A little boy was walking with a young woman down the street toward them. Though they were well dressed, they kept their eyes focused down and did not meet anyone's gaze. Did Lord Thornbeck mistreat the Jews? Many towns had laws that prohibited Jews from belonging to any of the skilled workers' guilds, thus preventing them from having any but certain types of jobs. Some towns, she had heard, had expelled entire populations of Jewish people, blaming them for plague, for poisoning the town well, or other disasters. Were the woman and boy, both of them obviously Jewish, afraid of the margrave?

Her heart constricted. She knew how it felt to have other people treat you as no one at all. It was a matter of course for a servant girl, the daughter of a crippled stable worker. But to be looked down on simply because you were born Jewish—that somehow seemed even more unjust.

Just then she caught Chancellor Jorgen writing something in a tiny book. Was he spying on them so he could report back to Lord Thornbeck? What was he looking for?

Magdalen was looking at Odette and the chancellor out of the corner of her eye. Was she also noticing that something was going on besides just a tour of the town?

Somehow Avelina had to figure out how to make Magdalen

stand out in Lord Thornbeck's eyes. But to do that, she needed to know what he valued, what he was searching for in a wife.

They passed on from the Jewish section of town and entered what Odette called the skilled workers' section. "This street over here is where you will find many butchers' shops." The air smelled faintly of raw meat.

Most of the ladies wore bored expressions, and some even slightly resentful. Avelina imagined they were irritated that they were not being entertained. Taking a tour of the streets of this town, encountering ordinary people who did not even know that they were the daughters of dukes, earls, and barons, was not their idea of being treated as they deserved.

Odette took them down a side street. "We shall leave our horses at the town stable and walk the rest of the way."

The ladies stared at each other with open mouths. One or two scowled and grumbled under their breath, but they all complied.

How would Lady Dorothea have reacted? No doubt she would have been as indignant as Fronicka and her friends appeared. Dorothea might have even protested, saying something like, "We are noble-born ladies. We are not accustomed to soiling our feet on the common streets of town."

But no one complained loudly enough to be heard, and they all dismounted, including Lord Thornbeck, who was only a few feet away, observing them.

She supposed she could not blame him for watching them, for wanting to know the character of the woman he would marry, wanting to make the wisest choice. Still, it made her feel a bit like cattle, lined up and waiting for the farmer to choose who to kill for the king's Christmas feast. But these ladies, especially the three or four who always had such passive expressions on their faces, were used to thinking of themselves as pawns to be married off to a powerful or wealthy man in order to benefit their fathers. They were well aware they had no say in the matter of who they wed. Therefore, they could have no say in how someone as powerful as the Margrave of Thornbeck chose his bride from among them.

Avelina had always imagined that someday she would be fortunate enough to marry someone who fell in love with her first. She had written about such a happening in many of her stories, imagining all the ways it might happen for her.

She was a poor servant girl. And even though it was unlikely she'd ever be wed to someone wealthy or powerful, no one was telling her who she must marry.

At least there was one blessing to being poor.

After handing off their horses to the stable workers, they set out on foot.

"It seems a pleasant town," Magdalen said as they walked side by side.

"Yes, it does." Avelina caught sight of Lord Thornbeck. She subtly tried to move Magdalen closer to him, hoping he would notice how pretty Magdalen looked today, with her pale, reddish-blonde hair only partially covered by her thin veil, wearing a silk dress that was a very attractive shade of light green.

Fronicka was at that moment calling out to the margrave, asking him to walk with her and tell her what to think of his quaint little town. "None of these buildings compare to Thornbeck Castle, of course, but you shall tell me the more favorable parts."

The margrave replied in a voice too quiet for Avelina to hear. He must have begged off, for he walked toward Chancellor Jorgen and talked privately with him. Fronicka did not look pleased.

As they continued on, Odette said, "Bakers Street is just ahead, and you can probably already smell the fresh bread."

Avelina took in a deep breath through her nose. The smell

reminded her of the kitchen at Plimmwald Castle, and she felt a tiny pang of homesickness. What mischief were Jacob and Brigitta up to today? She hoped they stayed out of trouble and did not annoy Father too much.

Father should not be too cross with them. Surely they knew to go to their neighbors if they got hurt or needed anything. Father was not the most tender man. Since Mother died, there had been much less order in all of their lives, and there would have been even less if Avelina did not provide it.

But surely they could survive three weeks without her.

". . . And this is the new Thornbeck Orphanage, which is in the old Menkels home. Our margrave has graciously established, with the help of the citizens of Thornbeck, a home for orphans who have no family to take them in."

Most of the other ladies were talking among themselves, but Avelina was staring up at the beautiful brick-and-timber house. She could not even imagine Lord Plimmwald wanting to establish an orphanage. Lord Thornbeck must be at least somewhat kind to care enough about poor orphans to start an orphanage.

She looked over her shoulder at him. He was staring straight ahead but then took a couple of glances at the home.

Through the open upper-floor window, Avelina could hear children's lively chatter. A laugh, then an exclamation, then more chatter.

She suddenly missed Jacob and Brigitta even more. Would they be proud of her for going to Thornbeck, for helping Plimmwald, for securing Lord Thornbeck's protection over their town and everyone she knew and loved? She imagined her father telling her, "Good work, Ava. And quick thinking, asking for the pork and goose for our table and dowry money for you."

Of course, that was assuming Lord Plimmwald made good on his promise. He might very well renege and pretend not to remember what he promised her. And it was not like her father to give her praise. Even so, she would have the satisfaction of knowing she had done something no other servant girl in Plimmwald had ever done.

A woman's face appeared at a third-floor window of the orphanage, smiled as though she had been expecting them, then disappeared.

They moved on down the cobblestone street, attracting the attention of everyone who saw them. Some people even followed them, staring curiously. It probably was not every day that the margrave came to town and walked the streets, along with ten—or nine, as it was—noble ladies who hoped to marry said margrave.

"And this is called Merchant Street," Odette went on, "because many of the people who live here are merchants and their families."

The homes were the most beautiful she had seen yet, besides the orphanage. They were truly impressive in their beauty, size, and artistry, and Avelina could not stop staring. There were not nearly so many wealthy merchants in Plimmwald.

Finally, they came to Thornbeck Cathedral, a massively tall structure with intricately carved spires ascending into the sky, and statues built into the eaves and walls. The front was dominated by an enormous stained-glass window that followed the shape of the door beneath and the roof above. Samson grappled with lions in the colorful depiction. Samson was a symbol of the region of Thornbeck and appeared on the town crest and on tapestries and paintings she had noticed in the castle.

"The *Dom* was completed seventy-five years ago," Frau Hartman said, "and took more than fifty years to build. King Ludwig the Fourth worshipped here on a visit to Thornbeck many years ago. He said there was no finer Dom in all the Kingdom of Germany."

Truly, the cathedral was beautiful. Odette continued to talk of all that made the church unique as three little boys ran up to them and started begging with their hands out. "Please, can you spare some money? I have not eaten in three days," one little boy said. All three of them had dirt smeared on their faces. Their clothing was ragged and patched.

They approached Fronicka and her friends, but the noble ladies actually cried out, stepping back and pulling their arms against their bodies, as if they were afraid the little boys would touch them and give them leprosy.

"Go away!" Fronicka shooed them with her hands.

The boys approached another of the ladies. "Please, give me something."

They went from one of the ladies to the next, but none of them gave them anything. Most of them only shook their heads or turned physically away from them, wrinkling their noses.

Avelina's heart sank, wishing she had something to give them, but she had nothing, only two small coins in her purse back at the castle.

When they approached Magdalen and Avelina, Magdalen had already reached into the purse she had tucked into her sleeve and was ready with some coins. She placed one coin in each of their hands. Avelina's heart swelled, so glad her friend had given them something. The margrave should give them something too.

"Cannot we buy them some food? Lord Thornbeck?" Avelina glanced around for the margrave, and he was suddenly by her side.

"Go buy some cakes at the bakery," Lord Thornbeck told the boys, taking Magdalen's coins out of their hands and replacing them with his own money. "Go on, now."

The little boys smiled and ran off toward Bakers Street, laughing playfully. And Lord Thornbeck gave Magdalen her coins back.

"Thank you for your generosity, but they will be provided for." He bowed and walked on.

What did he mean by "they will be provided for"? She had never seen beggars who behaved like those boys had—carefree and joyful, a ready smile on their faces. Something was odd.

She and Magdalen exchanged a look. Avelina glanced behind them. Just as she thought, Chancellor Jorgen was marking in his little book with his piece of charcoal.

Lord Thornbeck walked back and spoke quietly again with his chancellor, then the margrave announced, "Let us fetch the horses and return to the castle."

"Isn't it strange we didn't even make it to the *Marktplatz* and the town center?" Avelina leaned close to Magdalen's ear. "We didn't even see the *Rathous* or the guild houses."

"Perhaps he was afraid we were tired."

But that did not make sense. Also, she was beginning to think the begging was a mummery and the mud-smeared boys were players. But why?

9

LATER THAT AFTERNOON Reinhart sat at his desk in the library, Jorgen nearby at his own desk with Odette beside him.

Reinhart had not missed the way the ladies had more or less cringed away from the boys from the orphanage who had volunteered to put dirt on their faces and go begging to them. They had done a good job of it—it probably wasn't their first time to beg.

He also had not missed Lady Magdalen giving them coins and Lady Dorothea calling to him and asking him to buy them food.

And when they had passed the Jewish part of town, Lady Dorothea had had a look of great concern on her face and stared long at the little boy and young woman. It was very telling of her character, he thought.

"I shall write out my notes in a more legible form and get them to you later today," Jorgen said.

"Lady Dorothea and Lady Magdalen certainly have the most Christian charity toward orphans," Odette said, "and they never complained about having to walk in town."

It would be worth all the indignity of the testing of the ladies' characters if he were able to find a woman who had similar values. There was no reason why this process should not work well, no reason why he should not get precisely what he wanted.

Odette seemed to think his silence was a hint that she should leave, because she stood and curtsied. "I shall go now, Lord Thornbeck, and allow you and Jorgen to discuss his notes."

He nodded to her. "You and Jorgen have done well."

She curtsied again and left the room.

Reinhart tried to concentrate on the numbers and lists on his desk, of the expenses of the previous month, but his mind kept wandering, mostly to Lady Dorothea.

"Here are my notes from today's outing to town." Jorgen stood by his desk, holding out a sheet of parchment.

He took it from him. "I suppose you wish to tell me your impressions, which ladies you think distinguished themselves."

"Lady Magdalen and Lady Dorothea were the only ones who passed the compassion test in my estimation, my lord. And you, my lord? What did you think?"

Reinhart was not used to confiding in anyone. Growing up as a squire in a castle of men whose tastes and humor were often ribald and unrefined, he had avoided spending his spare time with them. And as a knight, he often found a quiet place to be alone, to read or study or pray. The knights who never seemed to want to be alone were often the troublemakers, and he preferred to spend as little time with them as possible. Perhaps that was why he rose so quickly to become the captain of the Duke of Pomerania's guard. The duke commented many times on his "serious" nature and his superior knowledge, how he did not carouse with the other men who had a penchant for women and strong spirits.

"They both seem like good choices for you, my lord."

"They are both good prospects, perhaps. Though Lady Magdalen is too young for me." Was he saying this because he already felt a preference for Lady Dorothea? Certainly Dorothea was beautiful, and he thought her appealingly forthright in her private audience with him. But he must not allow himself to be swayed by fickle, unreliable feelings. He did not want something as silly as beauty to cloud his judgment. After all, once he was married, beauty would mean little. But she was passing most of their tests.

There was the little matter of Lady Dorothea's father betraying him by telling the king that he believed Reinhart to have murdered his own brother. Could he trust the Earl of Plimmwald or his daughter? The king obviously thought it would be wise for him to heal the breach by marrying the earl's daughter, but might Lady Dorothea become like his mother, resentful and unfaithful?

"True, Lady Magdalen is a bit young," Jorgen said.

"We shall learn more about them both as the two weeks progress."

Jorgen nodded his agreement, a small smile on his face. Reinhart fought back a growl and cleared his throat instead. Jorgen and Odette were enjoying this wife search, as if they thought he was "falling in love" like an addled youth or a peasant farmer. He hardly found this enjoyable. For him, too much was at stake.

Avelina and Magdalen sat in the two cushioned, throne-like chairs in Avelina's bedchamber. The sun was going down and the windows were closed and shuttered against the wind that whistled just outside.

"I think the margrave, the chancellor, and Odette are setting up tests for us," Avelina confided.

"Tests?" Magdalen's brows lowered, then lifted. "Oh yes! You mean the way the chancellor and Lord Thornbeck were watching us when we were in town."

Avelina nodded, tapping her chin with her finger. "He has only a short time to choose a wife. He probably wants to find out how we will react in different situations. I can hardly blame him, I suppose, but it seems a bit . . . cold and deceptive."

"No." Magdalen shook her head. "I would not say cold. He doesn't want to marry someone who does not care about the same things he cares about. Perhaps it is a bit deceptive, but it is wise, and it shows he takes his marriage vows seriously. I think it is endearing."

Avelina hardly had the right to criticize him for being deceptive when she herself was deceiving them all. She lowered her voice a bit. "I think the tour of Thornbeck was a test. And they had the children begging because they wanted to see what we would do."

"I did remember thinking the children didn't look like beggars. They were dirty and their clothes were worn, but their eyes . . . they were cheerful. Not really sad at all."

"Yes, exactly." Avelina sat up and leaned toward Magdalen. "And did you see the way the chancellor was writing in his little book? And the way Lord Thornbeck took the money and gave it back to you, then gave the children some money himself and said that they would be provided for? I think they were from the orphanage that we passed, and he, or perhaps Odette, had the children come and beg for money and say they were hungry."

Magdalen's eyes were wide and her mouth hung open. She was so sweet and beautiful. She would make a wonderful margrave's wife. Avelina had already made up her mind that the margrave had not killed his brother. She simply could not believe anyone who was so particular about who he was going to marry, and who seemed so concerned about orphans, could have done such a despicable thing. At least, she hoped not.

"I think the margrave wanted to see if we cared about orphans—to see who among us would be kind to them and who would treat them as if they were offensive. And you, my dear Lady Magdalen, have surpassed their trial." Avelina clasped her hands and grinned. This was going to be easy. He might even choose Magdalen without any help from Avelina.

Magdalen shook her head. "He could have simply asked us what we think of the poor."

"He could have asked, but we might say whatever we think he wants to hear. By testing us he can be more certain of what is in our hearts. Our actions are more truthful. Do you not agree?"

"It does sound likely."

A knock came at the door.

"That is probably Hegatha worried about me getting to bed late."

Avelina opened the door to Magdalen's maidservant, who looked old enough to be her grandmother.

"Forgive me, Lady Dorothea, but Magdalen needs to be in bed soon. Come, Magdalen."

"I shall be there in a moment, Hegatha." Magdalen nodded to her, and the servant closed the door with a grumpy look.

Magdalen smiled apologetically. "Come to my room tomorrow. We can speak about it some more, before the ball."

They wished each other a good night and Magdalen left.

Irma wandered into the bedchamber and plopped down on Avelina's bed. "I thought she would never leave. I'm always afraid I will call you Avelina instead of Dorothea when other people are around. Keeping the secret that you are not an earl's daughter . . . I don't know if I can do it for two entire weeks."

Avelina expelled the breath from her lungs. "Don't even say a thing like that. You *must* keep the secret. Everything depends upon it—our very lives. Do you know what Lord Plimmwald will do to us if—?"

"Yes, yes, I know. I know." Irma waved her hands. "Do not bring about a resurrection of the saints because of it." She sighed. "I shall be careful not to say anything. The earl threatened me too, you should know."

Somehow it didn't seem that difficult to Avelina to keep the secret. She was already feeling less and less deceptive in her role as a lady.

"Irma, do you ever feel . . . as if you should have been a lord's daughter? I mean, did you ever feel as though you are the same as they are?"

She raised one eyebrow. "Humph! No, and neither should you. Don't be getting too high and mighty just because Lord Plimmwald was in a well of trouble and had no one else to send in his daughter's place besides you. Just because you get to wear Lady Plimmwald's old dresses and strut around like a princess and do nothing all day." Irma shook her finger at Avelina's nose. "You'll be back at Plimmwald Castle soon with the rest of us lowly servants."

Avelina put her hands on her hips, trying to think of an apt retort. Finally, she turned away and crossed her arms.

She should not have confided in Irma. Perhaps she *was* getting puffed up, being around earls' and dukes' daughters all day, being indulged and treated like a lady. But the truth was, for as long as she had known the daughter of the Earl of Plimmwald was vain and selfish and petty, Avelina had felt that she was no less noble than Lady Dorothea. A person's heart should be what she was judged by, rather than whose blood ran in her veins. She had told herself she could behave with as much nobility of spirit as any lady she had met so far.

Except for Lady Magdalen. Unlike Avelina, Magdalen was kind and gentle and probably never had a selfish thought in her life.

Magdalen deserved someone wealthy and powerful, and most

importantly, she deserved someone kind and good. And though Lord Thornbeck sometimes looked quite severe and frightening, and he had a bad temper at times, he was much better than most other noblemen Magdalen might end up married to. And if Avelina had anything to do with it, Magdalen would end up married to him.

⟿

"The truth is," Avelina told Magdalen the next day, "I cannot dance. I never learned."

Magdalen stared at her in shock. "How is that possible? Did no one try to teach you?"

"My father never hired a tutor for me." In the strictest sense, this was true. While Lord Plimmwald had made sure his daughter had learned every dance known to the noble class of the Holy Roman Empire, Avelina's father told her that her duty was to Lord Plimmwald and his daughter and had never let her go to the festivals with the other peasant girls, where they danced and played games. She should be grateful that she had a place in the earl's household and did not have to work in a field all day in the sun and rain and mud.

But she couldn't tell Magdalen that.

"Did your father never hold balls and parties at Plimmwald Castle? Did he not want you to attract the attention of a nobleman who would want to marry you?"

"No." Avelina shook her head, trying to look innocent. And there had been very few balls and parties for Lady Dorothea either. She had once heard the earl say that he planned to arrange Dorothea's marriage, and therefore there was no use in holding dances at the castle or sending her elsewhere to balls.

Perhaps that was one reason she ran off with Sir Dietric.

"What if Lord Thornbeck is angry with you for not dancing? You must let me teach you how." Lady Magdalen looked at her thoughtfully.

"Do you think you can teach me in one afternoon?"

"Perhaps not all the dances, but most of them are simple." Magdalen explained and demonstrated some of the dances, helping Avelina practice them.

"But how will I know which dance they are dancing?" Avelina asked. "I am certain to make a fool of myself in front of everyone. Besides, I told Lord Thornbeck that I would not dance, and he did not say anything."

Magdalen merely smiled in her pleasant, calm way. "You will have ever so much more fun if you dance. Come. It is not so difficult. We shall go through the steps again. You can learn these two dances, and if they are dancing something you do not know or recognize, you can say you are tired. But you must dance."

It did seem as if it would be fun, if she knew what she was doing. So they continued to practice until they were both laughing and out of breath.

Hegatha came into the room, a stern, disapproving look on her face. "Dear Magdalen, you must not tire yourself before the ball tonight."

"I shall go." Avelina clasped Magdalen's hand. "Thank you ever so much."

"You are most welcome." She leaned closer and whispered, "I am sorry Hegatha is so rude. You do not have to go."

"I should go get ready for the ball. Thank you again."

Avelina hurried down the corridor to her own chamber. It was a bit exciting to think of going to a ball and actually dancing.

10

He never should have let Jorgen and Odette talk him into having not one but two dances.

Reinhart stood in the large ballroom at the bottom of the stairs. Already the men were assembled. He had asked several young noblemen to come to the ball so the ladies would have enough partners for the dances.

He couldn't dance, with his permanent limp and injured ankle. But the ball was another of Jorgen and Odette's tests, a trial of vanity and pride. They would not have quite enough men for all the ladies to have a partner, so they would be able to observe how each lady dealt with this. Would they vie for partners? Or would they allow another lady to dance by sacrificing a dance or two? Would they compete for the best-looking and wealthiest men with the highest titles, or would they flirt with the margrave?

The second ball would take place on the last night of the two weeks. There he would reveal whom he had chosen to be his wife.

Already they were starting to come down the stairs to the ballroom floor.

The leader of the musicians was looking to Reinhart. He gave him a nod, and the musicians started to play, a sound that should draw the rest of the ladies from their rooms.

Jorgen strode toward him. "My lord, you are in a very good place from which to observe while everyone is dancing. Are you sure you do not wish some paper and a piece of charcoal for taking notes?"

"I shall rely on my memory."

Jorgen bowed and hurried away.

Reinhart spoke to his male guests. When they had all been properly greeted and stood talking with each other, he counted the men silently. Only nine, just as planned.

Lady Fronicka was coming toward him. No other ladies had dared to approach him, but he should know already that Lady Fronicka was not timid.

"Lord Thornbeck, your castle is perfectly suited for a ball. I am very eager to dance, for I love to dance and could dance all night." She smiled at him. At least her lips smiled, but her eyes seemed to be calculating exactly what kind of reaction she was getting from him.

She chattered on about balls and dancing. He signaled the musicians once again to announce the first dance.

"I shall find myself a partner," she said, "but I wish I could dance with you, my lord."

When he did not react to her statement, she turned away and approached a group of young men. One of them immediately led her to the middle of the dance floor. Quickly more couples followed. Soon the only person left was Lady Dorothea. She was standing alone on the other side of the room.

The music began. The dance was a rather complicated one, but the dancers all appeared to be proficient. For the first time Reinhart was glad for his lame ankle, since he was completely unfamiliar with the steps of this dance.

By the end all the ladies were smiling. There must be something about dancing that they enjoyed. Perhaps it was the way he used to feel when he had practiced sword fighting and jousting with the other knights—invigorated and alive. But with his lame ankle . . . he wondered if he would ever feel invigorated and alive, if he was always to feel somewhat weak and useless.

A second dance was immediately announced. The couples changed partners. One of the young men left the group and appeared to be asking Lady Dorothea to dance. She shook her head, smiling. He went back to his partner, and the dance began.

Reinhart started walking around the perimeter of the room and made his way to the other side and to Lady Dorothea. "So you do not wish to dance?"

Instead of smiling with all teeth showing, as Fronicka did, there was only a slight upturn to the corners of her lips.

"I never learned this particular dance, I'm afraid. Please do not concern yourself, though. I am perfectly content to listen to the music."

He was not so sure he believed her. After all, what lady had never been taught these well-known dances? But it might embarrass her if he pressed her to join the dancers. And since she wished to listen to the music, he said no more.

"Lady Magdalen looks very pretty tonight," she suddenly said.

He caught sight of Lady Magdalen dancing with a young duke's son. "Indeed."

Was she so unselfish that she would wish to draw his attention to another lady's beauty? Perhaps she did not wish to marry him herself and that was why she was trying to make him think of Lady Magdalen.

"Did you know that lady before you came here?"

"No, we only just met, but I like her very much. She is kind. There is no pettiness or jealousy in her, and she is very openhearted.

Those are very good qualities in a margrave's wife, I think, to care about her people in such a way. She is also a good dancer."

"Indeed. And do you not also have those same characteristics, Lady Dorothea?"

She looked up at him with wide eyes, her lips parted, as if his question had frightened her. "I . . . Me?"

The dance ended and the musicians announced the next dance. Lady Magdalen was coming toward them.

"Lady Dorothea, you know this dance," Magdalen said, a little breathless. "You should dance."

Just then, one of the young noblemen asked Lady Dorothea to dance. "Yes, I thank you," she said.

She let the young man lead her to the group of dancers, leaving Lady Magdalen standing beside Reinhart.

"I thought Lady Dorothea did not wish to dance." He eyed Lady Magdalen.

"I think she will enjoy this one." Magdalen had a very placid look on her face as she watched the dancers.

"Do you enjoy dancing?"

"Yes, but I did not think she could have wanted to stand here all night. Oh, forgive me." She turned to him with a sheepish look. "I did not mean to say that she would not have enjoyed talking with you."

He could not help a slight smile. "Do not distress yourself. I understand what you meant."

But his words did not seem to put Lady Magdalen at ease. Instead she turned a bit paler as she watched the dancers and chewed on her lip.

They were silent until the song ended, at which time Fronicka hurried over and nudged Lady Magdalen out of the way to get close to him.

"You must forgive us ladies for enjoying ourselves so much while we dance," Fronicka said.

The musicians announced another dance, but Fronicka turned so she was facing Reinhart, ignoring everyone else.

"I shall stay by your side for this dance, my lord, even though I do enjoy dancing very much. I would much rather talk with you."

He looked down at her. "That is very sacrificial of you."

She blinked, looking as if she did not know how to respond to that. She was not nonplussed for long. "I do love this room. The floors are beautiful and I've never seen such a perfect room for dancing."

Fronicka continued to talk about the room and the castle as everyone else started to dance. Everyone, that is, except Lady Dorothea, who stood nearby, talking with one of the young noblemen, the Duke of Wolfberg. Did Lady Dorothea think him handsome? He was younger than Reinhart, and as a duke, his rank was higher. Besides that, he had two strong ankles, unlike him. Was Wolfberg complimenting her as she smiled and glanced down at her hands? Why were they not dancing?

"What do you know of Lady Dorothea?" Fronicka suddenly asked. "There was some rumor I had heard about her from some travelers who came from Plimmwald. I'm sure it cannot be true."

"What rumor?" Reinhart purposely kept his tone bland.

"Oh, I would never repeat it. Something about Lady Dorothea and one of her father's knights, Sir Dietric. I am sure it cannot be true. People do gossip, especially the lower classes."

Reinhart forced himself not to react to her words. Calmly he said, "If you are sure it cannot be true, I am surprised you mention it."

Lady Fronicka opened her mouth to speak, closed it, then opened it again. "I do not know why . . . I say whatever comes to my mind. It is my greatest fault. But I cannot help it if someone blurts out such gossip in my hearing. I would not wish to hurt Lady Dorothea with such false gossip, which I am sure is exactly what it was. After all, if she truly were with child, it would show. I am sure it must not be true."

He glanced at Lady Dorothea as she spoke to the Duke of Wolfberg. Her face had such a look of innocence and modesty. Was it false? Was she pregnant with the child of her father's knight? Or was Fronicka only trying to make Lady Dorothea look bad? But the information was so detailed—she gave the name of the knight Lady Dorothea was supposed to be in love with.

His stomach churned. He hated that he was even considering that this rumor might be true, especially about Lady Dorothea. But he also needed to know if it was true.

11

Avelina stood with the Duke of Wolfberg. Even though she enjoyed talking with him, she reminded herself of the fact that he was not a stable boy or a manservant, but a handsome duke.

She had made it through the one dance with the young baron's son with the prominent front teeth. She only made two or three mistakes, including stepping on his foot. She'd been mortified, but he merely smiled and pretended not to notice. She never would have danced if not for wanting to give Lady Magdalen a chance to talk with Lord Thornbeck. He was so much less intimidating when one was speaking directly with him, with no one else around. She would almost say he was pleasant, and that there was gentleness, if one were able to get beneath his austere margrave facade. Perhaps Lady Magdalen would think so too if she had a chance to talk to him for a bit.

Surely he would fall in love with Lady Magdalen and choose her to be his bride. Who could not love her, with her sweet smile and calm contentment? She was sophisticated yet friendly and welcoming. She was everything a noblewoman should be. Lord Thornbeck must see that, if he spoke with her for even the length of time it took to dance one dance.

So Avelina had muddled through the dance. At least while

she was dancing, Lady Fronicka had stopped trying to poison her with every hate-filled glance she threw her way while Avelina stood talking to Lord Thornbeck.

But when the music began again, the baron's son moved away and asked someone else, and the Duke of Wolfberg had asked her to dance. She begged off, admitting to him that she was afraid she did not know the steps very well and would disgrace herself. He smiled most kindly—everyone was ever so kind to the woman they thought was Lady Dorothea—and stood talking with her, while Lady Fronicka dominated Lord Thornbeck's attention.

"Were you glad to get Lord Thornbeck's invitation to Thornbeck Castle?" the Duke of Wolfberg asked. "I was very glad to get away from home for a few days."

"Oh, I have been pleasantly surprised at how enjoyable it has been."

He opened his mouth as if to say something else, but a commotion seemed to be interrupting the musicians, who broke off their song on a discordant note.

Avelina and the duke both turned their heads to see who was shouting. A woman, looking very out of place in her dull-gray woolen kirtle and a bedraggled wimple covering her hair, was shaking her finger at the musicians.

"You should not be here," she cried. "You were never here before. Annlin! Annlin!" She turned and cupped her mouth with her hands. "Annlin!" she called up the stairs.

"The woman must surely be mad," the duke said quietly, as everyone in the room was now staring at her.

Lord Thornbeck, leaning on his cane, was walking toward her. Would he have her punished? Sent away with an angry rebuke for disturbing the ball?

"You there!" Lord Thornbeck shouted at a manservant. "Who's responsible for watching her tonight?"

Jorgen appeared from the other end of the room and hurried toward them. The chancellor took the older woman's elbow and nudged her toward the stairs. Lord Thornbeck said something near his ear, then turned and came back toward his guests.

The woman was still mumbling as though confused, but she complied with Jorgen and let him walk her up the stairs and away from the guests.

Lord Thornbeck nodded to the musicians as he rejoined Fronicka and several others at the perimeter of the room. The musicians soon announced another dance, but most of the guests remained clustered around Lord Thornbeck.

"Go back to dancing," he said. "We shall have our dinner soon, so make the most of the music."

"I wonder who that woman was," the Duke of Wolfberg commented.

The woman could not be his mother, since his mother was dead. He didn't have any sisters that she knew of, and the woman looked too old to be his sister anyway. Besides, she was wearing the clothing of a peasant or servant. But it was very strange to see a servant behaving in such a way. Lord Plimmwald would never have tolerated it. A servant like that would have been summarily sent away and ordered never to return to the castle. But Lord Thornbeck's chancellor escorted her upstairs.

The ladies slowly rejoined the dance. It was the simplest type of dance, one of the two Magdalen had shown her and that she had practiced, so when the Duke of Wolfberg asked her, she accepted. She didn't want to attract too much attention to herself, after all. If she only danced once, it might raise suspicions about her.

She concentrated on stepping correctly, keeping the other

dancers in the edges of her vision, making sure she was moving in the right direction.

Lord Thornbeck was once again talking with Fronicka. Was he falling for her charming friendliness and big smiles?

Avelina made it through the dance without stepping on the duke's toes. For the next dance, the Duke of Wolfberg asked Magdalen—they made a very good-looking couple—while Avelina stood alone, trying not to hear what Fronicka was saying to Lord Thornbeck.

However, she couldn't help noticing the margrave glancing in her direction occasionally. Truly, she felt out of place just standing there, the only person who was neither dancing nor talking with anyone. Would she stand here alone for the rest of the night?

When that song ended, Magdalen and the Duke of Wolfberg came toward her.

"We are tired of dancing," Magdalen said, "and decided we would come over and keep you company."

For the next dance, most of the young people wandered toward Lord Thornbeck and Fronicka, prompting the margrave to turn away from her and talk to some of his other guests. Only a few couples remained dancing. Fronicka's expression was quite dark as she glared at whoever dared talk to Lord Thornbeck.

Neither Magdalen nor the Duke of Wolfberg seemed to notice. They were near enough that Avelina could hear them talking about the time they had met each other as children, when his parents had come to Mallin. Magdalen's father was still alive then.

Lord Thornbeck was scowling and did not look pleased with having more than one person trying to talk to him at once. He signaled the musicians and they stopped playing. A few moments later a servant announced that it was time to move to the Great Hall for the meal.

Some of the ladies were smiling and even laughing, talking with the young men as they all moved toward the doorway. Avelina fell back a bit behind Magdalen and the Duke of Wolfberg, when someone touched her elbow.

"Lady Dorothea." Lord Thornbeck spoke in a quiet voice. "Will you step into the gallery with me for a moment?"

His face wore its usual brooding scowl, but there seemed to be something more than grumpiness in his eyes. What could he possibly want to say to her privately? Had he discovered that she was an imposter? How did he find out she was not Lady Dorothea?

Her heart pounded in her throat as she turned aside into the gallery.

His eyes bored into hers, but his expression was slack, as if he was trying to hide his thoughts. "Lady Fronicka said she heard a rumor that you were with child. I do not want to falsely accuse anyone or think of this rumor for one moment longer, so please tell me now if it is true or not, and I will accept your word."

"I—no! No, I . . . I am not with child." She shook her head as she had when she was twelve and Lord Plimmwald had accused her of stealing a pair of Dorothea's shoes. Avelina's hands trembled as she held them down by her sides, hiding them in the folds of her dress. "I cannot imagine where Lady Fronicka may have heard such a thing. I—"

"She said you were in love with one of your father's knights. If this is true, you may tell me and I shall not judge you or tell anyone. I only want to know."

"No, I am not in love with my father's knight." But wasn't she being deceptive? Everyone believed her to be Lady Dorothea, and if she were Dorothea, then what she was saying was a lie. But she was not. "I am not." She shrugged and shook her head, feeling breathless.

"She even gave me the name of the knight you were supposed to be in love with—a Sir Dietric."

"I—I have heard of him. He is one of my father's best knights. But I have never so much as spoken five words with him. I assure you, I am not in love with him, and I certainly am not carrying anyone's child." A nervous laugh threatened to escape her throat, which would have been quite out of place in this serious moment.

"Forgive me for asking and for bringing up such a thing. But she actually gave me the name of the knight."

"Yes, she must have heard someone speak of Sir Dietric, someone who had been to Plimmwald. Now that I think on it, I believe I heard my father say that Sir Dietric had gotten one of the maidens of Plimmwald with child. He was very displeased with his knight, as I remember. Someone must have overheard and thought they said Lady Dorothea was the maiden."

Avelina thought of how the real Lady Dorothea would react to this situation. She would be outraged—if she actually was not pregnant with Sir Dietric's child. But instead of feeling outraged, Avelina had the strangest feeling of regret that Lord Thornbeck would think even for one moment that she had been with a knight named Sir Dietric and was carrying his child. She couldn't bear to think she had disappointed him.

"Rumors often get started with a half-truth," he said. "Or a misunderstanding."

Was he thinking of the rumors that the Earl of Plimmwald had spread to the king himself about Lord Thornbeck murdering his brother?

"Of course. Very true." She should have told him she *was* in love with a knight, since that would have at least kept him from ever choosing her. But again, she could not bear to have him thinking ill of her. Besides, she was too afraid he would send her home in disgrace, and then Lord Plimmwald would certainly not reward her.

"Come." He held his arm out to her. "I shall escort you to the Great Hall before someone comes looking for us."

Her hands still shook a little from the shock of Lord Thornbeck asking her about Lady Dorothea's secret baby. But at least Fronicka did *not* realize Avelina was her maidservant in disguise. Lord Thornbeck seemed to believe Avelina and to believe that Fronicka's damning information about her was untrue. All was well as she managed to breathe evenly entering the Great Hall with the margrave. All the guests were already seated and talking amongst themselves.

Fronicka sat at the right of the head of the table, the place where she could best command the margrave's attention. All the places at that end of the table were taken. There was nowhere left for Avelina except at the other end of the table—which suited Avelina quite well, since Lady Magdalen and the Duke of Wolfberg were sitting there. The other ladies didn't seem to realize who the Duke of Wolfberg was—that he was a wealthy man with a higher rank even than Lord Thornbeck.

Avelina was not surprised that Lord Thornbeck began walking her toward that end. He halted beside Lady Magdalen, allowing Avelina to sit next to her. But then he sat at the very end of the table, with Avelina to his right and the Duke of Wolfberg to his left.

Everyone else turned, with a few gasps, to stare at the margrave.

"I hope my guests do not mind," he said, "but I shall sit at this end of the table tonight."

A murmur went through the room. Avelina did not dare look down the table at Fronicka, but she could well imagine that lady's face turning red.

A servant came and filled Lord Thornbeck's and Avelina's

goblets. The margrave stood and raised his goblet. "I wish to drink to the health of the noble ladies here tonight who have graciously come to Thornbeck Castle. I pray you all enjoy yourselves while you are here, and God will show me which worthy lady among you should be my bride."

Everyone smiled their approval of his words and they all drank, including Avelina. *God, show him that Magdalen is the worthiest of all.*

At least now he might see Fronicka as a mean-spirited person who spread untrue rumors.

The young squires served the food and the margrave talked to the Duke of Wolfberg about his uncle, who had taken over after the young duke's father died.

Magdalen leaned over and whispered, "Fronicka looks like she swallowed a burning Yule log."

Avelina laughed out loud but quickly covered her mouth and stifled the sound.

"Perhaps you should sleep in my room tonight," Magdalen whispered. "She may have one of her servants put a few snakes and spiders in your bed."

"I shall push some heavy trunks and chairs in front of all door-ways so no one can get in."

When Avelina's stomach settled enough that she could eat, the food was as delicious as always. She was reminded of Irma's blissful moans the night before when speaking of the sweet fruit puddings she had eaten with the other servants in the kitchen. Truly, the margrave's cooks had a gift for mixing just the right amount of spices and other ingredients into their dishes.

"Are you enjoying the story of *The Song of Roland*?" Lord Thornbeck suddenly asked her, his gaze on her instead of the Duke of Wolfberg, who was now talking to Magdalen.

She swallowed her bite of roasted pig. "I like it very much. I shall return it to your library tomorrow, since I finished it already."

No one else seemed to be listening, as those near enough to hear were having their own conversations.

"Tell me about one of your stories."

"Are you sure you want to hear about my stories? I think you would find them silly."

"I already know your views on love and marriage. Do you think you will surprise me with your stories?" He lifted a brow at her.

"No, probably not." She couldn't help but smile.

His brown eyes focused intently on her and glimmered in the light of the dozens of candles around the room. Birds' wings fluttered in her stomach. Not scowling, his features relaxed, brought out the square masculinity of his chin and the short stubble on his jaw. But it was the thought of him wanting to know about her stories that made her stomach tumble inside her.

"The story I am writing now is about a . . . a servant girl who falls in love with a wealthy merchant's son." They leaned toward each other to catch the sound of the other's voice in the noisy Great Hall.

"What happens next?"

"The merchant's son ignores her until one day when she saves his life from bandits who try to rob him."

"And that causes him to fall in love with her?"

"No, not quite yet. He still thinks she is too poor to marry him. But when he sees how she sacrifices herself to save a young child from being trampled by a horse, she is injured, and he marries her as soon as she is able to walk again." Avelina shrugged. "I suppose it is foolish to write such stories."

"It sounds like a good story."

She wasn't sure if she believed him. "I am sure you have spent your time doing much more worthy things besides writing stories."

"I have spent my life either preparing for battle or fighting. I am not sure if those were worthy pursuits or not, now that all my training is for naught. Even if I had not suffered this injury . . . I am a margrave now."

"What battles have you fought?"

"Not long after I turned sixteen, I was sent to fight during the siege of Castle Rotherholm. Then I was sent to defend the border by the Duke of Pomerania, who made me the captain of his guard." His jaw twitched and he glanced down at the roast pheasant a squire had placed on the table before them. He cut a large chunk from it, then placed it on her trencher. Then he cut himself a piece.

She ignored her food. "Did you enjoy your life of fighting?"

He shrugged. "I did what needed to be done. Fighting feels like a duty, not a chore, which I suppose is what keeps us from hating it. We defend the innocent, our allies, and each other."

She nodded. "Of course." She should not be talking so much with the margrave. She should draw Magdalen into the conversation. But she could not think how.

"Forgive me for not thinking of it before, but I will have some paper and a quill and ink sent to your chamber. You may want to write something while you are here."

"That is very thoughtful. I thank you."

"And you may borrow another book from the library whenever you wish."

Why was he paying so much attention to her? But he was only being a good host. He would speak this way to any of the other ladies, were they sitting beside him. But when he looked her in the eye and spoke quietly to her and only her, it filled an empty place inside her, and even made her eyes misty. It made her believe that she was just as worthy as a wealthy daughter of a nobleman.

Or perhaps she was only allowing herself to believe the pretense. Either way, she wanted to enjoy the feeling Lord Thornbeck's attention gave her, this warmth and sense of importance. Dangerous though it was.

She pulled Magdalen into the conversation as often as she could during the rest of the long meal. Sometimes the conversation went on between the four of them, including the Duke of Wolfberg, but then it would inevitably end with the duke talking to Magdalen and Avelina talking with Lord Thornbeck. But that was only because she was nearer to the margrave and the other guests were so loud.

When the final dishes of sweets had been served and consumed, concluding with an enormous subtlety made in the shape of a peacock, with candied fruits and nuts simulating its feathers, Lord Thornbeck announced the end of the ball and the night's festivities.

He fixed his gaze on Avelina. "I hope you enjoyed the ball, as you did dance twice, at least."

"I did." Avelina smiled and drew Magdalen forward so he could speak to her as well. "I thank you all," she nodded at the Duke of Wolfberg and Lady Magdalen, "for talking with me at the ball and not allowing me to stand alone and without a friend. Lady Magdalen is so kind."

"Lady Dorothea is the kind one."

"Oh no, I did nothing! You are the one—" But she was cut off before she could enumerate more of her friend's excellent character traits.

Lady Fronicka strode forward. "Lord Thornbeck, I—"

"I trust you enjoyed the ball, Lady Fronicka, and I bid you a good night." He bowed to her, turned, and strode away.

12

Avelina awoke to someone knocking at her door. Sunlight streamed through the edges of the shutters on the windows. She leapt out of bed and hurried to drag the heavy trunk away so she could open the door. When she had pulled it far enough to open the door a foot, she peered out at Frau Schwitzer standing in the corridor.

"Lord Thornbeck sent you these." She held out a portable desk—a wooden box with a slanted lid. "You will find paper, ink, and a quill inside."

"Thank you, Frau Schwitzer." Avelina took the box, tilting it sideways to get it through the doorway, and started to close the door.

"Lady Dorothea?"

"*Ja?*"

"Is something amiss?"

"No, all is well. Thank you." She closed the door on the servant's puzzled expression. She didn't bother to push the trunk either against the door or back where she had found it but walked over to the window seat and placed the wooden box on the cushion.

The heavy chair still stood against the door that connected Avelina's bedchamber to the small room where Irma slept. She stepped to her bed and threw the covers all the way back. No spiders or snakes anywhere to be seen.

Avelina sighed and lay across the bed.

Today was only her fourth day here. Ten more to go. She sighed again. But it wasn't all bad. She closed her eyes and relived her terror when Lord Thornbeck pulled her aside and asked if she was with child and in love with a knight. But squeezing her eyes tighter, she concentrated not on her fear but on his expression . . . his eyes . . . his lips . . . his dark brows and the way his dark hair hung over his forehead. She remembered his voice, the words he had spoken to her, and her stomach did that strange flip it often did when she thought about the margrave.

Magdalen was a fortunate woman if she married him. She would get to listen to that deep voice and look into those brown eyes for the rest of her life.

She sat up. "Irma." She went over and moved the heavy chair from in front of Irma's door. "Irma, get up and help me get dressed and fix my hair."

Avelina opened the door and Irma threw an arm over her face and groaned. "So high and mighty," she grumbled. "A week ago you were naught but Lady Dorothea's servant girl." Irma lay unmoving.

The scent of strong drink assaulted Avelina's nose. "What have you been drinking?"

Irma groaned again. "Stop shouting. I'll be up in a thrice." Still, she did not move.

"Have you been drinking with that Gerhaws woman again? I do not think she is a good influence on you."

Avelina got her own gown and began to dress. Then she hurried to Magdalen's bedchamber and knocked softly on the door.

In less than half an hour, Avelina was hurrying Magdalen down the stairs.

"Remember," Avelina whispered, "if Lord Thornbeck is in the library, tell him you want to read *The Song of Roland* and ask him if you may borrow it."

"Very well, Dorothea, but I do not think it is me Lord Thornbeck is interested in."

Avelina stopped abruptly and stared at her friend. "What do you mean?"

"You must admit, he did show a lot of interest in you at the ball last night, coming all the way around to the other side of the room to talk to you."

"Do you mean during the dance? That was only because I was the only one not dancing. He did not want to see me standing alone. He would have done the same for any of the ladies."

"And if I am not mistaken, he took you aside on the way to the Great Hall so he could sit beside you."

"*Nein, nein, nein.* He took me aside because . . ." Avelina glanced around. The corridor was still and silent. There seemed to be no one else nearby. She lowered her voice even more. "Fronicka had told him some gossip about me, and he was asking me if it was true."

Lady Magdalen gasped. "What kind of gossip? What did she say?"

Avelina probably shouldn't tell her, but Magdalen would not tell anyone. "He told me that Fronicka said I was with child and the baby belonged to one of my father's knights. I assured him it was completely false."

Magdalen shook her head, her eyes wide. "I cannot believe she would say such a thing. She truly is evil to make up a tale like that and tell it to Lord Thornbeck. He believed you, did he not?"

Avelina nodded, a shard of guilt piercing her at allowing Magdalen to think Fronicka had made up the story. "I think he believed me."

"You should take care. She has seen how he shows you favor, and if she would tell a lie like that to the margrave, she is capable of . . . terrible things."

"I would not say Lord Thornbeck shows me favor." Avelina's stomach sank. Surely it was not true. "He would do the same for any of the ladies."

"I do not think so." A little smile graced Magdalen's lips. "I think he favors you."

"Truly, Magdalen, I wish you would not say so." The sinking feeling grew more pronounced. "I cannot marry the margrave."

"Why not?"

Avelina swallowed and took a deep breath, pressing her hand to her middle. "I wish I could tell you." Did she dare trust her friend that much? It was not fair to tell her, to force her to keep such a secret. "Please, just believe me when I say that I cannot, nor do I wish to, marry Lord Thornbeck. It has been my intention all along for him to marry you, Magdalen. You are obviously the kindest maiden here, the most discerning, the most intelligent, the most beautiful—"

"Besides you."

Avelina expelled a breath through her pursed lips. "Nonsense. I am nothing compared to you."

"How can you say such a thing? Besides, I do not think the margrave would agree with you." Again, she had the amused smile on her face.

"I beg you not to say that." Avelina put her hands over her face.

"Very well, I shall not say it." She chuckled. "Come. You wanted to go to the library."

Avelina allowed Magdalen to take her hand away from her face, turn her around, and lead her toward the stairs.

They descended and turned away from the ballroom and went

down a wide corridor. On either side were doors, some of them open, some closed. They moved past two before coming to the open door of the library. Cautiously they stepped inside.

The room was dark near the door, as the windows on the opposite side faced the west and it was still morning. But at the far side of the room, in the corner surrounded by windows, Lord Thornbeck sat at a desk. He was writing.

He looked up. "Who is there?"

Magdalen grabbed Avelina's arm, her eyes wide at Lord Thornbeck's gruff voice. Would he be angry that they were there?

"Forgive us, Lord Thornbeck. It is I, Ava—uhh, Lady Dorothea and Lady Magdalen. We did not mean to dis—"

"Come in." He took hold of his cane and pushed himself to his feet.

Avelina's stomach twisted into a knot. Almost calling herself Avelina, coupled with Magdalen's words about the margrave's interest in her, sent her heart racing.

He moved closer, his cane thumping as he walked.

"Forgive us for interrupting your work, Lord Thornbeck," Lady Magdalen said, "but I saw Lady Dorothea reading this book and wanted to ask you if I could borrow it." Magdalen smiled at him.

"Why did you not ask Lady Dorothea?" He wore his usual stern look.

"Oh, I . . ."

"I have finished it," Avelina spoke up, "and before I returned it she wanted to ask if she might borrow it."

"You may."

"Thank you."

There was silence, then Lord Thornbeck locked eyes with Avelina. "Would you like another book? Shall I make suggestions?"

"Oh yes, of course. Lady Magdalen and I both like to read. What do you suggest for us?"

"This Book of Hours belonged to my mother."

He pulled a large book off the shelf and handed it to Avelina.

"And there is a Psalter here that the Duke of Pomerania gave to me. I have another Psalter that I read from. But perhaps you brought yours with you?" He peered down at her.

"I did not."

He took the book and laid it in Avelina's arms on top of the Book of Hours. "But if you prefer more books like *The Song of Roland*"—he searched the shelf and pulled out a smaller book— "you might like this one. It is *The Song of the Nibelungs.*"

Avelina had read Dorothea's copy of the Book of Hours as well as her Psalter, but she had long wanted to read *The Song of the Nibelungs*. She bit her lip. Magdalen and Lord Thornbeck should be talking to each other. This was not at all the way she had planned this to go.

They were both looking at Avelina. She had to say something. "Magdalen and I will enjoy reading these."

The margrave fixed first one, then the other, with an intense look. "Would you two like to go for a picnic? Winter will soon be upon us and we should enjoy the mild weather while we can."

They both seemed to be waiting for Avelina to answer. "Of course, we would be pleased to accept your invitation."

"I shall have some servants come along with us, to ensure safety and propriety. And you may also bring your own servants if you wish."

A few moments later Avelina found herself carrying three books while walking back upstairs to change into sturdier clothing suitable for a picnic. Magdalen whispered, "Do you think he will invite the other ladies, or only we two?"

"I don't know." She hoped he would invite everyone, and if he didn't, that Fronicka would not hear of it.

This was what meddling had gotten her. But perhaps it would still turn out well. Perhaps now Lord Thornbeck would get a chance to talk more intimately with Lady Magdalen. Surely he would see what a kind, worthy young woman she was.

⟋⟍

Reinhart stood at the bottom of the steps as Odette began to descend with Lady Dorothea and Lady Magdalen and her maidservant following her. Good. No one could accuse him of any impropriety with Lady Magdalen's dour-faced servant along.

Odette and one of the house servants also came, carrying a large basket of food. Just outside the castle, the stable servants had horses saddled and ready for them and a donkey loaded with supplies.

Soon they were on their way to the place Jorgen had assured him was an excellent spot for a picnic, in a clearing next to a stream. Odette knew the way, so he allowed her to lead.

Dorothea was glancing up at the castle, an anxious look in her eyes. The other ladies often seemed nervous around him, but Dorothea seemed almost afraid.

Dorothea and Magdalen rode side by side on the wide trail. When the trail narrowed, Reinhart ended up between them as they rode singly.

They arrived at the stream and the servants spread out the blankets and cushions for sitting and set out the food. Soon they were all eating and talking about the beauty of the quiet spot in the woods.

"There are still a few leaves on the trees," Lady Magdalen said.

"Which do you like better, autumn or spring?" he asked Lady Magdalen, but he was watching Lady Dorothea out of the corner of his eye.

"I think I prefer autumn. I love the brilliant colors of the leaves." Lady Magdalen took a bite of bread and cheese while propped and leaning back on her other hand, her legs drawn up beside her.

Lady Dorothea was seated similarly. She said nothing, so he asked her, "And you, Lady Dorothea?"

"Oh, I prefer spring."

"And why is that?"

Now she got that familiar look on her face, her hands curling in her lap as she drew her legs tighter toward herself, and she wouldn't look him in the eye. "As Lady Magdalen said, the leaves in autumn are beautiful, but spring holds the promise of new life and warmer weather."

He asked Lady Magdalen about her family, her mother and siblings. She spoke of her mother, her deceased father, and her younger siblings. As Magdalen spoke, Lady Dorothea's shoulders relaxed slightly, her hands uncurled, and she leaned on one hand while eating a bread roll.

He asked Lady Magdalen more questions. As long as she talked, Lady Dorothea nodded and looked at ease.

He finally turned his attention to Lady Dorothea. "Tell me about your family, Lady Dorothea."

"Oh, there isn't much to tell." She kept her gaze down and brushed off her skirt. "My father . . . he is consumed with . . . his responsibilities, and my mother died a few years ago." She shook her head, a slight movement, and her shoulders were high and tense again. She clasped her hands in her lap and finally said, "I'm sure Lady Magdalen and I would love to hear about your family, Lord Thornbeck."

Not that *she* would love to hear about his family, but that *Lady Magdalen* and she would.

He continued to focus most of the conversation on Lady Magdalen, since that seemed to help Lady Dorothea be less guarded when she did speak. They talked about the wolves that had recently claimed Thornbeck Forest as their territory, about their favorite books and writings, and they even managed to get Lady Dorothea to talk about the stories she had written.

By the time they were ready to pack up their things and go back to the castle, Lady Dorothea was talking as much as Lady Magdalen, and even laughed at something she said.

Once back at the castle, he parted from them and motioned for Odette to join him in the library, where Jorgen was working.

Jorgen looked up. "How was your picnic?"

Reinhart looked at Odette. "Did you notice anything strange about Lady Dorothea's behavior?"

"Do you mean how she seemed so nervous when you talked to her? And when you talked to Lady Magdalen she relaxed?"

"Yes."

"It was as if she wanted you to pay attention to Lady Magdalen and not to her, but I can't think why, unless she is very meek and timid, but she was not timid when she answered your questions that first day."

Reinhart tried to reconcile how her behavior had gradually changed. "Perhaps she simply does not like me."

"Then why would she want her friend to like you? Or you to like her friend? Did you not notice how she always tried to paint her friend in a positive light and herself as uninteresting? No, it isn't that." Odette sighed.

Jorgen said, "Perhaps she loves her friend so much, she wants her to marry you."

"But she's only known this young woman since she arrived here. No, it cannot be that, exactly."

Reinhart forced the scowl from his face. He hadn't known the girl long enough to care so much whether she liked him or disliked him, surely. He had believed her when she told him the rumor of her being in love with her father's knight was false, but it was possible she was lying.

"Either way," Odette said, "they both seem quite good-hearted. I should be very surprised if you do not choose one or the other of them."

Reinhart still had time to make up his mind. Besides, he didn't expect to fall in love with anyone, simply to make the best choice from the list of ladies the king had given him.

"How is Endlein?" Reinhart asked. "Is she calmer than she was at the ball?"

"She was calm when she made it back to her chamber and back to more familiar surroundings," Odette said. "I think all the strange people upset her. She seems better now."

Jorgen began telling him what he and Odette had observed and recorded the night of the ball. The people who stood out— the ones who always stood out—were Dorothea, Magdalen, and Fronicka.

His frustration rose as he thought of marrying someone he was not sure about, someone whose character turned out to be disappointing. But if all went as planned, that would not happen.

13

Avelina and Magdalen made their way down to the Great Hall that evening, since all the margrave's guests were invited to play games: chess, backgammon, and Nine Men's Morris.

Upon their arrival, the only people in the Great Hall were Fronicka and the two other ladies who were by her side everywhere she went—Otilia and Beatrix.

Fronicka lifted her head and smiled, showing a row of white teeth.

Magdalen gripped Avelina's arm a little tighter.

"Lady Dorothea and Lady Magdalen." Fronicka's smile grew even wider. "Come here."

Avelina hesitated, but she and Magdalen slowly made their way over to them.

Fronicka widened her eyes. "Tell us, how was your picnic with Lord Thornbeck? Were you frightened?"

"Why would we be frightened?" Magdalen asked.

The hair rose on the back of Avelina's neck.

Fronicka leaned toward them, as if to impart a secret. "Some people say," she whispered, "that Lord Thornbeck killed his brother in that mysterious fire in the west wing so he could be margrave. And that woman who wandered into the ballroom last night, calling for Annlin? She is the mother of his brother's lover. She went mad when the fire killed her daughter along with the previous margrave."

Avelina could not resist asking, "Then why would Lord Thornbeck keep her here if he killed her daughter?"

Fronicka raised her brows with a superior air. "For his guilty conscience's sake, or perhaps to make himself look innocent. I know not. I only know what the servants tell my servant. She always finds out truths about people that no one else knows."

"Like what you told Lord Thornbeck about me?" Avelina raised her own brows as she looked Fronicka in the eye.

"Are you accusing me?" Fronicka placed a hand over her chest.

"You should not gossip about people. Whatever you heard, it's not true about me."

Fronicka erased the shocked innocence from her expression and narrowed her eyes. "Is that so? Why do you hide the truth, Lady Dorothea? Do you hope Lord Thornbeck will marry you and will think the child is his?" Otilia and Beatrix looked shocked, then laughed, half covering their grins with their hands.

Magdalen tugged on her arm to pull her away.

"One thing is sure," Avelina shot back. "He is too wise to marry you."

Magdalen tugged harder and Avelina took a couple of steps back.

Fronicka turned her twisted glare into a haughty look. "I was only trying to warn you, to tell you what I had learned. Your own servant was too drunk last night to learn anything of any use to you."

"And why would gossip be of use to us?" Magdalen said.

Avelina stared at her friend, surprised at her speaking up.

"We do not care for gossip, as you seem to." Magdalen slipped her arm through Avelina's and turned away from Fronicka and her friends—just as several more people entered the Great Hall, including Lord Thornbeck.

A huge smile on her face, Fronicka hurried toward him. "Lord Thornbeck, do play the first game of chess with me!"

A backgammon board was set up on a nearby table, and as Avelina and Magdalen sat down to play, Magdalen leaned over and whispered, "They behave just like children."

Avelina rolled her eyes and nodded, then they both laughed.

Lord Thornbeck turned to look at them. What if what Fronicka had said was true, about Lord Thornbeck murdering his brother to become margrave? Lord Plimmwald had mentioned the very same thing. Would Magdalen be safe married to him? Avelina shivered and started setting up the game.

"Ladies," Lord Thornbeck said, suddenly standing beside them. "The servants found this necklace wrapped up in one of the blankets from the picnic." He held out a gold chain and locket.

"Oh," Magdalen said. "I forgot I was wearing it this morning. I should have been very sad to lose it. Thank you, my lord."

He gave her the necklace. "I hope I will be able to play chess with both of you, but to be honest, it seems unlikely to happen tonight." He glanced over his shoulder.

All the other ladies were looking his way, waiting for him to come back to the chessboard.

Avelina merely smiled, trying not to say anything, to let Magdalen do the talking.

"We can play chess with you another time," Magdalen said. "Thank you for returning my necklace."

He gave a slight nod and walked away to rejoin the others.

"Thank goodness." Magdalen held the locket close to her chest. "If I had lost this I would have been sad indeed. It belonged to my grandmother."

"It must have been a very honest servant who found it," Avelina said. "But I shall have to warn Irma to stay away from Fronicka's servants."

"Yes, you had better. Do you think a servant really said you were pregnant and in love with one of your father's knights?"

Avelina thought for a moment. Irma would not tell about Lady Dorothea, especially since they were both in so much danger if the whole truth came out. "I don't know, but I do need to warn Irma not to get drunk again, and to be careful not to say anything that could be used against us. Magdalen?"

"Yes?"

Avelina whispered, "Do you think the margrave killed his brother?"

Magdalen whispered back, "Of course people will say that he killed him, but how can he prove it was an accident?"

"I don't suppose he can."

"And the king obviously trusts him."

"Perhaps it is simply easier to believe him than to replace him. And yet, I don't believe he did it either. Though it is possible."

The two exchanged glances. "It is impossible to know for sure, I suppose"—Lady Magdalen's eyes were wide—"but I am inclined to believe him innocent." Magdalen looked down at their game. "You may go first."

They played backgammon, but Avelina's mind wasn't on her moves and she lost to her friend. They then switched places with two other ladies who were playing Nine Men's Morris.

Avelina grew tired of playing the games and listening to the other ladies try to flirt with the margrave. Magdalen did not seem to be enjoying herself either.

"Shall we leave and go to our rooms for the night?" Avelina asked.

"I do not think anyone will mind."

They both stood, caught Lord Thornbeck's eye as he was sitting across the chessboard from one of the ladies, and curtsied to him. He nodded and they hurried out of the room.

They headed up the stairs and down the corridor to Avelina's room. As soon as they opened the door, they smelled something foul and put their hands over their noses.

"What is that?" Avelina went over to the bed and pulled back the coverlet. There, smeared all over the sheet, was some kind of filth that smelled of horse manure. Very fresh horse manure.

"Ugh," Magdalen said, while Avelina gagged and had to turn away.

Avelina ran to the adjacent compartment where Irma slept and yanked open the door. Irma was no longer lying there, as she had been most of the day.

With her arm over her nose, Avelina hurried out of the room, Magdalen leading the way.

Out in the corridor, Magdalen whispered, "Will you tell Lord Thornbeck?"

Avelina gulped in the cleaner air of the corridor. "What would I tell him? 'My bed is full of horse manure'? No, I will simply have to find clean bedding and throw out these. I can remake the bed and it will be well enough."

"Shouldn't you get a servant to do that?"

Avelina opened her mouth, realizing her blunder. "Of course, I will not change the bedding. I will get a servant—Irma, she can do it."

"I shall send Hegatha to find Irma, or to have some of the other servants clean up the mess." Magdalen went to her own bedchamber and soon came back with Hegatha, who walked past them down the corridor without even glancing at Avelina.

"We will have it cleaned up in no time."

Avelina shuddered. She did not want to admit it, but her insides were all churned up to think someone would do something like this. Fronicka had brought several servants with her, and she must have had them do the vicious deed.

Avelina wanted to hurt her, to do the same thing back to her, and to add a few stinging nettles. But of course, as the priest in Plimmwald had said, God demands forgiveness, and vengeance does not belong to man. For now, she had to concentrate on keeping one step ahead of Fronicka.

Magdalen shook her head. "Who knows what she might do next. I think we should tell Lord Thornbeck."

"Perhaps." Avelina tapped her chin with her finger. "But I don't want to run to him with such a petty . . ." She sighed. "I simply have to get through these next ten days. Surely we can do that."

"Very well. Do you want to sleep in my bed tonight? I sometimes let my sisters sleep with me."

She did not relish sleeping in the bed where Fronicka had left her such a disgusting offering, but she also did not wish to have Magdalen's old nursemaid giving her sour looks. No, Avelina was a grown woman. "Thank you, but I think I shall be well."

Hegatha came back just then, an even sterner look on her face than usual, with Irma in tow, carrying clean bedclothes and grumbling under her breath. She brushed past them and entered Avelina's bedchamber—and exclaimed in a high-pitched voice.

"Come to my room." Magdalen took her by the arm, leading her.

Avelina spent the next hour with Magdalen, until they heard the other ladies coming up the stairs. She hurried back to her room. She checked the bed, throwing back the sheets. Then she knelt and checked under it. Nothing was there. Surprisingly, there was no lingering stench, only a strong herbal smell of lavender and pennyroyal.

She took off her outer clothes, crawled into bed, and lay staring at the canopy above her with all the curtains pulled back to let in as much light as possible. Was it her imagination that something was touching her leg?

She threw the covers off and sat up. All she saw was one of her own long brown hairs by her leg. She laughed out loud at herself.

She lay down again and tried to close her eyes, but she kept seeing the mess that had been in her bed. Finally, she got up and went to Irma's little room and opened the door.

"Irma?"

"Yes," answered the lump on the bed.

"Do you mind if I leave your door open?"

"Afraid of that nasty Lady Fronicka, are you? I warned you she was a malicious one. What did you do to make her hate you?"

"Nothing!"

"From what I hear from the other servants, the margrave fancies you. You had best make sure—"

"That is not true. He favors Lady Magdalen."

"That's not what I hear."

Avelina rubbed her face. "What do you hear?"

She sat up in her small bed. "I hear that Lady Dorothea is in love with her father's knight and is with child."

"For all the angels in heaven's sake, Irma, keep your voice quiet."

Irma went on in a loud whisper, "And that Lord Thornbeck took you and Lady Magdalen on a picnic, just the three of you."

"That is a lie. Odette Hartman went with us, as did several servants. They were with us the whole time."

"Ach, well, some of the ladies were very jealous."

"Who have you been talking to? Who told you all that?"

"Gerhaws. She knows all the gossip. And there is talk of you and Lady Magdalen being his favorites."

"I fully intend that he shall choose Magdalen to marry, as well he should. She is by far the most suitable lady for him." But even as she said the words, a voice rose up inside to accuse her. *You think he would be happier with you. You wish he could marry you.* But Avelina shoved the voice away.

"Just be careful he doesn't end up choosing you, *Lady Avelina.*"

"You know you should not call me that." And wasn't she doing all she could to make sure Lord Thornbeck did not choose her? She discouraged his conversing with her, and he had started showing a preference for Magdalen, she was sure of it. What did Irma and those servants know? They weren't there with them at the picnic or when Lord Thornbeck brought Magdalen her necklace.

No, the margrave was going to marry Magdalen.

"Irma, I want you to be extra careful around those other servants. Do not say anything about me, anything at all. You know what danger we are in if anyone discovers . . . And please don't get drunk anymore. You might let our secret slip—"

Irma's lip curled and her eyes narrowed. "Look who thinks she's an earl's daughter. Just because you wear fancy clothes, you cannot tell me what to do," Irma hissed. "So don't forget that we are equals, you hear me? Equals. And I will do as I please when I am eating and drinking with the other servants, which is what you'll be again, soon enough." Irma flopped down on the bed and turned over to face the wall.

Avelina stood there, motionless for several minutes, except for her chest rapidly rising and falling.

I am only a servant, nothing more. Not a lady. Not the daughter of an earl. Only a servant. But she could make the margrave fall in love with her if she wished. She could. She felt it in the way he looked at her and spoke to her. And what was just as bad was, she could fall in love with him too.

14

"Choosing a wife this way is humiliating."

What was supposed to be a calm evening of playing games turned into six ladies all vying for his attention and nearly coming to blows. Four of the ladies had gone off and played games between themselves, including Lady Dorothea and Lady Magdalen, but the six who were left crowded around him, asking to be the next to play with him and commenting on every move he and his opponent made. Lady Fronicka was the most vocal.

Reinhart rapped his cane on the floor. "I should much rather be doing something more productive, like ridding the forest of wolves."

Odette was quick to say, "There is nothing humiliating about choosing a bride by getting to know her first."

"It will all be well in nine days, after you make your choice." Jorgen sent him a hopeful expression.

"I think I must inform you, my lord," Odette said, "that someone placed something very disgusting in Lady Dorothea's bed last evening."

Reinhart stared at her.

"Horse manure."

His chest tightened. "How did such a thing get past the servants and guard?" He gripped his cane and gave in to the urge to bang it on the floor again. "This should never . . ." Steam seemed to rise into his forehead.

"No one will tell who did it." Jorgen frowned.

He clenched his teeth. When he could trust himself to speak, he said, "Have a guard assigned to watch Lady Dorothea and Lady Magdalen's corridor. No one is to go in or out of any of the ladies' bedchamber doors besides their maidservants."

"Yes, my lord," Jorgen said. "I shall see to it."

"And ask Lady Dorothea if she would like a different bed-chamber."

"Yes, my lord." Odette and Jorgen were looking to him.

"And set up the hunt for this afternoon. Have the huntsmen make sure the dogs are ready, and the stable workers should have the horses saddled. Notify all the guests and get a count of how many intend to go. That is all. You may go."

How dare someone inflict cruelty on Lady Dorothea in Reinhart's own castle. If he found out who was responsible, he would expel them immediately.

~~~

The next day was Sunday, and Avelina and Magdalen walked to the chapel together.

Lord Thornbeck was already there, kneeling near the front of the nave, which quickly grew crowded with the guests, all the serv-ants of the guests, and Thornbeck Castle's servants and workers. Even many of the margrave's guards were there, kneeling before the chancel, bowing reverently, or gazing up at the large crucifix over the altar.

The early morning sun was shining through the stained-glass

windows in brilliant colors. A yellow bit of glass was lighting up Lord Thornbeck's head like a halo. But Avelina bowed her head and closed her eyes to block out his image.

After silently reviewing her sins from the past week, Avelina prayed for her father, brother, and sister in Plimmwald, that she would get through the next eight days without having to lie, and that Lord Thornbeck would choose to marry Magdalen.

After Holy Eucharist and Communion, some hymns sung by a boys' choir, and a brief homily from the priest on the importance of showing kindness as Jesus did, everyone filed out of the chapel and headed to the Great Hall, where they would all break their fast.

Lord Thornbeck's voice came from just behind Avelina and Magdalen. "I hope you found an interesting way to spend your day yesterday during the hunt."

"Yes, my lord," Magdalen said. "We talked and read."

"Talking and reading." He nodded. "That can certainly be interesting."

Avelina peeked over her shoulder to see if he was being sarcastic, and he was looking straight at her. Other people were all around them, but they seemed to mostly be having their own conversations.

"Yes, Lady Magdalen read your book and enjoyed it. Did you do well on your hunting trip?"

"We did not do as well as we'd hoped. There seems to be a shortage of deer just now."

Someone coughed on the other side of Lord Thornbeck. Avelina turned her head and saw his chancellor, Jorgen, and Odette walking beside him. Odette wore a look of chagrin and Jorgen was trying to hide a smile behind his hand.

They walked together—Lord Thornbeck with Magdalen and Avelina—and talked until they reached the Great Hall. Lord

Thornbeck indicated that they should sit beside him, but Avelina purposely placed Magdalen by the margrave's side and she sat on the other side of Magdalen.

During the meal, Lord Thornbeck said to Magdalen, "I was sorry you did not join us for the hunt."

Avelina's heart fluttered. That certainly indicated interest in Magdalen.

"Please forgive me, but Odette said it would not be taken amiss if I did not go. I simply do not like the hunt."

"There is nothing to forgive. You were not obligated to go. But if you do not mind me asking, why do you not like the hunt?"

Magdalen explained that she had cried on the first—and last—hunt she had ever gone on. "I did not want to ruin anyone else's enjoyment of the hunt yesterday."

"Lady Dorothea," he said, looking past Magdalen. "You told me you would not be going on the hunt. Was it because you do not shoot a bow?"

"It was because I do not ride well." She had told him that her first day in Thornbeck.

"Perhaps it is because you were thrown as a child?" He raised his brows.

"No, I—" She stopped herself before saying it was because she had never owned a horse. "I've just never had a liking for horses."

He stared at her, as if thinking of something else. Then he turned back to Magdalen. "Do you like horses, Lady Magdalen?"

"Oh yes, I like animals of all kinds. I had a pet dog as a child. When he died, I couldn't bear to get another one."

Avelina pretended great interest in her food as she listened to their conversation. But when Lord Thornbeck leaned toward Magdalen and said something low in her ear, too low for Avelina to hear, her heart thumped harder.

When the meal was over, Lord Thornbeck bid them a good day. As soon as Avelina and Magdalen stood and left the table, several other ladies, including Fronicka, crowded around Lord Thornbeck. One young lady actually asked his opinion about her dress.

Avelina hurried Magdalen away. As soon as they were in the wide foyer at the junction of the stairs and the grand ballroom, Avelina whispered, "What did Lord Thornbeck say?"

"When?"

"You know! When he leaned and whispered in your ear."

"He did not exactly whisper. He—" Magdalen leaned over to look past Avelina's shoulder. That's when she heard a woman's footsteps swishing toward them on the marble floor.

Fronicka was coming, alone. "There is something strange about you, Lady Dorothea." She clasped her hands behind her back, as if to look demure. "You don't know how to dance, you don't ride well and therefore could not go on the hunt with us, and your servant said she had never been a lady's maidservant before she came on this trip with you. Sometimes I wonder if you're even a lady at all."

Avelina's breath seemed to leave her, and her heart pounded as Fronicka looked down at her through half-closed eyes. Her nose pointed high as she turned away and went back into the Great Hall.

"She's more of a lady than you will ever be," Magdalen said under her breath, but Fronicka was already too far away to hear.

But Fronicka was right. Did she even know how right she was? Avelina's heart gradually slowed. Surely Fronicka had not discovered the truth. If she had, she wouldn't hesitate to tell everyone.

"Oh, so what Lord Thornbeck said . . ." Magdalen started up the stairs and Avelina hurried after her.

"What? What?"

"He said . . ." Magdalen drew out the words dramatically, then she whispered in Avelina's ear, "he wants us to meet him in the rose garden just beyond the south side of the castle in the morning."

"Oh. But surely he meant only for you to come."

"No, he specifically said for me to bring you with me. And I shall not go at all if you do not come."

"Oh, but you must! He wants to talk to you."

"He wants to talk to you too. He said so."

If Lord Thornbeck was taken with Magdalen, as he obviously was, he would surely want to get to know her better, and having Avelina around would be uncomfortable. However, he might fear it would be improper for Magdalen to be alone with him, so for that reason, Avelina would go along with her.

⁓

Avelina heard the soft knock at her door and quickly opened it. Magdalen stood there smiling. "Are you ready?"

"Let me put on my shoes." The old pair of Dorothea's slippers were so thin they nearly had a hole worn in them. She only needed them to hold up for seven more days.

They slipped out the door, not speaking until they had made their way down the stairs and out through a side door that led to the kitchen.

The morning air was crisp and cool and Avelina wrapped her shoulders in Dorothea's old velvet cloak. "How did you sneak away from Hegatha? Did she allow you to go without her?"

"She was out, so I left her a note."

"Won't she be angry?"

"Probably." Magdalen's frown turned into a grin. "It will be worth the guilt she will heap on me to sneak away to meet the margrave with you."

"Are you falling in love with him, then?" Avelina held her breath, waiting for her answer.

Magdalen's half grin turned into a half frown. "I am still hoping you will fall in love and decide to marry him."

"Magdalen! You know he favors you now."

Her brows shot up. "I do not think he fancies a wife as young as I am. You are closer to his own age. But we shall not argue about it. We shall simply enjoy his company. Agreed?"

"Very well."

The air was misty with fog as they entered the small rose garden. Vines clung to the stone wall, and there were only a few roses, one here and there, that were still in bloom so late in autumn.

Lord Thornbeck suddenly appeared in the mist ahead, standing next to the family mausoleum. He came toward them and cleared his throat. Avelina got the idea that he was trying to think of something to say. Perhaps one reason he was so gruff sometimes was because he had not spent much time with ladies and did not know how to make polite conversation. And this morning he did not have Odette to help prompt conversation.

"Did you see the flowers that are still blooming?" he finally asked.

Avelina let Magdalen walk ahead of her. "I like the yellow rose with pink around the edges." Avelina stopped and leaned down to get a better look. When she straightened, Lord Thornbeck and Magdalen were staring at her.

Avelina pretended not to notice as she turned and wandered away to find another fully bloomed rose. When she glanced over her shoulder again, the margrave and Magdalen were talking. Avelina resumed examining the roses and bushes and trees. Her plan was working perfectly. So why did a pang of regret shoot through her middle?

"Lady Dorothea, come and join our conversation." Lord Thornbeck was seating Magdalen on a wooden bench between two large rosebushes.

Avelina walked forward and sat beside Magdalen, then the margrave seated himself on the bench facing them. He was not smiling.

Silence stretched between them until Magdalen said, "We were just speaking about how difficult it is for our lord to choose a bride from among his guests."

"I did not say it was difficult," Lord Thornbeck said. "I said it was uncomfortable to invite ladies to one's home for the express purpose of choosing from among them whom to marry."

"Then why do it?" Avelina wished she hadn't been so quick to speak, but she couldn't take back the question.

His expression was stern as he stared back at her. "I am doing it because I do not wish to marry someone who will be . . . less than what I am expecting in a wife. I do not wish to have the king choose my bride for me. If I can find a suitable wife, one that he approves, I shall not be forced to marry someone whose character may be less than exemplary or someone who may not wish to marry me and therefore will be unhappy in our marriage."

"That makes sense."

"Do you think so?"

His obvious interest in her opinion surprised her. "Yes. You are the margrave. You can do anything you want, and if you want to find a wife you consider to be suitable and a woman of good character, then you should use any reasonable means to do so." Again, she probably should not have said so much. She sounded terribly impertinent. Once she returned to Plimmwald she would have to watch what she said, lest she speak her opinions the way she had here and offend Lord Plimmwald.

Before that happened, Irma would put her in her place, no doubt.

"I do not wish to force anyone to marry me who does not wish to."

Was he thinking of Magdalen? She did seem a bit un-enthusiastic around him.

"I am sure you know that a woman of good character, modesty, and prudence would not make her wish to marry you very obvious. She will not be hovering around you, trying to force your attention to her every moment." She spoke carefully, hoping he would see the contrast in her description between Lady Magdalen and Lady Fronicka. "She would not try to make you look unfavorably upon another woman to make herself look good. She might seem quiet and reserved, but that is only her Christian meekness and sobriety shining through."

Magdalen was staring at her with wide eyes and a wisp of a smile on her lips, and Lord Thornbeck's expression was nearly the same.

"Are you saying that if a lady does not show great interest, it does not necessarily mean she does not wish to marry me?" He lifted one brow, waiting expectantly.

He had never looked so handsome. *Ugh.* She should not be thinking such a thing.

"Precisely. You are a man of great character yourself, are you not? Wishing to show kindness to the poor, a man of godly ideals in every area of your life?"

"I try to be."

"Then a woman of good character will be very attracted to you, will consider you a wonderful potential husband, even if she does not show it." Avelina had to swallow the lump that rose into her throat. "She will count herself fortunate to have secured your good opinion."

He stared back at her, unblinking.

"Is it getting warmer?" Avelina stood. "Perhaps we should walk around and see all the roses before the sun burns through the fog and overheats us." She turned away and wandered toward the wall behind them. Truly, there was little likelihood of it becoming that warm, but she needed to free herself of his penetrating stare, and a sudden fear had gripped her. Could he have thought she was speaking of herself instead of Magdalen?

She wandered over to the climbing rose clinging to the stone wall and fingered the soft red petals of a stray rose, closing her eyes as she tried to slow her breathing. Behind her, the voices of Lady Magdalen and Lord Thornbeck drifted toward her, but she could not make out the words.

She could not have faced him another moment. When she was with Lord Thornbeck, it was so difficult to keep from talking to him. She was so drawn to him, to his opinions, his deep-brown eyes, and his rich, rumbly voice—which was exactly why she needed to stay away and let him talk to Lady Magdalen.

She leaned closer to the rose, so close that the cool, velvety petals caressed her cheek. She breathed deeply of the scented flower, pressing this moment into her mind so she could remember it in the future when she was a servant again, cleaning up after someone else, or helping in the kitchen now that Lady Dorothea was gone, or building a fire, or leaning over a boiling pot of pea-and-oat pottage she was cooking for her family.

She wanted to remember being in the company of the Margrave of Thornbeck—a noble man who was so conscientious about choosing an equally noble wife that he would go to such lengths as this. And to remember the sweet and proper Lady Magdalen, who never put herself forward and would not even do so now, when the margrave obviously was thinking of marrying her.

Footsteps were approaching behind her. She straightened and continued to wander down the path.

"My mother always said," Lord Thornbeck said, "that a lady could only sleep in a bed and could never sleep in a chair or on the ground. And a lady would never be able to sleep on a dirty mattress at an inn, where peasants had slept."

Magdalen laughed. "I may not be a lady then. I get a backache if I am not sleeping in a bed, but when forced to it, I can sleep almost anywhere."

Avelina had slept on the floor many times or on the cot in the little adjoining closet next to Lady Dorothea's bedchamber. But she already knew she was not nobly born.

"My mother said a lady could feel even a tiny pea if it was underneath her."

"What did you say to your mother?" Lady Magdalen asked.

"I said that was nonsense. She was only picking up on the fact that ladies generally expect, and are accustomed to, the finest and softest beds, not that they have any sort of special ability to feel lumps in their mattresses. What do you say, Lady Dorothea?"

She was forced to turn and join their conversation. "I say a lady is no different from a peasant. They—we—all have flesh and bones and feelings and desires. The same blood flows through one's veins as the other's."

There she went again, expressing her fanciful opinions that no one else agreed with. Her face heated.

"Perhaps you are right," Lord Thornbeck said quietly.

"Will you test us, then?" Magdalen said, "and put a pea under our mattresses and see who is able to sleep and who is not?"

"I suppose my mother might have done something of that sort," he said, "but I would not even try the experiment to discount it. Besides, I do not care about whether or not you can feel a pea under your mattress."

"But you have been testing us, have you not?" Avelina couldn't resist asking. "When we were walking through Thornbeck, did you not have those children come and ask us for food? To see how we would react?"

The margrave hung his head. When he looked up, he had a faint smile on his manly face. "You have found us out. Odette and Jorgen arranged to have the children from the orphanage perform that mummery for you all. And only you and Lady Magdalen passed that test."

"Only Lady Magdalen gave them anything," Avelina pointed out.

Lord Thornbeck gave her a hard stare. "But you were the one who demanded something be done for them. Were you not?"

Perhaps she was trying too hard to make him like Lady Magdalen.

But then he focused his attention on Magdalen and asked her about Mallin.

Avelina's heart constricted inside her as she realized Lord Thornbeck might actually be thinking of her as a possible bride. After all, he said she and Magdalen had passed that test, and now he was alone with the two of them. What could she do to make him think only of Magdalen?

Her stomach churned and her head ached. She did not want to think about it anymore now. Instead, in listening to Magdalen speak of her home, Avelina thought about her own little sister and brother. What were they doing? Were they being well cared for? Did they have enough to eat? Were they staying warm at night now that it was getting colder? Did they miss her?

She stayed within hearing while Lord Thornbeck spoke of his older brother.

"He was ten years older, and I came back to Thornbeck because he was making me the captain of his guard."

It was strange that his brother had brought him back to Thornbeck to lead his guard. Younger brothers were sent away as children, as Lord Thornbeck surely had been, to train as a knight, probably so things like this would never happen—a younger brother being rumored to have murdered the older one to take his inheritance.

"You and your brother must have been very good friends, then," Avelina couldn't resist asking, "for him to ask you to be the captain of his guard."

The margrave turned to her. "You, along with everyone else, have heard the rumors that I murdered my brother to get the margravate and Thornbeck Castle." He looked away. "The fire happened only a few days after I arrived. I saw the smoke coming from underneath his chamber door. I ran in to save him. I ran to the bed and picked him up. I was throwing him over my shoulder when the bed collapsed on my ankle. I was able to get him out, but the smoke had already overcome him. I did not kill my brother, Lady Dorothea, even though your father seems to believe I did. My brother was the last of my family members."

Avelina's cheeks heated again at the mention of the earl's offensive letter to the king. "I am very sorry."

A noise came from behind them. When she turned, Fronicka was opening the small iron gate and walking down the path toward them.

"This looks like an interesting group." She smirked as she picked a rose off a bush and twirled it between her fingers.

Lord Thornbeck's lips formed a tight line and his brows lowered. Fronicka flitted around him, smiling and asking him questions about the garden and about what they would do today. Lord

Thornbeck gave her one-word answers, then said, "I shall escort you ladies back to the castle now. I have duties."

Avelina and Magdalen walked together while Lord Thornbeck was forced to walk by Fronicka's side. As soon as they were inside, he excused himself from them and walked away, his cane tapping the marble floor as he went.

15

THE SUN WAS barely up, and Irma was not, when Avelina glanced down at the note that had been slipped under her door the night before, still amazed at what it said.

She made her way quietly down the corridor to softly knock on Magdalen's door. She opened it without waiting, but just as she slipped inside, she caught sight of the guard at the end of the corridor, watching her.

"Dorothea," Magdalen said. "I am almost ready. Hegatha, will you finish lacing up the back of Lady Dorothea's dress?"

Hegatha frowned as she came around Avelina's back and laced up the last few inches of her gown and tied it with little jerky movements.

"Thank you." Avelina gave her a smile, but the woman simply walked away to assist Magdalen with the last touches to her hair.

When she was finished, they hurried out into the corridor and walked toward the stairs. The man who had been standing at the end of the corridor was still there.

"Magdalen?" Avelina whispered. "Do you not think Lord Thornbeck is also taking the other ladies on outings like this?"

"He might be," Magdalen whispered back. "He might be doing it secretly, two ladies at a time, so no one will be jealous."

Avelina nodded. It seemed likely. "I don't think he likes crowds."

At the bottom of the stairs, Lord Thornbeck stood waiting for them.

"You got my message, then. Good. Let us go." They made their way down the hill via the stone steps to the stable. The early morning sun was spilling between the tree limbs and painting everything with a pale light. Lord Thornbeck wore a leather mantle, but his slightly wavy dark-brown hair was bare. He had a couple days' growth of beard on his face, which made him look rugged and even more masculine than he normally did. Her heart beat strangely. When she went back to Plimmwald, she hoped she could remember exactly what he looked like at this moment.

Lord Thornbeck checked both of their saddles carefully while his horse was being saddled beside him. He helped Lady Magdalen onto her horse, then it was Avelina's turn.

His grip on her elbow was strong as she stood on the mounting stool and put her foot in the stirrup. Lord Thornbeck lifted her onto the saddle. He looked her in the eye, and her breath stilled in her chest. There was such an intense expression on his face, but there was also something else . . . tenderness.

He turned away from her, as though reluctantly, and limped up to his horse. He mounted while the stable boy tucked his walking stick into a loop on his saddlebag. Then they were off, riding slowly down the side of the castle mount.

The manor house on Red Stag Hill was built of pale-pink stone. It stood just south of Thornbeck Castle and was the home of Jorgen and Odette.

They dismounted and were greeted at the door by Chancellor Jorgen and his wife, whose servants took their cloaks. Next they were treated to a large breakfast of eggs, cold meat, and pastries with various kinds of sweetened fruit fillings.

"Are there any cherry ones?" Avelina whispered to the servant who was offering them on a large platter.

The servant pointed to one, and Avelina took it and bit into it. She sighed. Tart but sweet.

"Is cherry your favorite?" Odette, who was sitting beside Avelina, asked.

"Favorite pastry, favorite tart, favorite fruit." They were all looking at her.

"You do not eat them raw, do you?" Magdalen was staring at her. "Hegatha says uncooked fruit will make you sick, and she never lets me eat them uncooked."

"I confess I do. I have only sickened once from eating cherries, and I think that was because I ate too many." Odette and Magdalen chuckled and Lord Thornbeck graced her with his slight smile.

They talked and laughed, listening to funny stories from Jorgen, Odette, Lord Thornbeck, and Magdalen. Avelina even told her own story, about a servant boy who had stolen a bracelet from another servant, then tried to sell it to the young man who had given it to her in the first place. She told another story, a true one, about a puppy she tried to hide from her father. She had to change a few minor details, but they all laughed.

She was not so different from noble men and women, and neither were Jorgen and Odette, even though they were not born into noble families either. But if they all knew that her father was a stable worker and she was a servant . . .

They had long finished their meal and continued sitting and talking. Avelina wasn't sure she had ever enjoyed herself so much. But was Lord Thornbeck truly singling Magdalen and her out, or was he taking other pairs of ladies out like this? Perhaps he truly did prefer Magdalen over all the other ladies and had taken them to Chancellor Jorgen's home to escape Fronicka's prying. But if that were the truth, why did he take Avelina with them?

They spent nearly the entire day at the chancellor's house, and by the end of their visit, it felt as if the five of them were longtime friends.

As they prepared to leave for the castle, Avelina found herself standing near Lord Thornbeck. She would probably regret it later, but she decided to ask, "Are you prepared to accept the consequences of leaving the other ladies behind today?"

He met her eye and after a few moments, he said, "I hope you are not being subjected to consequences."

"There was the incident with the horse manure in my bed."

"I posted a guard at the end of your corridor since that happened."

"So that's why that man stands there all the time."

"I will send you and Lady Magdalen and Odette ahead and I'll come later."

"I don't think that will fool Fronicka. But do not worry. I think Lady Magdalen and I had such a wonderful time that it was worth all of Lady Fronicka's jealousy. Why don't you bring her and Lady Otilia tomorrow?"

He leaned forward. "I will not be bringing Lady Fronicka here." His look was fierce, his brows drawn together and down. "Why would you speak of Lady Fronicka? Why would you want me to bring her here?"

Avelina's heart pounded and her breath shallowed.

Lord Thornbeck turned away from her. He ran his hand through his hair, causing it to stick out in a few places, and blew out a huff of air.

What had she said that bothered him so much?

Just then, Odette called out, confirming that they were ready.

Avelina tried not to look back at him as she hurried away, but somehow she could not resist turning. He met her eye. His expression was more questioning than angry.

⁓

The next day, Lord Thornbeck left another note under their doors for Avelina and Magdalen to meet him in the solar. When they arrived he showed them his collection of sculptures and paintings that were not of his family members and therefore were not in the gallery. They were mostly scenes of nature—trees, animals, birds, and people working.

Avelina and Magdalen stood admiring the works of art and pointing out various aspects of the paintings and sculptures. The margrave commented here and there or answered their questions.

"It is a beautiful view, is it not?" Lord Thornbeck stood beside Avelina as she stared out the window at the rugged land below. In the distance she could see the spire from Thornbeck Cathedral.

"It is very beautiful. Plimmwald is rather flat, and I think I prefer these beautiful mountains."

"Truly?" His face held such a tender look. It made her heart trip over itself.

"There is no place like home, of course, but the mountains and valleys are so wild and exciting compared to level places. Do you not think so?"

"I do."

A shiver went up her spine. Part of her wanted to lean toward him so she could see deeper into his brown eyes, to put her arms around him and feel his warmth and strength.

How could she even think such a thing? He was to be married to Magdalen and very soon. She would only be here for five more days.

The truth was, she liked Lord Thornbeck so very much. The disloyalty to Magdalen made her stomach feel sick. After all, her friend was so kind and generous. But could she help it if she thought Lord Thornbeck was everything a woman might desire in a man? He was not perfect—he was peevish in the way he hardly ever smiled or laughed, and he was harsh sometimes to his servants—but beneath that severe exterior, she sensed an earnest intention to do what was right. And that longing in his eyes, that conscientiousness in his every action, took her breath away.

She turned away from him, closing her eyes to get her thoughts under control.

A horrible pang of guilt—and something else she shouldn't try to name—snaked through her chest.

Soon Lord Thornbeck excused himself. "Some correspondence I must attend to." He left them in the solar.

Tamping down those ridiculous feelings, Avelina said, "What do you think of Lord Thornbeck?"

"He is a good sort of man." Magdalen stared distractedly at a painting of Thornbeck Castle in winter, with bare-limbed trees all around it. "Why do you ask?"

She spoke so dispassionately, she could not be in love with him. *Oh God, please let her fall in love with him.* She couldn't bear to think of either Lord Thornbeck or Magdalen in a dispassionate, less-than-joyful marriage. But they were both good people. Surely the love and joy and passion would come, in time.

Magdalen turned and looked hard at her, her brows drawing together, as if she was about to ask her a question.

"Let us go exploring the castle." Avelina grabbed her arm. She couldn't bear to answer any probing questions or tell her friend a lie right now. "It is so big, and I have not seen nearly all of it. Perhaps there are some hidden passageways and lost rooms somewhere."

"You make it sound fun." Magdalen laughed. "I suppose it cannot do any harm."

They left the solar, which was on the third level, and walked through a corridor Avelina had not been down before. "This must be the way to the west wing."

"Maybe we should not go there," Magdalen said, her voice hushed. "I do not think Lord Thornbeck would want us to."

"Did he say we couldn't go to the west wing?"

"I don't remember, but I got that impression. Is it not where his brother died?"

"I had not thought of that." Would it be completely destroyed after the fire? Or still mostly intact?

The corridor was lit by small windows about ten feet apart along the wall facing east. They stopped to look at the view, as it was different here. Then the corridor took a sharp turn and there were no more windows to let in light.

"Do you know where you're going?" Magdalen asked.

"No, but if it gets too dark, we'll turn around and go back." And get a torch.

They walked until Avelina could no longer see her feet.

"Maybe we should go back," Magdalen whispered.

Just then—"I see a light ahead." It was faint but Avelina headed toward it. When they reached it, she could see that the light was the glow around a doorway at the end of the corridor. In fact, there were two doors—one at the end of the corridor and the other along it, to the right.

Avelina reached for the glowing door. She pulled on the iron handle and it creaked open a crack, letting in more light. As she eased open the door, she gasped and stepped back, bumping into Magdalen.

She was looking into open space and sky. On the other side of the door, there was no floor, no walls, only . . . sunlight.

Magdalen clutched Avelina's shoulder, pulling her back. "Dear heavenly saints!"

They both stared as they looked out the open doorway. That's when Avelina noticed the smoky black covering the walls. "The fire must have destroyed whatever used to be behind this door."

"Perhaps it was a balcony."

The door to their right suddenly opened. A woman stood staring at them, then said, "Annlin?"

It was the woman who had wandered around the ballroom floor the night of the ball. She stared at them with vacant gray eyes.

"Good day. I am Lady Dorothea and this is my friend Lady Magdalen."

"Have you seen Annlin?"

"No, we have not," Avelina said.

The woman motioned for them to come inside, and Avelina followed her in.

"Dorothea?" Magdalen whispered rather urgently behind her, questioning whether she should be doing this.

Inside was a room littered with half-burned furniture, including a bed frame that was broken and blackened, its curtains nearly entirely burned away. The window at the opposite wall was thrown open, letting in the cold air.

The walls were all covered in soot, and piles of ash and half-burned cloth lay in the corners and on the floor.

"Are you not cold?" Magdalen approached the woman and took her hand. She looked back at Avelina. "Her hand is as cold as ice." She turned back to the woman. "Please come with us. We will take you somewhere warm."

The woman followed them a few steps, then stopped and pulled her hand away from Magdalen. "No, I must stay here. Annlin might come back. She was here. She might come back."

"Do you not want to go search for her in the kitchen?" Avelina asked. The woman was so thin, she seemed in need of a good meal.

The woman placed her hand against her cheek and stared into the near-empty room. "I don't know."

"What are you doing here?"

Avelina startled, spinning around.

Lord Thornbeck stood in the doorway. "It isn't safe in this part of the castle." He glanced from Avelina to Magdalen and back again. Then he held his hand out to the woman. "Endlein. Come. You should not be here either. People are looking for you."

"Where is Annlin? Did the margrave take her away somewhere?"

"No, Endlein," he said, as she took his hand and followed him out.

Frau Schwitzer was behind him. She took the woman's hand and led her away, talking softly to her.

Avelina held her breath as Lord Thornbeck turned to Magdalen and her. "You should not be in the west wing. Why did you come here?"

"Please forgive us."

"Let us go." He ushered them out, placing his body between them and the door that led to a sheer drop to the ground far below, and then followed close behind them. When they were past the end of the corridor, he mumbled, "Need to have someone seal up this entrance."

They stood in front of the solar, back where they had started. Would he berate them for their curiosity? Was he angry?

"The third floor of the west wing is a dangerous place. You could have been killed if you'd stepped out that door."

"Forgive us," Magdalen said again.

"It was I who wished to go to the west wing," Avelina said quickly. "I dragged Lady Magdalen with me."

Lord Thornbeck sighed and ran his hand over his eyes. "The bedchamber where I found you is where my brother died. I tried to save them, but it was too late."

"Them?" Avelina asked.

His face was angled slightly away from them as he stared at the floor. He nodded, an ever-so-slight movement. "My brother, Henrich, and Annlin. She was his . . . they were lovers, even though she was . . . a servant." He rubbed the back of his neck and grimaced, as though in pain. "The absurdity of a margrave and a servant . . ."

Avelina's stomach churned. No doubt that was how he would feel if she fell in love with him. "*A servant.*" He said it as if it was the worst thing in the world. "*Absurd.*" But she couldn't let Magdalen or him know how his words twisted inside her heart like a knife.

"We argued about it the day he died. I tried to convince him to give her up, to realize how wrong the relationship was. He was angry with me—and very drunk—when he went to bed that night. I can never seem to forget that. It was partially my fault he died. If I had not been so harsh in what I said, if he had not been so drunk . . ."

Avelina's heart seemed to actually be breaking inside her chest at the pain in his voice and in his face. "I am so sorry." Her words sounded empty.

"The woman is Annlin's mother, Endlein, a kitchen servant. She became very addled, as you have seen, after the death of her daughter. She wanders up here sometimes to this room, as if she knows this was the last place where her daughter was alive." He shook his head. "Even though she is no longer able to work, I cannot send her away."

"That is kind of you," Avelina said.

He stared down into her eyes. If Magdalen had not been

present, she would have thought he was thinking about kissing her, the way he seemed to be staring at her lips.

How he would hate her if he found out she was a servant, that he was opening his inmost thoughts to someone so far beneath him.

Lord Thornbeck drew back and cleared his throat. "I need to have someone build a wall over the doorway to the burned balcony, and close off that entire corridor. But in the meantime—" He focused his eyes on Avelina. "Do not go near it."

"How did you know we were there?" Avelina asked.

"I didn't. Odette came to tell me the servants couldn't find Endlein, so I went up there to look for her."

"Lord Thornbeck?" Chancellor Jorgen rounded the corner. "Are you ready to sign these documents?"

"Ladies, excuse me."

He went to attend to his duties, while Avelina and Magdalen went back to their bedchambers. He did have a temper. She had seen it displayed when her horse had those sharp shards of pottery underneath its saddle and he'd shouted at his servants and guards, and she'd seen anger in his eyes and heard it in his voice when he found them in the west wing. What would he do if he discovered she'd been deceiving him all this time?

16

AVELINA SAT LISTENING to the local musicians and singers Lord Thornbeck had invited to the Great Hall. A woman sang and was accompanied by a man playing a hurdy-gurdy, another playing the lute, as well as a flute player and drummer. They were quite good, and Avelina enjoyed the music. It was not often she was allowed to listen in when traveling musicians came to Plimmwald Castle, though she usually found a way to sneak into the shadows to hear some of it.

Magdalen, seated beside her, looked so peaceful as she listened to the music with her eyes closed. Avelina closed hers too. The music seemed to surround her. It was as if she could hear each instrument separately, as well as together. The woman's voice sounded richer, fuller, and she found herself taking a deep breath and sighing without even meaning to. She sighed again.

When the song was over, she opened her eyes—and Lord Thornbeck was standing several feet away, watching her.

Her heart skipped as his lips twisted up on one side and he turned away.

She glanced over at Magdalen. She was speaking to the Duke of Wolfberg, who sat on the other side of her.

She wanted to shake her and say, "Don't talk to Wolfberg! You are supposed to be making Lord Thornbeck love you."

She needed to have a talk with her friend. There were only three more days left!

Just then, Endlein wandered in. Her gaze roved around the room, and she wore a very confused, frustrated look.

Avelina rose and quietly walked to where Endlein was standing at the back of the room. "May I help you, Endlein?" she whispered.

"I am looking for my daughter, Annlin. But I don't understand. Who are all these people?"

She looked so thin, Avelina said, "Why don't you come with me to the kitchen and I'll get you something to eat."

"Oh. I never feel hungry. I'm looking for Annlin."

But she allowed Avelina to lead her out and down the stairs toward the kitchen.

"Where are we going?"

"To the kitchen, to find some food. All is well, do not worry." Avelina tried to speak soothingly. "After we get some food, I will help you to your room."

The kitchen servants looked up when they entered.

"Can we have some food, please? Whatever you have."

Two of the servants gathered some cheese and bread and some fruit pastries and brought them to a table and coaxed Endlein into sitting down to eat. Avelina thanked them, then stayed with her while she ate and the servants went back to work.

Endlein actually ate quite a bit. Then she suddenly stood. "I need to find Annlin."

Avelina touched her arm and said gently, "We cannot find her tonight, Endlein. Can I take you up to your room? Come. Let me take you there."

The only problem was, she didn't know where the woman's room was. She asked one of the servants, who explained, and Avelina took her arm and led her up.

When they finally reached Endlein's narrow little bedchamber, Endlein turned and smiled at her. "When I find my daughter, we shall do something kind for you. What is your name?"

"Av—Dorothea. Dorothea."

"Dorothea." Endlein turned and went toward her bed.

Avelina closed the door. It was sweet of Endlein to want to do something for her. Poor Endlein.

Avelina meandered back to her bedchamber after praying alone at the chapel. Only two more days until the ball.

She had prayed for forgiveness for all of the half-truths and deceptions of the past two weeks, and for favor with Magdalen, that she would not hate her when Avelina told her the truth. And she prayed that she would not embarrass herself with tears at having to leave this place—at how much she would miss Lord Thornbeck and Lady Magdalen.

When she opened her bedchamber door and went inside, she saw a familiar-looking piece of paper on the floor. Another note under her door. Avelina picked it up and read it. *Meet me on the balcony at the end of the gallery next to the ballroom after dark.*

Her heart leapt at the thought of seeing him again. She had not seen Lord Thornbeck all day. Probably he was spending time with some of the other ladies. But she only felt slightly jealous thinking about that. Now she would see him on this clear night, with the moon and stars above.

Avelina hurried to tidy her hair. Irma was almost never around to help her with her hair, her dress, or anything else. Irma had confessed the night before that her new friend, Gerhaws, had introduced her to another servant—a man with whom Irma was obviously infatuated, as she was now not even coming back to her room overnight to sleep. Avelina wanted to warn Irma that the manservant would break her heart when they had to leave, but she couldn't imagine Irma would be eager to hear any advice from her.

She scurried to Magdalen's door, but before she could knock, she noticed a piece of paper attached to the door.

I am waiting for you at the balcony.

M.

She glanced at the end of the corridor. The guard was not there. Where had he gone? And if Magdalen was waiting for her at the balcony, then she must already be with Lord Thornbeck. A pang of jealousy attacked her like a bird of prey, its talons gripping her heart.

No. She stomped her foot to force her heart to listen. *I will not allow jealousy to get hold of me.* Magdalen was her friend, and Avelina could never have Lord Thornbeck anyway.

She hurried toward the balcony. She would be joyful for Lord Thornbeck and Magdalen.

So why did she have to blink away tears as she walked?

When she arrived at the gallery, the long, narrow room's only light came from the windows and the moonlight outside, as all the torches and candles had been snuffed out. As she walked the only sound was the swishing of her skirts and scuffling of her slippers on the stone floor. The portraits seemed to watch her as she passed, their eyes following her. Her heart beat faster, and she was thankful when she reached the open door at the other end of the long room.

Avelina wrapped her arms around herself, as the air was quite cold, and stepped onto the balcony. She looked to her right. A young woman was there, alone, leaning against the railing, but she was not Magdalen.

"Good evening, Lady Dorothea." Fronicka said her name slowly, drawing it out. "Come and have a talk with me."

Avelina took a step forward, then stopped. Something was amiss. Where were Magdalen and Lord Thornbeck? Why was Fronicka here?

"It is a beautiful night, is it not?" Fronicka smiled in a friendly way—almost too friendly.

"It is."

"A little warmer. Quite warm for this time of year."

"Hm, yes."

"The sky is beautiful. Did you notice?"

Avelina gazed up. Perhaps Lord Thornbeck and Magdalen decided they wanted to be alone. Another pang smote her breast, taking her breath. They would be married soon. Of course they did not want her around.

Fronicka motioned her closer to the railing. "If you stand over here, you can see a few of the lights from the town, and also a few more stars."

How strange that Fronicka was behaving this way. Did she want something? "What are you doing out here gazing at the lights and the stars?"

"I had nothing else to do." Fronicka smiled.

Cautiously Avelina approached the railing and looked out. She did not see the lights Fronicka had spoken of, but she did not care enough to ask her about them.

"So, is it you or Lady Magdalen who will marry Lord Thornbeck?"

Avelina started to say, "It is not I," but she stopped herself.

Fronicka was up to something. So she said, "I suppose only Lord Thornbeck knows the answer to that question."

Fronicka looked over the balcony railing. "This is such a beautiful place, is it not? I can see the rose garden from here. Look."

Avelina took another step closer. She laid her hand on the railing and looked down. The rose garden was visible to their right by the light spilling out from the lower-floor windows inside the castle. But straight down was a sheer drop, a ravine with small trees and bushes growing out of it, so deep she could not see the bottom. She looked back at Fronicka. The hair on the back of Avelina's neck prickled and she shivered. She should have brought her cloak.

"Who are you, Lady Dorothea? Are you truly that lady? Or are you someone who has come here to take her place?"

Avelina stepped away from Fronicka, and the railing pressed into her lower back. "Why would you say such a thing?"

"No reason, except that I recall hearing that Lady Dorothea had golden blonde hair, and yours is brown. And that Lady Dorothea's eyes were green, but yours are blue."

"Many people's hair darkens when they get older." *Let Fronicka not see panic in my face.* "I don't know why you are so suspicious, Lady Fronicka."

Fronicka started fingering the embroidery on her belt. "I wanted to marry Lord Thornbeck, but he barely looks at me. He's too busy spending time with you and Magdalen."

"Why did you want to marry him so badly? There must be another titled man to whom your father could betroth you."

"I had a reason to want to marry Lord Thornbeck." Fronicka's smile was cold and sent a shiver down Avelina's spine.

"Are you in love with him?"

"What a naive thing you are. Of course not. Love has nothing to do with marriage." Fronicka stared up at the sky for a moment.

"I wanted to marry him to get Thornbeck. It rightly belongs to my father, and once I married him . . ."

"You would kill him, and your father would take over."

"You are not as foolish as I thought." Fronicka stepped toward Avelina.

She leaned back against the railing.

It suddenly gave way behind her.

Avelina cried out as the night air embraced her. She flailed out both hands and grabbed the part of the railing still attached to the balcony.

Her feet dangled below her. She was going to die.

She opened her mouth to scream but no sound came. *O God, help me!*

She clung to the railing with all her strength, her hands gripping the broken railing, the only thing keeping her from plunging to her death into the ravine below. She tried to pull herself up. She was not strong enough. Her heart jerked and pounded, her breath came in painful gasps.

She finally forced in enough air and screamed, short and high-pitched.

She held on tight, the muscles in her arms clenching painfully. If she let go, she would fall into the deep ravine below. She would never survive such a fall. She screamed again.

How long could she hold on?

Fronicka hovered over her, staring at Avelina's hands where they gripped the wooden railing. The cool, assessing look on her face made Avelina's stomach sink.

Fronicka stood and ran away, saying, "Help! Someone, help!"

Her hands were slipping. The darkness below seemed to be pulling her, sucking her down. She no longer had enough breath to scream. She closed her eyes. What would happen to Jacob and

Brigitta and Father? How would they get food without Avelina's wages? How cruel for her to die now. Would Lord Thornbeck and Lady Magdalen find out she'd lied? Would they hate her?

The sound of footsteps made her open her eyes. The balcony vibrated with the steps, and suddenly Lord Thornbeck was standing over her.

He fell to his knees and grabbed her arms, just above her wrists. "I've got you. Let go."

He was holding her arms with a grip so tight it hurt. *Please don't let go.* But she was still dangling. She would have to let go for him to pull her up. How could she? Fear gripped her even tighter than his hands, fear of plunging to the ground below. What if he lost his grip and dropped her? She couldn't let go.

"Look at me," Lord Thornbeck demanded, his voice strained and gruff. "Let. Go. Now."

Avelina squeezed her eyes shut. She let go, her heart pounding.

He pulled her up as she raised her knees, scraping them on the edge of the stone balcony. Then her legs touched the solid, flat surface.

She clung to him without even opening her eyes. He wrapped his arms around her and held her tight as he sat back on the floor of the balcony.

Her breath was coming hard. She pressed her cheek against his chest. His heart beat in her ear, thumping nearly as fast as her own.

"You are safe now. I have you. You are safe." He held her even tighter.

Avelina squeezed her eyes shut and concentrated on his solid warmth to push back the thought that she almost died.

"Are you all right?" Fronicka was behind them. "She leaned against the railing and it gave way. I was so frightened. I ran to get help, but I couldn't find a guard."

Avelina shuddered and pressed her face into Lord Thornbeck's shoulder. He held her tight against him. If only she could stay like this forever, safe and warm and protected, or at least until she stopped shaking.

She forced herself to pull away from the delicious warmth of his chest and sat up, unable to look into his face.

"Are you well?" He still held her with one arm around her back. He reached out and brushed the hair that had come loose out of her face. She finally looked into his eyes.

"What happened?" he asked.

"I leaned against the railing and it broke. I fell." Her lip quivered and she pressed her hand against her mouth. "I fell, but I grabbed the railing and held on. I was so afraid."

A violent shudder shook her whole body.

"You are not well," he said.

"I am well." She stared down at her feet. "But I lost my shoes. They were my only pair." Tears dripped from her eyes as her teeth started to chatter uncontrollably.

"I'll get you new shoes." Lord Thornbeck caressed her shoulder.

She kept her head down, hoping he would not see that she was crying. "I-I think I-I sh-should lie down." Her vision was spinning. She didn't want to faint.

Lord Thornbeck turned to one of the guards. "Carry her to her chamber."

The guard came over and helped her to her feet, then lifted her in his arms. She felt herself growing even dizzier, and her vision began to blur and darken.

Her head fell back against the man's shoulder and she kept her eyes closed. She should probably feel very embarrassed, but she was too close to fainting to care how she looked. She could hear Lord Thornbeck's footsteps and walking stick thumping beside her.

When they reached her chamber, she peeked through her nearly closed lids. Lord Thornbeck opened the door and the guard carried her straight through to her bed and laid her down.

Lady Magdalen's voice came from near her doorway. "What happened? Is Lady Dorothea sick?"

Someone took her hand. Avelina opened her eyes and Magdalen was standing at her bedside.

"She has had a terrible fright," Lord Thornbeck said. "I shall send for Frau Schwitzer to see if she needs a doctor."

She expected Lord Thornbeck to leave the room, but he was still standing there. He stepped toward the bed. "This never should have happened," he said in a quiet, deep voice. "I had no idea the railing was loose."

She wiped her cheek and tried not to sniff. "Thank you, Lord Thornbeck, for saving me."

"I thank God I was able to reach you in time." He reached over and squeezed her hand, the one Magdalen was not holding.

Guilt froze the tears behind her eyes. She had no right to enjoy his touch. She was a terrible friend in that moment, because she wanted him. Oh, how she wanted him to love her! To always be near to hold her and protect her. She turned her head away from him and made sure her hand stayed limp inside his.

"I shall leave you alone, then." Lord Thornbeck turned away and walked out of the room with the guard who had carried her in.

⁓

Reinhart rubbed his face with his hand. He could still smell her light, flowery scent, like springtime and lilacs, could still feel her in his arms, and his heart skipped a beat. Seeing her dangling from the balcony, hanging over that deep ravine, knowing she was one moment away from death, sent a bolt of lightning through his veins. *Thank You, God.* He had arrived in time.

He limped back to the balcony. Thankfully, his lameness had not prevented him from saving Dorothea. He must have thrown down his walking stick when he heard her scream, and a guard retrieved it for him when he was holding her on the balcony.

He made it to the balcony and approached the railing. He got down on his knees to examine it, but most of it was gone, and unless he was mistaken, even the part that Dorothea had been clinging to was gone. There was only a broken bit farther over on the balcony. Had someone done something to the railing, possibly cutting it, so it would break when someone leaned on it? They could have broken off the part that was cut and gotten rid of it.

But who would do such a thing?

He would discuss it with Jorgen. They could send someone to fetch the broken pieces of the railing from the ravine below and possibly discover if this was an accident or a deliberate attempt at murder. First the pottery shards, now this. Was someone trying to harm Lady Dorothea?

Reinhart pushed himself up with the walking stick, remembering again how he had pulled her from the edge of death. He closed his eyes and relived how she had clung to him, burying her face in his shoulder. Later, when Lady Magdalen had held her hand, she'd clung to her, but when he tried to hold her other hand, it had laid in his like a wilted flower.

He still had no idea if she cared for him or not, and the ball was tomorrow night.

He turned and went to find Jorgen.

Avelina raised her hand to her face, the one Lord Thornbeck had squeezed a moment ago, and was overcome by his familiar scent—the smell of evergreen trees and mint leaves the servants put in his laundry. Warmth washed over her as she remembered how he had held her tight, much tighter than necessary, sitting on the balcony floor.

Surely it was only a reaction to the frightening situation. Surely he did not love her.

"Dorothea, what in heaven's name has happened to you tonight?"

Avelina had a sudden urge to tell Magdalen her secret, to tell her everything. "I . . . ." No, she should wait until all this was over, after the ball. "I fell off the balcony. The railing gave way behind me and I . . . ." She swallowed past the dryness in her throat and forced herself to go on. "I was holding on to what was left of it. I could barely breathe but I managed to scream, at least once. If Lord Thornbeck had not come and pulled me up, I would have fallen from the balcony." She shuddered and closed her eyes.

"You poor girl." Magdalen pulled her hand up to her heart. "That is terrifying. It is no wonder you are still shaking."

"I am well, but I lost my shoes." She lifted her skirts, revealing her bare feet.

"Do you not have any more?"

"No." Who would believe an earl's daughter did not have another pair of shoes? But Lord Thornbeck had said he would bring her some.

"Perhaps I have some that will fit you."

"Do not worry about it tonight, please. It will not be the first time I have walked in bare feet." She grimaced. Though Magdalen had surely been shod all her life, Avelina had many times been without shoes.

"Where is that servant of yours, Irma?" Magdalen said, with

the closest thing to irritation on her face that Avelina had ever seen. "She is never around when one needs her."

Magdalen's maidservant suddenly entered the room.

"Hegatha, go get a pair of my shoes for Lady Dorothea."

A tear ran down Avelina's cheek. She hastily wiped it with her hand.

"Please don't cry, Dorothea." Tears welled up in Magdalen's eyes. "You're safe and well now. Do you want to talk about it some more?"

Avelina took deep breaths to force back the tears. "Forgive me. I don't want to make you sad. I am well now."

Magdalen surprised her by climbing up into the bed beside her and hugging her arm. "Now tell me exactly what you feel. I make my little sisters do this whenever they cry."

What was Avelina feeling? "Afraid. Tired. Shaken. Guilty. Sad." She sniffed.

"What were you doing on the balcony . . . in the dark?" Her brows drawn together in a look of bewilderment, Magdalen propped on one elbow to stare down at Avelina.

"That is what I don't understand. I came back to my bed-chamber after praying in the chapel and there was a note on the floor saying to meet on the balcony tonight. When I went to your room, there was a note on the door saying you were waiting for me there."

"Where?"

"On the balcony at the end of the gallery. It was signed 'M.'"

"It was on my door? I never wrote that."

"Did you not get a note from Lord Thornbeck to come to the balcony?"

"No. I've been in my bedchamber for the last few hours, and I did not get a note."

"Someone wrote that note and the one on your door. I went to the balcony and no one was there except Fronicka." *Fronicka.*

"She must have written those notes. But why?"

"I don't know. Maybe she . . ." Maybe she wanted to accuse Avelina of not being the real Lady Dorothea. She obviously suspected something was amiss.

"So how did you fall off the balcony? Did Fronicka . . . ?"

"I was leaning back against the railing and it gave way behind me."

"What if she did something to the railing? What if she wanted you to fall?"

Surely even Fronicka was not evil enough to do something like that. "She called for help as soon as I fell." But she remembered the cold look on her face while she was hanging there and shuddered again. And as though through a fog, she also remembered Fronicka saying something, just before Avelina fell, that shocked her very much. She said she wanted to marry Lord Thornbeck. Avelina asked her why. What had Fronicka said? For some reason, she could not remember. Perhaps it was the shock of falling off the balcony and the terror of nearly dying, but it made her want to warn Lord Thornbeck. She couldn't remember why.

"It seems very suspicious." Magdalen hugged Avelina's arm tighter. "I will be staying with you tonight. I'm not letting you out of my sight until after the ball, and I will not let anyone hurt you."

"Thank you," Avelina whispered, the tears starting to leak from her eyes again. "You are the best friend I've ever had."

But after nearly falling to her death and feeling so guilty for her deception, she had decided to tell Lady Magdalen the truth, the complete truth about who she was. As soon as the ball was over. Lady Magdalen would be hurt and would never speak to her again, but at least she would hear the truth from Avelina and not from someone else.

17

It was the night of the ball. The hour had finally come. Avelina put on her best dress—a silk cotehardie that was half pink and half green, with one pink and one green false sleeve that hung straight down from her upper arms. Her hair hung down her back with tiny braids interspersed. On her head she wore a circlet of gold filigree that Lady Magdalen had insisted she borrow. Avelina had prepared her hair herself, since Irma never came to help her get ready for the ball.

"You must send that Irma to the kitchen. Truly, Dorothea, you are an earl's daughter. You should not accept such deplorable behavior from your personal maidservant."

Avelina nodded. When she was finally ready, her feet shod with Magdalen's shoes, she looked in the mirror. Her hair was lovely, her clothing was becoming, and there was a bit of color in her cheeks. *Not bad . . . for a servant.*

"Oh, Dorothea, you look beautiful." Magdalen clasped her hands, her smile stretching all the way across her face, her eyes glowing.

"You should be getting yourself dressed," Avelina told her. "Don't look at me. You're the one who should look beautiful tonight."

Magdalen gave her a sideways stare, her brows arching high. "Me? Do you think so?"

Was she trying to be coy? "Of course I think so. Tonight is the night Lord Thornbeck will choose his wife."

"Mm-hm." Magdalen was smiling again, her brows still arching.

Avelina had a strange feeling in her stomach. "I am hoping he will choose you, so don't look at me like that." Irritation welled up inside her. No, she should not be angry with Magdalen. Magdalen, who was so kind and was so concerned about her. Magdalen, who was by far the best choice for Lord Thornbeck.

Except me. Avelina would be good for him. She could make him stop scowling, could make him believe in love and goodness. She could love him out of that dark thought pattern he seemed to be in, thinking about his lame ankle and about his poor dead brother and how he could not save him.

But it was wrong to even think about it. He would marry Magdalen and that was that. Two weeks ago she would have never even dreamed of such a thing as marrying the Margrave of Thornbeck. But now . . .

Tears welled up in her eyes and she turned away from her friend, pretending to adjust her embroidered belt. She should tell Magdalen now. She should get it over and done, ignore the sick feeling in her stomach and just tell her.

"It is time to go downstairs." Magdalen headed toward the door.

Avelina hesitated. But the words didn't come, and she found herself walking through the corridor beside Magdalen.

Avelina could not help looking at her friend as they made their way down. This was the last time Magdalen would think of her as an equal, since she would tell her the truth—she would—as soon as this was over.

As they descended the last section of the stairs, everyone was already in the ballroom, and they all watched as Lady Magdalen and Avelina joined them.

Lord Thornbeck was also watching, but his gaze seemed to be on Avelina. He should have been looking at Magdalen. She was beautiful tonight. Her strawberry-blonde hair was crowned by a circlet of dried flowers. She wore a pale-blue silk cotehardie with a long-sleeved yellow underdress. She was much prettier than Avelina, and she was truly the daughter of a baron.

Avelina refused to meet Lord Thornbeck's gaze.

She pasted on a smile, even when she saw Fronicka smirking up at her. Her father, the Duke of Geitbart, stood beside her, not looking at anyone in particular, his gaze darting around the room.

She smiled and greeted everyone who came near her, but it was as if there was a fog over her eyes and ears, dulling everything. The music was indistinct and a mist lay over the beautiful people and their beautiful clothing. Her legs were weighted down with the same dullness and she didn't think she could dance. And yet, she did not want to draw attention to herself as she had at the last ball. Lord Thornbeck himself had come to her side so she would not have to stand alone.

But tonight there were more people, parents and guardians who would be escorting their daughters home in the next few days. Perhaps she could hide amongst them.

Lord Thornbeck suddenly appeared in front of her. He took her hand and bowed over it and kissed it so quickly she did not realize he was going to do it until it was done. His brown eyes were piercing as they stared straight into hers. "Are you well?"

"Yes, of course." She blinked, hard, to rid herself of the dullness.

Lord Thornbeck looked very handsome. He seemed to have

burned away the mist, with his bright-blue outer tunic and white sleeves, his thick dark hair combed across his forehead.

He squeezed her hand before letting it go. "You look beautiful, Lady Dorothea."

Truly, she should blurt out the truth to him right now, at this moment.

She glanced around for Lady Magdalen. She was standing just behind her. Avelina stepped back to join her. Lord Thornbeck took the hint and greeted Magdalen, but he did not kiss her hand.

People seemed to be crowding around them, wanting to speak to Lord Thornbeck, so Avelina hurried away, farther into the room, her breath suddenly coming faster.

A few moments later Magdalen caught up with her.

"Dorothea, why did you run away? Lord Thornbeck wanted to speak to you." Magdalen chewed on her lip, a look of concern in her eyes. "Don't you like Lord Thornbeck?" she whispered close to her ear.

Avelina studied her friend's expression. "What do you mean? Of course . . . I-I like him very much. Who wouldn't? But that is certainly not important—"

"Stop saying things like that!" Magdalen shook her head and looked as if she might laugh.

Avelina's face burned. A rock seemed to settle in the pit of her stomach.

"Magdalen, I have to tell you something. I should have told you already, and I can't go another—"

She turned to face the Duke of Wolfberg.

"Good evening, Lady Magdalen. Lady Dorothea." He nodded to them both.

The music started. The Duke of Wolfberg asked Magdalen to dance, and with an anxious glance at Avelina, she moved with him to the middle of the floor, along with many of the other guests. But there was still a cluster of people around Lord Thornbeck.

One of the young nobles from the first ball approached Avelina and asked her to dance. Since she was familiar with this dance, she agreed. It was much easier to forget what was looming ahead of her while she was forced to concentrate on the steps and on what her partner was saying to her. But always in the back of her mind was Lord Thornbeck, in his blue outer tunic, looking very handsome, and soon to be a distant memory.

For now, she was Lady Dorothea, dancing with a nobleman, smiling and dressed like all the other ladies in the room.

As they performed the rather slow steps of the dance, her partner said, "You look beautiful, Lady Dorothea."

"I thank you, Lord Dreigers. And you dance very well."

"I thank you, Lady Dorothea."

They smiled and complimented each other a few more times until the dance was over. She simply had to keep this up for the rest of the night. One last night to pretend. One last night to feel important and beautiful.

Carefully, she stayed in the small crowd of older people, except for the three dances she danced. She chatted with Lady Applonia's mother. For a moment she thought Lord Thornbeck was coming toward her, but he was stopped by Lady Otilia's father, who spoke with him for several minutes, then they were joined by two more fathers.

When Magdalen finally stopped dancing, she came over to Avelina. "Have you spoken to Lord Thornbeck?"

"No, why?"

A worried look came into her eyes. "Perhaps you should talk to him. I am sure he wishes to speak to you."

"Why would he wish to speak to me?"

Magdalen bit her lip again, as if in frustration.

"What is wrong?" Something was bothering Magdalen. "I'm sorry if I was rude to Lord Thornbeck, but Magdalen, there is something I need to tell you."

Just then, the music stopped and everyone turned toward the head of the room, near the staircase. Jorgen Hartman and his wife, Odette, were standing with Lord Thornbeck.

"May I have your attention, please," Jorgen said.

All conversation ceased.

"You all know that for the past two weeks, Lord Thornbeck has been deciding who he will marry from among the ten ladies here tonight."

Avelina and Magdalen glanced at each other. Magdalen had such a strange look on her face.

"And now, before we retire to the Great Hall for the feast that is prepared for you, Lord Thornbeck's guests, our margrave would like to announce his choice."

Avelina's next breath stuck in her throat as her heart beat fast and hard.

Lord Thornbeck thanked Jorgen, then turned his eyes on Avelina. "I wish to thank all the ladies who came to Thornbeck Castle for these two weeks."

Why was he staring at her?

"I expected to learn a little of each lady's character and temperament. I did not expect . . . to be so impressed, by one lady in particular."

Avelina's heart pounded. If only he would hurry and get it over with.

"I choose to be my wife the noblest and most worthy lady . . . Lady Dorothea of Plimmwald."

The floor seemed to give way underneath her, and she was

dangling once again above a cavernous ravine. Her stomach plummeted even as her heart trembled in excitement. Could Lord Thornbeck have truly chosen her? Love *her*? It was the most wonderful moment of her life, and the worst possible thing that could happen.

Her vision was so blurred, she could just make out Lord Thornbeck standing as if he was waiting for her to come forward and join him.

Magdalen hugged her from the side and giggled, an overjoyed smile on her face.

"No, no," Avelina whispered to her friend. "This can't happen."

"What do you mean?" Magdalen whispered back. "He's waiting for you. Go." She gave Avelina a gentle push.

She started forward, putting one foot in front of the other. What would she say? Her heart squeezed inside her. *O God in heaven, I don't want to hurt him!* She must simply wait until they were alone. She could not tell him in front of all these people. It would be too shameful, for both of them.

His face was blurrier than ever. People were murmuring all around her, a few of them saying, "*Glückwünsche*," or some other congratulatory word, but she concentrated on walking straight ahead.

When she had nearly reached him, Odette embraced her, smiling, even whispering into her ear, "I knew you were the one for him."

Avelina felt a stab. She would tell them—Lord Thornbeck, Magdalen, Odette, and Jorgen—as soon as this evening was over and everyone else had dispersed to their chambers.

She finally looked up at him. *I'm so sorry.*

Suddenly, Fronicka was speaking. "That woman is not who she says she is. She is not Lady Dorothea."

The room quickly hushed. Avelina felt the blood drain from her face.

"Explain yourself." Lord Thornbeck stood rigidly beside her.

The Duke of Geitbart said, "We have discovered that this woman is not the daughter of the Earl of Plimmwald. She has been deceiving everyone for the past two weeks. Not only is she not the Earl of Plimmwald's daughter, she is only a servant, Lady Dorothea's maidservant."

"Prove it." Lord Thornbeck's voice was raspy and harsh.

"I don't have to prove it." Geitbart pointed at her. "Just ask her. Just ask . . . Avelina Klein."

Avelina sensed rather than saw Lord Thornbeck turn and face her. "Is it true?"

She did her best to hold her head up and meet his eyes. "Please forgive me. I was going to tell you."

No one spoke for the longest moment. *Father God, do not let me faint.* She could barely breathe and the air was so hot and suffocating. What would he do now?

He said quietly, "Take her to the library."

Someone took hold of Avelina's arm.

She lifted her head enough to find Magdalen in the crowd. She was crying.

"I—"

Jorgen led her away as Lord Thornbeck said to the crowd in an even voice, "It is time to go to the Great Hall."

Avelina had to hurry to keep up with Jorgen as he held her by the elbow and propelled her forward. Soon they were turning into the dark library.

Jorgen let go of her to light some candles. "You may sit." His words were curt and his expression hard.

The closest chair was at Lord Thornbeck's desk, and she sat

down and laid her head on it. Lord Thornbeck would be so angry. How would he punish her? Would he yell at her? Beat her? Throw her in the dungeon? But worse was the thought of his strained voice, and Magdalen crying among all the strangers.

Her own tears flowed.

After what seemed like hours, she heard the *step-step-tap, step-step-tap* of Lord Thornbeck coming down the corridor and getting closer.

18

Reinhart neared the library, his breath coming fast. How dare she humiliate him? A servant. How could this be? How could he have chosen to marry *a servant*? He had tried to choose the woman with the best character and the most integrity, and instead, he'd chosen the deceitful one. An imposter. Pretender. Servant.

The back of his neck burned as he entered the room. There. She had the audacity to sit at his desk? After what she had done? "Get up."

Jorgen moved to his right.

"Jorgen, you may go."

Dorothea—but that was not her name—sniffled and stood as Jorgen left the room. How dare she try to gain his sympathy by crying? It would not work.

"What is your name?" he demanded.

"Avelina Klein, my lord." She was wiping her face with her hands, keeping her head down so he couldn't see her face.

"Get away from my desk. Come over here, to the light."

She moved toward the table where the candles were lit and stood on the other side of it from him.

"Look at me."

She lifted her head. Her eyes were puffy and red. Her chin quivered. A pang went through him and he clenched his teeth. She had made a fool of him.

"I would never marry you." He infused as much coldness into his voice as possible. "I just declared my intention to marry you in front of all those people . . . You deceived me."

"I had no choice. I—"

"You had no choice but to pretend to be someone you were not? You came here pretending to be Lady Dorothea. But you are only a servant. This is true, is it not?"

"Yes, my lord."

She bowed her head, clasping her hands in front of her. "I am sorry. I do not expect you to understand. I must seem despicable."

Why wasn't she defending herself? Expressing those strong opinions of hers?

His insides twisted to think he had fallen for a servant, just like his brother, whom he had so criticized for the very same thing.

"Why did you do it? Did you want to humiliate me? Was that Lord Plimmwald's plan? Did he send you to make a fool of me in front of half the country's noblemen?"

"No, he did not—that is, he did send me, but he was not try-ing to—"

"Why did he send you?"

"He wanted you to help us. He was afraid of Geitbart—the duke—taking over Plimmwald. He did not want to offend you. And the real Lady Dorothea could not come."

He gritted his teeth. He was a fool to even listen to her at all. Heat exploded in his head. He'd confessed to everyone there tonight—half the noblemen in this part of the empire—that he wanted to marry a servant girl.

He should ask her more questions, demand to know every detail, but he was losing his grip on his temper. He imagined yelling at her, shaking her. If she were one of his guards, he'd send her immediately to be punished—locked in the dungeon. Listening to her explanation for why she had deliberately deceived him would cause him to do something he would regret. Still, he could not allow himself to soften, and to add fuel to the fire inside, he had one question for her.

"What would you receive if you succeeded in tricking me?"

She met his eye, her head rising. "I asked Lord Plimmwald for a dowry so I could marry."

"And whom did you want to marry?" Was there someone at home, a servant boy she was in love with? He clenched his walking stick so hard it dug into his palm.

"I had no one particular in mind, if that is what you are asking."

"But you wanted to marry."

"Yes. I wanted a husband who would love me." Defiance was in her eyes, but there was a slight tremor in her voice, and her jaw twitched, as if she was clenching her teeth.

"So you did all this—risking my wrath, risking that I would find out you were not a rightful earl's daughter—all for a dowry so you could marry well?"

She tilted her chin up. "I also asked for a goose and a side of pork every month for my family."

He turned his back on her and ran his hand through his hair. To think that she would ask for such a thing, for a basic provision of food for her family . . . or perhaps she was lying again.

He could not allow himself to feel sympathy for her. He must keep his wits about him.

He must not be like his brother.

"I might have married you. I might have made you my wife,

thinking you were Lady Dorothea. What kind of fool do I look like in front of every powerful noble . . . All this, after I condemned my brother for sleeping with a maidservant."

Why could he not have chosen some other woman? Why Avelina? But he knew why. It was because she had seemed good and kind and had expressed her thoughts without any false pride or pretense. He had admired her forthrightness and her compassion. And although he had never thought a wife with strong opinions was a good thing, he actually found he liked her opinions—or at least admired her for having them. He wanted to get to know her, to know everything that was in her heart. He wanted to marry her and, surprising even himself, to love her. Yet . . . she had deceived him.

"I was not trying to make you choose me."

He turned around to face her again. Her arms were crossed over her chest and her lips were pursed.

"I would not have let you marry me, thinking I was Lady Dorothea. I would have told you the truth."

"You wanted me to marry Lady Magdalen." He expelled a breath, suddenly realizing the truth. "I thought you were only being modest, frightened by my attention." He had hoped, deep down, she felt the same way about him, that she was just as drawn to him as he was to her. But he had deluded himself.

She looked at him with wide eyes and an open mouth. "*I* could not marry you. Of course I wanted you to marry Mag—Lady Magdalen. She is kind and noble and she needed a powerful husband like you, since her father died and there is no one to defend her castle."

That sounded logical, at least. And it was just as logical for him to send her away and never think of her again. Just as logical for him to choose someone else to marry.

"Go to your bedchamber. Do not come down to the Great Hall. I do not wish to see you again."

He turned and stalked out of the room and down the corridor—and felt as if he'd just been punched in the gut.

In her bedchamber, Avelina sat on the floor by her door, listening for Magdalen to walk by on her way to her room. After a few minutes she heard footsteps. Avelina jumped to her feet and yanked open the door, but it was only a kitchen servant, bringing her a tray of food.

Avelina stepped back and let the servant in, who eyed Avelina askance as she set the tray on her table.

After the servant left, she lifted the cloth covering the food. The smell that wafted up to her made her stomach turn. She laid the cloth back over it and went back to the door and sat, drawing her knees up and laying her head on them.

Was Lord Thornbeck able to eat? Tears stung her eyes again. *Dear God, please . . . comfort him. I'm so sorry for hurting him.* She sat, alternately praying and crying.

Someone was coming down the corridor. Avelina stood too quickly and had to reach out a hand to steady herself. Before she could open the door, someone knocked.

Avelina opened the door to Magdalen.

"Oh, Magda—Lady Magdalen, please forgive me. Please let me explain."

"May I come in?"

"Yes, please. Come in." She closed the door. "Please forgive me for deceiving you."

"I forgive you, of course." Magdalen's expression was sad, and she sighed. "But I would like to know why."

"My lord, the Earl of Plimmwald made me feel as though I was doing it for the good of our people." She sighed. "He told me people would die if I did not strengthen our alliance with Lord Thornbeck."

She proceeded to explain the whole story while Magdalen stared, shook her head, and nodded for her to go on.

"I am so sorry for lying to you. I never wanted to deceive anyone. And once I was here, it seemed rather easy to assume Dorothea's identity. No one questioned that I was her."

"So this is why you said you could not marry Lord Thornbeck!" Magdalen slapped a hand over her mouth. "Oh, Avelina. How can you ever forgive me?"

"Forgive you?"

"For not believing you. I thought you were only trying to be kind to me, to sacrifice Lord Thornbeck so I could marry him. I didn't understand when you said you couldn't marry him. I knew he was planning to choose you."

"How could you know?"

"I could tell by the way he looked at you. And then yesterday he told me so himself."

"He told you?"

"Yes, but he was worried that you didn't care for him, and I assured him that you did." Magdalen put her hands up to her face. "I'm so sorry."

"No, no, you couldn't have known. Besides . . ." Avelina blew out a breath, trying to push back the tears. "I did care for him . . . very much." And he cared for her. Her breath hitched and she pressed her hand over her lips to keep them from trembling.

"He fell in love with you. Perhaps . . . perhaps he will still marry you." But even Magdalen looked doubtful.

"No. He told me tonight that he would never marry me."

How good it had felt to be chosen by him, even in the midst of her horror at what was about to happen, at his discovering she was an imposter. It was like being in his arms after he rescued her from falling off the balcony, his fine woolen tunic against her cheek. So much heaven . . . but it could never be. Not for her. She was Avelina the servant, not Dorothea the earl's daughter. *Dear heavenly saints. How she wanted him to love her, wanted his love.* The pain was so great she doubled over.

Lady Magdalen put a hand on her shoulder.

She couldn't think about how much it hurt to be so close to having his love, only to lose it. She should think of Lord Thornbeck and how humiliated he must feel for asking her to marry him in front of everyone.

And what about Magdalen?

"You must hate me for deceiving you."

"It sounds as if you had little choice. I do not hate you, Doro—Avelina. Do not be so hard on yourself."

"But I am only a servant. You must be so angry—"

"I am surprised, but I am not angry. You have a noble heart. You always did seem too kind and openhearted to be the daughter of an earl."

Avelina might have laughed if she had not been so miserable. "I know I have no right to ask for your friendship anymore, Magda—" She stopped and corrected herself again. "Lady Magdalen."

"Nonsense! You shall always have my friendship." Magdalen squeezed her shoulder.

"I felt so guilty for deceiving you, I am glad I can tell you now. Even though . . . everything is ruined. But perhaps something good will come of this. Now that he knows I am not Lady Dorothea, perhaps he will want to marry you."

Magdalen smiled and shook her head. "I never wished to marry Lord Thornbeck. And when I saw the way he looked at you, I knew, even if you didn't, that he was falling in love with you. Besides, I am still hoping I may end up betrothed to the Duke of Wolfberg."

"Oh! Yes, of course. When the two of you were dancing and talking at the ball . . . I should have known." But she had been too busy trying to make sure Lord Thornbeck noticed Magdalen.

"It is too cruel Lord Thornbeck can't marry you."

"Even if he wanted to, it would not please the king. The king wants him to marry someone who will help him form an alliance, who will keep the kingdom stable. Marrying me would not please anyone. And he does not want to marry me now. He made that very clear."

Avelina rubbed the back of her neck, which had begun to ache. "I was going to tell you the truth tonight. I would not have parted from you without telling you."

Magdalen gave her a gentle smile. "I believe you. I am only sorry . . ." She shook her head and sighed. "Sorry things did not work out for you and Lord Thornbeck."

Avelina shrugged. "It was never to be. I never expected to marry the margrave."

Magdalen gave her a sad frown.

Seeing the compassion on Magdalen's face, Avelina's composure started to unravel. She bit the inside of her lip to try to gain control. "I will let you go to bed since it is very late. Thank you for letting me explain and apologize."

They walked to the door together and Magdalen gave her a hug. "Please know that you will always be my friend. If I can ever do anything for you, please . . ."

"Thank you." It was all Avelina could trust herself to say. She squeezed her tight, then Magdalen slipped out and went down the corridor to her own chamber.

Avelina walked back to the bed and curled up in a ball, too weighed down to even undress or get under the covers.

19

Avelina heard the door to Irma's small room open. She lifted her head from the bed. She must have finally cried herself to sleep. Her eyes were gritty and her head ached.

Irma hurried toward her. "I see you are taking this hard, but this is no time to pity yourself. We have to leave, now."

"Now? In the middle of the night?"

"It's not the middle of the night. It will soon be morning. And we have to leave before Lord Thornbeck throws us out in the cold. Come on. Get your things together."

"He wouldn't throw us out while it's still dark." At least, she hoped he wouldn't.

"I have heard from the other servants that he is furious." Irma glared down at her.

Avelina did not bother to sit up. Her face felt heavy and her eyes burned. "Why should we hurry back? We will not exactly be welcomed at Plimmwald, now that we have failed so thoroughly."

"Listen, Avelina. You are not thinking clearly." Irma started gathering things from around the room and stuffing them in bags. "Let me make the decisions. If we leave now, Friedrich can go with us and we won't have to ride by ourselves all the way to Plimmwald."

"But did Lord Plimmwald not send guards to escort us back?"

Irma huffed. "We cannot depend on them. They will have heard, like everyone else, that you are only a servant girl. They're probably halfway back to Plimmwald already to tell the earl the news. Besides, Friedrich has arranged it all, and he will lend his protection."

"Friedrich? Is that your love's name?"

"Yes, that is his name. While you were enjoying yourself with the margrave and pretending you were a princess, I was ... enjoying myself as well. At least Friedrich loves me and is willing to help us."

"Can't we wait until morning?" Another tear leaked out as she pressed her hand over her face.

"It's nearly dawn now! You cannot tell because it is snowing."

"Snowing? When did that start?"

"During the night. Now get up and help me. You aren't an earl's daughter anymore."

Avelina sighed and pushed herself up. What would happen to them once they were back in Plimmwald? Nothing good.

She helped Irma pack up their things. "Do you think we will make it safely back to Plimmwald with no guards?" Traveling presented many dangers.

"We have to, princess. Now let us go."

They hefted the bags to their shoulders and left the room.

No one was around the dark corridor, with only one torch burning. Irma headed to the back stairs, the ones the servants used, and Avelina followed her. Irma certainly was in a hurry. Avelina had never seen her move so fast.

She probably should not be leaving without Lord Thornbeck's permission. He had sent her to her chamber and expected her to stay there until he told her to leave. But he would surely not care that she was sneaking away early in the morning. He would be glad to get rid of her, of the reminder of his folly of choosing to marry the only maiden among ten who was a mere servant.

"Oh, wait! I have to say farewell to Lady Magdalen." She turned and started back up the stairs.

"No!" Irma whispered. "We need to go now. Friedrich will be waiting; the horses will be waiting."

Avelina hesitated. No, she could not go without telling Magdalen. "I'll only take a minute." She hurried to Magdalen's door with her heavy load, then laid it on the floor by the door and knocked.

Hegatha answered, her lips pursed in a sour frown. She just stared at Avelina.

"Please, may I speak to Lady Magdalen, only for a moment?"

Magdalen came up behind Hegatha in her underdress. "I am here."

Hegatha moved away.

"I wanted to tell you I am leaving, and to say thank you for your friendship."

"Why are you leaving?"

"We have the chance to go back with a man to guard us, but we have to go now."

Magdalen reached out and embraced her. "I will miss you, and I hope I see you again. Are you sure you should be leaving now?"

"Yes, I must go. Farewell, and thank you." Avelina turned to leave so Magdalen would not see her cry.

"Come, make haste," Irma said when she returned. "We have a long way to go."

Irma's gaze darted to the side, and she would not look at Avelina.

When they got to the bottom floor of the castle and walked outside, the cold hit Avelina in the face, along with huge flakes of snow that clung to her eyelashes and the dampness on her cheeks. The moon was nowhere in sight, obscured by the snow and clouds. Irma was ahead of her and she plunged forward into the darkness toward the stable.

Irma seemed to know just where to go. They came to three saddled horses, which Avelina did not even see until she was only a few feet from them. Irma tied her bag to the back of her saddle, and Avelina did the same. Friedrich helped Irma to mount, then Avelina. As they were covering themselves with the fur robes slung over the horses' saddles, a howl, long and wild, came from the woods. Another howl joined it.

Avelina shivered. "Could that be wolves? They sound close."

Irma did not answer her. She was sitting sidesaddle on a large black gelding, while Avelina was riding a brown mare, which was small and docile. Friedrich mounted his horse and the three of them set out into the cold, predawn, snow-white forest.

"Aren't we going the wrong way?" They seemed to be headed away from the town of Thornbeck, instead of toward it.

"Friedrich knows a shortcut."

Her head still ached from all the crying. Stupid thing, crying. It changed absolutely nothing about the circumstances, but it made your eyes burn, made your face puffy and blotchy, and gave you a headache.

She had cried most of the night. The cold feeling of moisture in her hairline and the tightness of the drying salt water on her cheeks kept her awake until a new thought or memory would start the tears afresh. Now, every step her horse took made her head pound.

She could only hope the horses didn't lose their footing in the snow, as sections of the rocky roads were steep and narrow leading down from the castle mount. And what about the wolves? *Father God, let them stay far enough away to not spook the horses.*

Friedrich led them, and Irma was just in front of Avelina, as they made their way down the hill.

No one spoke. Avelina was grateful for the fur robes, as she was not sure they could survive the cold and the snow without them. She had the protection of the hood of her cloak, but how long would it be before the snow soaked through to her scalp?

Every time she thought of Lord Thornbeck or Magdalen, she felt like crying. And since she didn't want her face turning to ice or her lashes freezing together, she forced them out of her thoughts and set her mind on her little brother and sister. But would they even be glad to see her when they found out that she was responsible for Plimmwald having no allies to help them defend themselves against Geitbart?

If only she could numb her mind so she wouldn't think of anything at all. If only she could sleep all the way to Plimmwald so she couldn't think. Or perhaps she could stop in Thornbeck, find work and a place to sleep, and never go back to Plimmwald. But that was impossible. She could not abandon her family.

They had made it down the castle mount and were on the narrow forest road that led to the walled town of Thornbeck. Dawn was beginning to spread a pale light over the snow-covered world around them. The whiteness made the ground brighter than the sky, and there was a special hush that came only with snow. Somehow it did create just that numbness she was longing for, at least for the moment.

After they had been riding for quite some time, Irma broke the silence. "I am sorry for what I am about to do, Avelina. I made an agreement with Friedrich and Lady Fronicka."

The back of Avelina's neck prickled. "What?"

"Friedrich works for Lady Fronicka's father. I can go and be with Friedrich in Geitbart if I do this one thing for Lady Fronicka." Irma still had not looked at her.

"What? Do what for Lady Fronicka? Irma?"

Irma waited for Avelina to catch up to her. When their horses were side by side on the road, Irma reached out and snatched Avelina's fur robe off. Then she lifted her leg and kicked Avelina in her side.

Avelina tried to hang on to the reins, but her legs slipped right off the saddle. She hit the ground almost before she knew what was happening.

Irma grabbed Avelina's horse's reins, slapped the horse's rump, and galloped away with Friedrich down the road.

Avelina jumped up off the snow-covered ground. "Irma!" How could she do this? How?

Her heart lurched into her throat. What would she do? She was stranded. Wet snow clung to her clothing. She shook her skirts, brushing the snow off, but already it was soaking through and wetting her legs. And her feet. The cold immediately seeped through the thin little dancing shoes Lady Magdalen had given her the night before.

She had no fur to keep her warm. She was probably about a half hour's walk from the castle, and she suspected there was nothing but forest for miles in the other direction, so she turned around and started walking back to the castle. She wrapped the cloak tightly around herself, ignoring the cold, wet snow biting into her feet.

Lady Fronicka obviously wanted Avelina to die out here in the cold. And suddenly she remembered what Fronicka had said on the balcony. She wanted to marry Lord Thornbeck because she wanted Thornbeck Castle. She would have killed the margrave had he married her. She believed it rightfully belonged to her father, and they wanted it.

She needed to get back and warn Lord Thornbeck.

But that did not explain why she still wanted to kill Avelina.

Obviously, the margrave could not marry her now, so it wasn't out of jealousy. It must be pure vindictiveness.

She quickened her pace, walking as fast as she could up the hill. The rocks hurt her feet, but she walked faster, and soon her feet were too numb to feel much pain.

Suddenly a howl, then another and another split the dark forest and sent a shiver across her shoulders. Wolves. White-hot fear stabbed through her middle.

Avelina forced her shaking legs to run. She ran along the side of the road until she tripped over a fallen tree, hidden in the snow. She pushed herself up and kept moving. Her skirts were wet and clinging to her legs, but she held them up the best she could and continued running.

Would she make it to the castle before the wolves reached her? She still could not even see the castle. How close were the wolves? If she screamed, would anyone hear her? But she would have to slow down to catch her breath enough to scream. She kept running.

Some movement to her left made her turn her head. A wolf was trotting through the trees alongside her, about forty feet away. A second wolf trotted just behind him.

She looked about for something she could use as a weapon, but everything was covered with snow. Up ahead on the road were some limbs their horses had stumbled over earlier. She ran, glancing back and forth between the limb ahead of her and the wolf beside her. Was he getting closer?

She reached down and snatched up a limb that was just small enough to get her hand around. Thankfully, it was not too long or unwieldy. She had been told that a wolf would sometimes not attack if you faced him and refused to flee, and since she could never outrun a wolf, she stopped and turned toward him, trying to draw in a deep enough breath to scream.

A third and fourth wolf appeared a few feet away from the first one. They all kept their eyes on her, their ears erect. They stalked toward her as a fifth wolf appeared from the edge of the trees.

She forced a deep breath into her burning lungs and screamed. It didn't sound very loud. She tried again. The screams seemed to have no effect on the wolves at all. She held up her stick, panting, her chest heaving. Fear seemed to be strangling her, stifling her breathing worse than running had.

The wolves stopped too. They spread out in a semicircle around her. Their terrifying eyes and mouths seemed to be laughing at her, hating her with vicious intent.

"Get away!" Avelina screamed. "Get away!" She shook the stick at them, but they just kept watching her.

The wolves started moving closer, very slowly. The closest one suddenly bared its long, pointed teeth and growled.

"Get away!" Avelina screamed, a deep, throaty sound. She could not let them know how terrified she was. She raised her stick over her head, yelled, and took a step toward them. The wolves stopped and eyed her, but they did not retreat.

"Get out of here! Go!" She shook the stick, but the wolves started moving toward her again.

Should she run toward the castle? If she did, they would chase her. If she ran toward them, they would probably attack her. All her life she'd heard stories of wolf attacks, of people being killed. The only time someone escaped was when they had help from other people, or had a weapon like a sword or bow and arrow. How could she possibly escape a pack of five wolves? *God, help me. Please, help me.*

She backed away up the road, holding her stick in front of her. The wolves came toward her, twice as fast as she was moving. Now two of them were baring their teeth. Some movement in the trees showed there was a sixth wolf.

She moved slower, and still the wolves stalked closer. "O Father God, if You don't do something to save me . . . Jesus help me, please save me." She began speaking randomly, not even knowing what she was saying, to keep herself from sobbing. "Jesus . . . holy saints . . . Save me, holy God," she rambled, her voice growing more and more high-pitched. "Spirit of the living God, save me . . . save me."

Still the wolves stalked closer. She turned and yelled at the wolf behind her, raising her stick, but when she turned back around, the wolves had stalked closer, so close she could see the yellowish color of their eyes.

Suddenly something tugged at her skirt. She screamed and struggled to turn around, slamming the stick against the wolf's head. The wolf grabbed the stick in its mouth, snarling. She tugged but could not pull it free.

A second wolf moved stealthily forward. It bared its teeth and growled. The wolf let out a bone-chilling snarl. Then he suddenly sprang at her, its eyes locked on her neck.

She let go of the stick and lifted her arm, crouching at the last moment. The wolf sailed by her shoulder, but its claws raked her forearm as he passed.

The pain in her arm barely reached her consciousness. She was surrounded on every side. All six wolves were closing in, their movements as smooth and flowing as a river, snarling and baring their fangs, their hungry yellow eyes trained on her.

This was the end. There was no mercy in their wolfish faces. She had no weapon with which to fight them. Still, she shook her skirts at them, then clapped her hands and yelled, which turned into a scream. They simply continued to stare and move ever so slowly toward her.

Terror gripped her tighter, turning her blood to ice. She shook so hard she could barely stand upright. Would she die of the cold before the wolves decided to kill her? Soon they would go for her throat again, and then her blood would spill on the snow.

Perhaps this was for the best. After all, she had no future. Everyone would hate her now. She had failed. But who would look after her father and little sister and brother? *O God, You know. Provide for them.*

The wolf near her feet snarled and lunged forward. It sank its teeth into her ankle.

Avelina screamed in fear and pain. The animal held her fast in its jaws.

The animal to her left, the wolf that had already leapt for her throat, suddenly crouched, preparing for a second leap.

Horse's hooves sounded behind her. The wolf kept its eyes on her, but its ears flattened back against its head.

The horse rode hard and fast. It neighed, high and loud, very close by, then stopped. A loud growl sounded behind her—a man's growl this time.

The wolf's eyes bulged as it jumped, propelling itself toward Avelina.

She closed her eyes and waited for the impact.

20

REINHART PLUNGED TOWARD the group of wolves surrounding Avelina. One of the wolves was crouched and ready to lunge.

He unsheathed his sword and leapt off his horse. The wolf lunged at her throat and Reinhart brought the sword down on its head, knocking it to the ground.

Reinhart dove at the wolf that was holding Avelina's ankle in its jaws. He brought the blade's edge down on the wolf's neck, severing its head from its body.

The other four wolves advanced on them. Reinhart stepped toward them, raising his sword. One animal leapt at his head. He stepped to the side and the wolf's teeth latched on to his shoulder.

Reinhart stabbed it with his sword and it fell to the ground.

At the same time, another wolf caught his sword arm in its teeth. He switched his sword to his left hand and slashed the blade across the wolf's belly and slung it to the ground.

The remaining wolves backed away, whining, slinking into the trees.

"You're hurt," Avelina said behind him.

He turned around. Her ankle was still trapped inside the wolf's jaws, even though it was dead, and blood surrounded her, bright red against the white snow. Her arm was also bleeding through her sleeve, but she was staring with wide, dazed eyes at his injured shoulder and arm.

"I'm so sorry," she said.

Reinhart dropped his sword in the snow and fell to his knees at her feet. He took the wolf's jaws in his hands and pried them open, gently removing them from her ankle, then threw the head on the ground.

More blood dribbled down her ankle. He grabbed a handful of snow and pressed it against the puncture wounds, and Avelina collapsed backward onto the ground. Her lips were blue and her face was deathly pale. His heart twisted inside him, as if it were being clenched inside a fist.

"I have to get you out of here, out of the cold, and stop the bleeding. Put your arms around my neck." He bent over her.

She blinked up at him as if she did not hear.

"You're hurt," she said again, reaching toward his shoulder.

He slid his arms underneath her and picked her up, trying to ignore his own pain.

Her teeth started chattering, just as they had after he pulled her up from the edge of the balcony, as he carried her to his horse.

More horses topped the hill above them—Jorgen, Odette, and two guards. The guards reached him first and dismounted.

Reinhart handed her to the first guard. "Hold her while I mount my horse." He glanced at the others. "Jorgen, Odette, go after them. They went east, at least three."

Reinhart mounted his horse and reached for Avelina. The guard handed her back to him. He turned his horse toward the castle and started up the hill.

He held her tightly in his arms. She was so pale. How much blood had she lost? She seemed to be losing consciousness. She needed to stay awake.

"How did this happen?" he demanded. "What were you doing out here?"

Her teeth slammed together so hard he wasn't sure she could speak. She huddled against his chest. "Irma s-said w-we had to l-leave. Fronicka . . . sh-she t-told Irma t-to leave me . . . in the s-snow. Th-the wolves came."

She clung to his shirtfront, blood soaking through her sleeve, but he feared her ankle was her worst injury.

"You're hurt," she said. "I'm so sorry. I'm so sorry."

She had that dazed look on her face, a dangerous symptom he had seen once before in a soldier who had been badly injured. And if she did not get warm . . .

He urged the horse to go faster as they came to the steepest part of the road to the castle. The horse's hooves slipped on the snow but kept fighting upward. They finally made it to the castle steps.

Reinhart managed to hold her as he dismounted. He carried her toward the castle.

A guard ran down the steps and took Avelina from his arms, several more guards behind him. He carried her into the castle, with Reinhart just behind them.

"Fetch Frau Schwitzer. Send someone for the healer in the cottage in the forest. Fetch a bucket of hot water and clean cloths and bandages, and build up a fire in the front room."

A maidservant scurried into the room ahead of the guard who carried Avelina in. A fire was blazing in a small fireplace and the servant was already throwing more wood on it.

"Put her on that couch next to the fire," he said.

Avelina sucked in a quick breath, as though a sudden pain struck her. The guard laid her on the couch in a sitting position, with her legs stretched out on the cushions. Reinhart grabbed a large fur and laid it over her, pulling it up to her chin, then he knelt at her feet and found them bare. She must have lost her shoes in the snow.

Shoes. He told her he would get her some more shoes after the balcony incident. He'd forgotten.

Her feet were like blocks of ice, and her toes were purple. He started rubbing her right foot between his hands. She inhaled another sharp breath. At least she was waking up and no longer had that dazed, vacant look in her eyes.

Another woman servant came in. Reinhart ordered her to rub Avelina's other foot.

Avelina bit her lip, probably to keep from crying out.

Two more women servants came in and he ordered them to take over the intense work of rubbing her feet between their hands.

Frau Schwitzer hurried into the room. Reinhart ordered, "Go find some dry clothes for her."

Avelina's teeth were chattering worse than ever as she huddled underneath the fur. It must be the wet clothing she was still wearing. He turned to the maidservants in the room.

"Get those wet clothes off her, now. Frau Schwitzer is coming with some dry ones." He left the room and waited outside.

It wasn't until that moment he realized he did not know where his cane was, and his ankle was throbbing almost as bad as the wolf bites to his shoulder and arm.

She had been so close to being killed . . . His stomach clenched again. *Thank You, God, I got to her in time. Again.*

~⁓

The maidservants were undressing her. Avelina was nearly helpless—stiff with cold and shaking uncontrollably. The women quickly and efficiently divested her of her clothing and pulled a new, thicker underdress over her head, followed by a rich velvet cotehardie. Then they covered her again with the fur robe. It was all over in a matter of moments.

Avelina's teeth still chattered. But at least the fog was finally clearing from her mind and she focused on the here and now and pushed away the terror and the attacking wolves from her mind.

Lord Thornbeck came back in and he and another servant went back to rubbing her feet, a grim look on his face. He had come and rescued her from the wolves, risking his life in the process. Did he still care for her? She had been so dazed, she had not really understood what was happening during the attack. But now . . .

O Lord God, let him not suffer any lasting effects from having saved me. Let his wounds heal and not fester. She could not bear it if any lasting harm came to him because of her.

"S-someone m-must see to your w-wounds, my lord."

He looked at her with that unreadable but intense expression, as more people poured into the room.

"I have sent for a healer. She will be here soon. But first we must get you warm." He moved away from her and spoke to a guard at the door, while the maidservants were still taking turns rubbing her feet. The stabbing pain was beginning to subside to a sharp ache.

An older woman came in dressed like a peasant. She carried a bag and set it beside Avelina and shooed the servants away. The woman touched Avelina's toes, then squeezed them. She pushed Avelina's skirt up enough to examine her ankle.

Avelina jerked her feet out of the woman's grasp, pulled them in, and covered them with her skirts. "I refuse to l-let you treat m-my injuries until you look at Lord Thornbeck's wounds." She tried to clamp her teeth together, but they just would not stop chattering, especially when she talked.

"That is not for you to decide," he said.

She hugged her knees. "I will not s-submit t-to anything until she l-looks at your wounds."

He lowered his brows at her. "Avelina . . ."

Her heart leapt inside her. He called her by her name instead of Lady Dorothea, but his tone had an edge of warning.

"Your injuries are the most severe."

She tried to shake her head, but it was difficult when her head felt so heavy and her movements were jerky and difficult. "N-not until sh-she looks at your arm and shoulder."

"She has to get warm," the healer said in a no-nonsense voice, as if she did not notice the tension between Avelina and the margrave. "She's shivering and her lips are blue. If she doesn't get warm, she will die. Her ankle can wait."

"What must we do to warm her?"

"She is already close to the fire, but it's not enough. Another person's body heat is the best way."

He glanced around. "Everyone out of the room, except Frau Schwitzer and Susanna. Don't let anyone else in."

The guard nodded. Everyone quickly exited the room except for Frau Schwitzer and the healer.

"No." Avelina shook her head. "She has to examine your shoulder and arm first." Tears threatened, since she knew she was too weak to force her point. Besides, she was no longer the respected daughter of an earl. She had no right to order the margrave about. He could strike her and no one would care. He could ridicule her and scoff at her and laugh her to scorn if he wished, and he would be well within his rights. But she could not rest until he had his wounds taken care of.

He stared down at her. She knew he must see the tears swimming in her eyes.

"I will get you warm. Susanna can look at my shoulder and arm at the same time. Scoot up."

He stepped toward her, and she scooted forward on the couch. He sat down behind her, then wrapped his arms around hers, pulling her back firmly against his chest.

His warmth instantly seeped through her borrowed clothing to her skin. His chest warmed her back while his arms held the fur securely around her arms and shoulders.

Avelina sat stiffly, her shaking nearly stilled by the margrave's nearness. She could feel his breath against her hair, his big hands holding on to her elbows. She was as snug as a moth in its cocoon.

"Cut the cloth on my arm and shoulder." His voice rumbled near her ear.

The healer took some shears out of her bag and came to the side of the couch. She cut the sleeve of his surcoat and his shirt. When his arm was bare, Avelina shifted her head to his left shoulder to see the teeth marks and the blood matting up his arm hair. She cringed at the painful-looking injuries.

"Puncture wounds, mostly, but not deep enough for serious damage," the old woman said. She sent Frau Schwitzer to get some hot water and clean cloths. "I shall clean it so I can see if anything needs to be stitched up."

Next she moved to the other side of the couch and cut away the cloth at his left shoulder while Avelina leaned her head forward so she could see. He was so warm, already her teeth had ceased chattering.

His shoulder was bloody, but there was not quite as much blood and the wounds did not look as deep as the ones on his arm.

Susanna grunted. "Not very bad, especially for a wolf attack."

"My leather mantle protected me."

Again, she felt his breath against her hair, his voice sending pleasant sensations all through her. She closed her eyes for a moment, trying not to sigh at how pleasant it was.

Frau Schwitzer returned with a bucket of hot water, cloths, and a clean bowl.

"Attend the lady's ankle and arm first," he said.

Avelina opened her mouth to protest, but he squeezed her arm, as though to warn her. And why had he called her a "lady" when he knew now that she was naught but a servant? She kept quiet as Susanna examined her ankle.

Susanna set the bowl on the bench. She placed Avelina's foot in the bowl, pouring the hot water from the bucket over it. The water felt good even as it burned her half-frozen skin. But as the hot water touched her open wounds, the pain of the puncture wounds caught her full attention and she drew in a breath through her clenched teeth.

Lord Thornbeck's big hands gently squeezed her arms, as though to comfort her, at least taking her mind off the pain for a moment.

"These puncture wounds are deep," Susanna said. "We shall hope the teeth did not do permanent damage. I'll not sew them shut, to allow any bad humors out. But best to keep it loosely covered, except for a few hours a day to let the fresh air in."

Frau Schwitzer wrapped the clean cloths around her ankle while Susanna pulled back the sleeve on Avelina's arm. "Scratches, that is all. Clean and wrap them and they should heal."

She came back to Lord Thornbeck's arm and cleaned it in the same way she had cleaned Avelina's ankle. He didn't even flinch as she rubbed off the crusty dried blood from the wounds.

"Should heal without a problem, but if either of you have any red streaks or swelling or pus, fetch me and I'll bring my septic salve."

Susanna finished up his shoulder while Frau Schwitzer brought back some woolen stockings for Avelina's feet, which still burned like they'd been stung by bees. Avelina pulled the thigh-high stockings on, then Frau Schwitzer brought her a warming pan.

"She should rest her feet on this," Susanna said, to no one in particular. "I don't want her feet getting cold again for at least a week. But as soon as she stops shaking, she should be able to warm up on her own. Just give her something hot to drink."

And with those words, Susanna packed up her things and left.

Frau Schwitzer was tidying up. What would happen now? Lord Thornbeck still had his arms around her and his chest pressed against her back.

She closed her eyes, since he was behind her and couldn't see her anyway, and seared this last kindness into her memory, this feeling of warmth and safety.

For a moment in time she had been a lady, someone who was wanted . . . by the Margrave of Thornbeck, a man who was easy to talk to, even when she was trying not to talk to him, a man who would risk his life to rescue a woman who had made a fool of him and who was only a servant. He would have married her. She was wanted.

But now . . . what would he do with her? She had no reason to stay at Thornbeck Castle, and he had no reason to care.

21

REINHART SHOULD NOT be holding this maiden. He should have let someone else hold her and impart the necessary body heat to stop her shaking and get her warm again. She was a servant, and it was improper for him to touch her at all, improper to risk his life to save her from wolves, to spill his own blood for her, and to hold her in his arms and wish with all his heart that . . . what?

He was thinking like a fool.

The king would never approve his marriage to this servant girl. The king wanted him to marry someone who could solidify relations and strengthen German alliances. His whole purpose was to find someone like that, but someone with whom he could have a life.

But she had turned out to be deceitful and, for a margrave, not eligible for marriage. She and the Earl of Plimmwald had made a fool of him.

He removed his arms from around her and stood, then stepped away from her. "Frau Schwitzer, you may go."

She nodded and left the room.

He faced away from Avelina, crossing his arms in front of him. "Why did you leave like that?" He had to know. "What were you doing going out in the snow before anyone was awake?"

"I . . . I thought you would want me to go." She spoke quietly. "I knew you would hate me for deceiving you, and Irma talked me into it when I was still half-asleep. She said if we left immediately, Friedrich could go with us and protect us. But just before she kicked me off the horse and galloped away, she said she had made an agreement with Fronicka. Irma could go and live in Geitbart with her new lover, Friedrich, if she left me there in the snow. She must have known the wolves were nearby."

"Everyone knew it. Did you not hear them howling?" He turned to face her.

She shrugged. "I wasn't thinking about wolves."

"How did Fronicka know who you were and all the details of your secret, that you were a servant and you were taking Lady Dorothea's place?"

She stared down at the floor. "The only person who knew everything and could have told her was Irma. It must have been Irma. She was willing to give up everything for Friedrich."

Yes, that made sense.

"Lady Fronicka must have discovered the truth about Dorothea's pregnancy from one of the guards who escorted Irma and me to Thornbeck. I'm not sure. But the other things she must have found out from Irma."

There she sat, calm and quiet after nearly being killed twice in the last few days. Any other woman would still be sobbing hysterically, or at least still in shock after facing down a pack of wolves, especially with the serious injury to her ankle.

"What will you do with me?"

He rubbed his shoulder, but that only made it hurt worse.

"I know I have no right to ask, but please . . . do not be angry with Lord Plimmwald for sending me in his daughter's place. If he loses your protection, the people will have no one to defend them from their enemies."

The sincerity and pleading in her expression made him pity

her, but he had to harden his heart. "Word will certainly get back to Lord Plimmwald. You may lose your dowry." The ugly sound of sarcasm was in his voice. Jealousy and pain warred inside him, as if trying to tear his heart in two.

She lowered her head even more. She was silent for several long moments. "I am sorry for causing you pain. And I'm sorry you were hurt, saving me from the wolves."

He snorted. As if that pain was worse than finding out she had deceived him. No, the wolves had nothing to do with this pain in his heart, this pain that had kept him awake all night.

"But please." Her voice quavered. "Please forgive me. And please do not allow Geitbart to destroy Plimmwald. Please promise me you will save Plimmwald."

His heart was thumping and his arms were suddenly aching to hold her again.

He turned and fled from the room, nearly falling when his lame ankle gave way. Where was his walking stick?

He found two guards outside the door. To the first one, he said, "Carry this woman to the servants' quarters and have Frau Schwitzer find her a bed with the kitchen servants."

"Yes, my lord."

"And you, bring my cane. It may be in my saddle or at the stable," he said to the second guard.

Reinhart stood leaning against the wall as the guard carried her away.

The second guard brought him his cane. He went to his desk in the library, but feeling restless, he wandered out to the balcony. Maybe the cold air and whiteness of the snow would clear his head. But that was where he had first held Dorothea—Avelina—in his arms, right after he'd seen her dangling from the balcony, just a moment from death.

Fronicka had tried to murder Avelina.

According to Avelina, Geitbart had threatened to attack and take over Plimmwald. Perhaps he intended to take over Thornbeck as well. After all, the present duke's father had lost both Plimmwald and Thornbeck when he married a woman the king did not approve of. What would he do when Reinhart banished his daughter from Thornbeck? Geitbart might prove to be just as murderous as his daughter.

⌒

Avelina lay in the narrow servant's bed trying to process all she had experienced in the last day. She was alone in a large room full of similar beds. All the other servants were working.

She should be afraid. She should try to figure out how to get out of the mess she was now in. But she was so exhausted, the thin straw mattress actually felt good, and soon she fell asleep.

When she awoke she hopped to the window on one foot. It had stopped snowing and the sun was brightly shining in the noon sky.

A knock came at the door.

"Come in."

Magdalen entered and shut the door behind her. "One of the servants told me you were attacked by wolves. Can this be true?"

Avelina sighed. "I will tell you all about it, but you should not be here. Your mother certainly would not approve of you visiting the servants' quarters." Even Avelina wasn't used to sleeping in a place like this. She was a lady's maidservant, not a kitchen servant.

Magdalen huffed. "I can't believe Lord Thornbeck sent you down here. He could have at least allowed you to stay in your own room until you leave." For only the second time since she'd met her, Magdalen looked angry.

Avelina started hopping back toward the bed.

"You're hurt! Is it bad? You must tell me immediately what has happened to you this morning."

Avelina told her all about Irma's betrayal, about the wolves' attack, and Lord Thornbeck saving her. She showed her the bandaged ankle. "It doesn't hurt as much now. I can still walk on it if I have to."

Magdalen threw her arms around her and hugged her tight. "Thank You, God," she breathed, her voice fervent, "for protecting Avelina, and for Lord Thornbeck."

Tears sprung to Avelina's eyes at her friend's sincere concern for her safety.

Suddenly another knock came at the door. A maidservant was there with a piece of paper. "From Lord Thornbeck for Avelina."

Magdalen took the note and brought it to Avelina, who unfolded it.

Do not think of leaving again. You are to stay until your ankle
heals, and until I have had time to consider your request.
Thornbeck

She handed the note to Magdalen. "At least he's not throwing me in the dungeon."

Magdalen read it quickly. "What was your request?"

"I asked him to save Plimmwald if the Duke of Geitbart attacked. I know he must hate Lord Plimmwald after he sent me in his daughter's place, but I begged him not to be angry with him . . . . What?"

Magdalen was shaking her head. "No. No begging. And no

behaving like a servant girl around Lord Thornbeck. You are a person just like me, like the Earl of Plimmwald's daughter, like anyone else at this castle."

Avelina had never heard Magdalen sound so forceful or look so adamant.

"None of this was your fault. You simply followed the orders of your lord, and the margrave should understand that. If he doesn't, then . . . that's not your fault either." She ended with a firm, quick nod. "He chose you from among all these ladies, and he cannot discard you like a worn-out garment or treat you like a lowly . . . It just will not do."

"But he has to send me away. He cannot marry me. The king would not allow it."

"He doesn't have to marry you, but he does have to treat you with respect."

"I like the way you think, Magdalen, but I cannot make demands on Lord Thornbeck. I have nothing to bargain with, no leverage. I need him to save Plimmwald. I have a father and a little brother and sister whom I dearly love. I cannot let anything happen to them if I can help it."

Magdalen simply did not understand what it was like to be a servant. It was a different life, a different way of thinking. If begging saved her family and her people, then she would beg.

"Even a servant can demand respect, Avelina. Look at Hegatha. Everyone respects her. She demands no less."

"I'm no Hegatha," Avelina said ruefully.

"You don't have to be exactly like Hegatha to demand respect."

It was something Avelina had never thought about, and yet, she had very often thought about the disparity between the way Lady Dorothea was treated and Avelina herself was treated. Was the difference more because she did not insist that people respect her, instead of the fact that she was born the daughter of a stable worker?

"Remember what I am telling you, Avelina. If my mother has taught me anything, it's that a woman must demand respect."

What she said made sense. "But I don't think Lord Thornbeck has any reason to care about me anymore. To him I'm only a servant. And he'd only known me for two weeks."

"It was long enough for him to decide he wanted to marry you."

But short enough for him to forget about her and send her to the servants' quarters.

"I will not have you sleeping here tonight," Magdalen said. "I'll be back soon."

She left, and after perhaps half an hour, Magdalen returned with one of Lord Thornbeck's guards.

"Carry her gently," Magdalen instructed the guard. "She's injured."

Magdalen gave Avelina a wink.

She submitted to being carried for about the fifth time in the last few days. She was beginning to get used to it.

The poor guard had to carry her up many stairs and two floors to the bedchamber she had slept in since her arrival. Magdalen walked up with them.

"Did you get Lord Thornbeck's permission?" Avelina asked as soon as she was back in her bed and the guard had left.

"Yes. I told him you were injured and he should not leave you in the servants' quarters, which you were not accustomed to even when you were Lady Dorothea's own maidservant. I was very indignant, and he consented for you to stay in your room until your ankle was healed."

Her stomach did a little flip. What did Lord Thornbeck think about Lady Magdalen coming to her defense? But her friend would soon be going back home to Mallin, and Avelina would have no one to prevent Lord Thornbeck from taking out his anger on her, or sending her back to the servants' quarters—or forgetting about her entirely.

———⁓

Avelina had watched evening descend out her window. It was only the first day of her confinement—no longer an earl's daughter, she had nowhere to go and nothing to do.

She wrote the beginning of a story on the paper Lord Thornbeck had given her several days before. But she soon got tired even of that task. Besides, her ankle had a tendency to throb when it hung down, so she'd crawled back in bed, lying with her head at the foot of the bed so she could stare out the window.

As the moon rose and shone eerily down on the white world, she got up and limped to the door of her chamber. Perhaps she would go visit Magdalen.

She stood undecided. Hegatha no doubt would give Avelina her disdainful look. And soon Magdalen would leave to go down to the Great Hall for the evening meal. She might try to convince Avelina to go down with her, as she had for the midday meal, and Avelina simply could not bear to face anyone after what had happened. Besides that, no one would welcome her presence, especially Lord Thornbeck, who said he never wanted to see her again.

A sound came from the corridor, muffled by her closed door. It sounded like someone scratching against her door. Avelina hobbled to the door and opened it. Endlein was standing in the corridor, calling for her daughter, Annlin.

"The men." Endlein motioned toward the west wing and looked worried and confused. "I think they did something with Annlin."

"Men?"

She gestured for Avelina to come closer. Avelina limped into the corridor. "You seem kind," Endlein said. "Come with me. You will help me, won't you?"

"Yes, of course."

Avelina followed Endlein—slowly and with the woman holding to her elbow and helping her along—through the corridor toward the west wing.

Avelina heard footsteps and voices as they neared the chamber where Lord Thornbeck's brother had died. Endlein placed a finger to her lips and led Avelina in through an open doorway. They stood listening as footsteps approached, passed the doorway, and entered the room near the end of the corridor.

Avelina peeked out, and when she did not see anyone, she walked up to the door where the voices were coming from and placed her ear up to the keyhole.

"I brought you all here," a man's voice said, "because I fear Lord Thornbeck's mind is addled. He has chosen a . . . *servant girl* . . . for his wife instead of one of our daughters. And there is still the suspicion that he is the one who caused the death of the previous margrave so he might take his place as lord of this region."

Who was speaking? Who would dare say these things?

"He also is responsible for the lack of game in the forests of Thornbeck, the king's forests, allowing poaching of the king's own deer. His chancellor actually married the notorious poacher who was killing all the deer in Thornbeck Forest."

What? Odette was a *poacher*? That couldn't be true, although she had seen Odette and Jorgen just after the wolf attack, with a faint memory of Lord Thornbeck instructing them to go after the wolves.

Other men's voices murmured, but nothing she could make out. Who else was there? She stuck her eye up to the keyhole but could only see the men's backs.

Someone said, "What do you propose we do? All of these things are only gossip, hearsay."

"We will capture the margrave, subdue his guards, and look into this gossip, as you call it."

She could hear the sneer in his voice. Her heart started pounding. Wouldn't someone protest? But there was only silence.

"I have brought my guards, knights, and soldiers with me to assist. We cannot allow any dissention of this sort. We must uphold our alliance to each other and the king, and ensure the safety and security of the Holy Roman Empire. We cannot allow sedition and murder to abound in Thornbeck. This is an important border and must be guarded. A margrave who intends to marry a servant and appoints a chancellor who consorts with a poacher—it is a disgrace."

Avelina listened, but again, no one protested what he was saying. No one spoke on behalf of Lord Thornbeck—the traitors!

She had to open the door and see who was there, who was speaking against Lord Thornbeck, and who was going along with it. She had to warn Lord Thornbeck.

"All of you must pledge your loyalty to me. You must tell your guards to join with mine in the fight against Thornbeck. He must be stopped. If you are loyal to our king, you must join me in this fight."

How dare he say such things? She pulled the iron door handle, as carefully as possible, while the men were talking. She opened the door just a crack and put one eye up to it.

Geitbart stood in the middle of the group. Several noblemen who had come to take their daughters home were there, probably seven or eight men, though she could not see very well through the tiny crack. Her heart was pounding. If she was caught . . .

"We are all agreed, then." Geitbart was turning in her direction.

Avelina stood and darted down the corridor toward an open door, ignoring the pain in her ankle. She hurried silently in her stockinged feet into the next room, but she was not sure Endlein was following.

Behind her, men's footsteps entered the corridor.

"What are you doing here?" The men must have encountered Endlein standing in the corridor.

"It is only the lack-witted woman Lord Thornbeck lets roam the castle—another reason to doubt his sanity."

They seemed to be ignoring Endlein and walking on by, as Avelina plastered herself against the wall inside the room so they wouldn't see her.

The men were soon gone, their footsteps growing fainter.

Where would Lord Thornbeck be at this time of day? "Please let him not be in the Great Hall." She didn't want to face all those people.

Endlein was staring at her.

"Don't tell anyone about those men and what they said." Avelina looked into her eyes to make sure she understood. Those men would kill her if they thought she might tell someone what they were plotting.

"Very well." Endlein stared back at her with that vacant look.

Avelina turned and took two steps before pain shot from her ankle up her leg, reminding her to walk slower.

She limped, her heart still pounding, heading toward the stairs. Perhaps she should tell Magdalen so she was not the only one who knew of this treachery. The two of them could split up and find Lord Thornbeck faster.

She limp-hopped through the long, winding corridor, making her way from the west wing to Magdalen's door and knocked. She waited. Then she pushed the door open and called softly, "Magdalen. Magdalen, are you here?"

No one answered, and there was no sound.

Avelina closed the door and hurried away as fast as she could, painfully making her way down the stairs, holding on to the railing and walking down sideways, leading with her good foot.

First she would try Lord Thornbeck's library. If he was not there, she'd try the Great Hall, then the chapel. Then she'd risk asking someone for help. But if Geitbart was able to take over Thornbeck, they were all doomed. Avelina—and Lord Thornbeck—would be at Fronicka's mercy. There would be nowhere to turn for help, like staring down into a deep ravine from a balcony with only a broken railing to hold on to.

22

REINHART PULLED HIS chair away from his desk and sat staring out the window at the snow-covered forest. From this secluded alcove behind a curtain, he was all but hidden from the rest of the library, should anyone come in to look for him. He should be in the Great Hall, feasting with his guests, but he was not in a festive mood. Let them feast without him.

Because of the snow, all of his guests were staying at least one more night, in the hopes that the sun would burn away the clouds and melt the snow. But when should he send Avelina home? Should he wait until her ankle was better enough that she could walk on it? Or should he send her home tomorrow on a cart?

His chest still ached every time he thought about her. But when an arrow had struck a warrior, he did not wait to pull it out. He immediately took hold of it and yanked it out. Just so, it was not wise to keep her here. He should send her away as soon as possible. The longer he waited, the more painful it would be.

He would never do what his brother had done—ask for the love of a servant who was obligated to do as she was told. Never. But he had to admit, even though he was still very angry with her, Avelina could be a temptation to him.

He still wanted her.

And he was no closer to choosing a bride than he had ever been.

A shuffling sound came from near the door, then moved closer. A rat, perhaps. He would have to have the servants set some traps for it.

"Lord Thornbeck?" someone called softly.

This was the problem with having guests. One could never get any peace with so many people around.

Reinhart carefully pulled the curtain back a bit to see who was there.

"Lord Thornbeck? Are you in here?" It sounded like Avelina's voice.

He pulled the curtain back some more. She was turning to leave, limping on her injured ankle.

He should just let her leave. She was nearly to the door.

"What do you want?"

She turned around. "Lord Thornbeck, forgive me, but I must speak with you." She was still talking in a hushed tone. She limped toward him. When a bit of light fell across her face, he saw the urgency of her expression—or perhaps it was pain from her ankle that made her face so tense.

He stood. "What is so important that you would walk on your injured ankle?"

"I overheard . . . Are we alone?" She glanced around the room.

He went toward her, struck with the irony of how similar her gait now was to his. "What did you overhear?"

She looked up at him. "The Duke of Geitbart," she whispered, "was talking to several of the noblemen in the west wing. He plans to capture and take over Thornbeck Castle."

Hadn't she claimed Geitbart planned to do the same thing to Plimmwald? "Why would he say that? And what were you doing in the west wing?"

"Endlein led me there. I suppose Geitbart was looking for a place where no one was around and where you would not hear of their private conversation. But he was telling the other men that you . . . that your mind was addled because you had chosen a servant to marry."

Heat rose into his face. "Yes, I suppose he would."

She looked away from him, and he imagined she was blushing—he couldn't tell in the dark room. But she set her jaw and went on.

"I wanted to warn you. If you do not wish to hear how they plan to attack you, I will go."

So, she had not lost her spirit.

"You may go on."

"Geitbart mentioned the rumor that you had killed your brother, that you did not stop some recent poaching, and you allowed your chancellor to marry a notorious poacher. He told the men if they were loyal to the king, they should pledge their allegiance to Geitbart and join with him in capturing you and subduing your guards."

So that's how it was. He had to act, and quickly.

"Do your guards outnumber Geitbart's?"

The only region wealthier than Thornbeck was Geitbart. It was very likely the duke's guards did outnumber his. And no doubt he would have built up his force by hiring every mercenary and stray knight, baron, and thief he could find as he planned for this. Reinhart's best hope was to send word to the king and ask for help. But what if Geitbart had already poisoned the king against him as well?

Surely the duke's influence did not reach that high. If it did, then Reinhart's cause was already hopeless.

Avelina was staring up at him, waiting. There was such a look of trust and belief on her face. He imagined reaching out and caressing her cheek.

"Did anyone see you? Do they know you heard them?"

"Only Endlein was there with me. I was listening through the keyhole."

They stood in the middle of the library, neither of them speaking for several moments. "Avelina, will you do something for me?"

"Of course."

"Go to the kitchen, ask for Frau Schwitzer, and tell her I need her to find Sir Klas right away and have him come here to the library. I will wait for him here."

"Yes, my lord."

"No, wait. You have an injured ankle. I need someone fast."

"I will be fast, and I shall send a boy from the kitchen, someone who can run, to fetch Sir Klas."

"Very well." He had little choice. He dragged his chair back to his desk. "But do find someone to send as soon as you can to—"

But she was already to the door, hobbling faster than he might have imagined.

He had obviously grown too trusting and complacent. He should have known something like this would happen sooner or later. He had trained for battle, then was relegated to a diplomatic role as margrave and permanently injured on the same day. Still, he knew what to do—if he could keep from getting captured by Geitbart.

Avelina hurried as fast as she could toward the Great Hall, beyond which was the kitchen where a lot of pages and squires would be serving and going back and forth.

She swept around the last corner before reaching the Great Hall and nearly ran into a young squire.

"I need your help," she told him. He could move much faster than she could.

She lowered her voice, forcing herself not to look around and thereby seem suspicious and draw attention. "Lord Thornbeck wishes for Sir Klas to come to him in the library at once."

"Yes, my lady." Apparently he had not heard that she was not a lady anymore.

"I shall wait for you here."

She sat on a bench in the dark corridor and he hurried away. Her ankle was throbbing, and she lifted it onto the bench, propping her shoulder against the wall. The bandage on her ankle was turning red in two different spots. All the walking must have reopened the wounds.

While she waited, she covered her face with her hands and prayed.

After what seemed a long time, the squire returned. "I'm sorry, my lady, but I could not find Sir Klas. I asked another guard and he said he had not seen him all day."

Perhaps they had already captured Lord Thornbeck's captain.

"Very well, then." She tried to smile and look as if nothing was amiss. Should she ask the boy to fetch another guard? She was risking him finding a guard who was not loyal to the margrave, but Lord Thornbeck needed help.

"Will you fetch one of Lord Thornbeck's guards and tell him the margrave needs to speak to him in his library?"

The boy stared at her a moment, then nodded and ran in the other direction.

Avelina sighed. If only she didn't have this frustrating injury. Perhaps *she* could help the margrave. She could spy for him and discover Geitbart's devious plans. She could redeem herself in his eyes and he would not think entirely ill of her when she had to go away.

She pushed herself up off the bench and started walking. Her ankle hurt more than ever, pain stabbing her like knives. She limped slowly, biting her lip as she shuffled toward the staircase. Painfully, she made her way up the steps and to Lord Thornbeck's library.

"Did you find Sir Klas?" He stood up from his desk. He was waving a letter in the air to dry the hot wax he'd just sealed it with.

"No. I sent a squire to find him, and he said no one had seen him."

Lord Thornbeck grimaced.

"But I told him to go fetch another guard and tell him you wanted to see him in the library. Was I right to do that?"

He nodded, staring at the wall.

Avelina found a stool and sat down. She would rest a moment and then go back to her room. Her ankle was throbbing terribly.

A guard suddenly entered the room. "Lord Thornbeck." He paused to bow.

"Sheinlin. Take this missive to the king. It is very urgent that you not let anything deter you. This letter must find its way to King Karl."

"In Prague, my lord?"

"Yes, as far as I know, the king is at his home. Here is some money. Change horses as often as you need to, but get this letter to the king as quickly as possible. And it is equally important that no one know of this. You must not even tell your fellow knights where you are going or what you are doing."

"Yes, my lord. I shall succeed." The guard turned and strode quickly from the room, barely giving Avelina a glance as he passed.

Lord Thornbeck stared down at the floor while leaning on his cane. Avelina stood, planning to slip quietly out of the room. She was limping heavily now.

"Wait."

She turned. Lord Thornbeck stared at her with brows drawn together in that severe look of his.

"Sit down. I'll find a servant or guard to carry you back to your bed."

"But first—is there anything else I can do?"

He sighed. "I need to get word to Chancellor Jorgen. He will have to send letters to round up enough of my allies and soldiers from town and the outlying areas to fight."

"Perhaps I can go fetch him." Avelina started to stand.

"Sit."

She sat.

He went into the hallway and called out to a servant. He came back in and said, "Let me see your ankle."

She gazed up at him. He did not look as if he'd accept any sort of argument, so she carefully inched her skirt up to reveal the bandage. She flinched at the amount of bright-red blood soaking her bandage.

For a long moment Lord Thornbeck did not say anything. She glanced up at him.

"I should not have allowed you to go down the stairs and back up again. I shall send for the healer."

"My lord, do not trouble yourself. All I need is a bandage change."

"I shall send Frau Schwitzer to see to it."

"Thank you, my lord."

A guard came into the room.

"Carry her to her room, then ask Frau Schwitzer to see to her wounds."

The guard lifted her in his arms and carried her out.

Lord Thornbeck did care for her a little or he would not have saved her from the wolves and looked so regretful when he saw her bloody bandage. But it only made her heart ache for what might have been, how much more he would have cared if she had been an earl's daughter.

"Avelina!" Someone called from behind. Magdalen hurried toward her to keep up with the fast-moving guard. "Why are you out of bed?"

"I have to tell you something," she said quietly, "when we get to my room."

They walked the rest of the way in silence until they were in Avelina's room and the guard had left.

While Magdalen pulled a chair up to her bedside, Avelina told her what she'd heard Geitbart say.

"We have to keep Geitbart from capturing Lord Thornbeck and throwing him in the dungeon, or worse." Avelina's stomach twisted and her mouth went dry at the "worse" things that could happen. "And from taking over Thornbeck."

"But how? What can we do?"

"I don't know." Avelina tapped her chin. "Lord Thornbeck and Jorgen will be asking men to come and help fight Geitbart's guards. But I was thinking you and I could spy on Geitbart, find out what he is doing and planning."

Magdalen leaned over and lifted Avelina's hem, then inhaled a noisy breath. "Your ankle is bleeding terribly. Blood is getting on the blanket. You won't be going anywhere."

Avelina felt a little sick at the sight of the red-soaked cloth.

A knock came, then Frau Schwitzer opened the door and bustled in with a basket of clean cloths and a pitcher of water.

They stayed quiet until Frau Schwitzer had washed off the

blood, changed the bandage, and left. Then they discussed what they might do to help save Thornbeck from Geitbart. Their ideas ranged from the practical to the fanciful, about how to spy on Geitbart, and how to kidnap him and Fronicka.

Finally, Magdalen declared, "I'm sleeping in your room tonight. I don't think I should let you out of my sight, with Fronicka hating you like she does."

"Thank you, but I don't think she would—"

"No arguments. I won't take no for an answer."

All Avelina could do was smile meekly. "Thank you, Lady Magdalen."

23

Hegatha could not have been pleased with the arrangements, but she would never have allowed Magdalen to sleep in Avelina's room without her, so she slept in Irma's little closet, with the door open.

When Avelina awoke, the sun was shining and she and Magdalen were still alive. Someone knocked, then a maidservant entered the room with a tray of food. The smell of fried meat and stewed fruit awoke her appetite, and she threw back the covers to get up.

"Oh no." Hegatha set down the tray and shook her finger at Avelina. "Frau Schwitzer said you must keep your foot up. You shall eat in bed."

There was good and bad to everything, even having a grouchy older woman in her room taking charge.

It seemed strange to be sitting in bed eating like a queen when Lord Thornbeck was in so much danger. But for now, Geitbart could not know that the margrave knew of his treachery. He was surely still trying to muster support from others and amassing troops for his attack.

Magdalen and Avelina talked while they ate, and Avelina told her about her own brother and sister. Then the talk turned to Lord Thornbeck.

Magdalen asked, "Do you think he is handsome? Or do you still think he is too severe looking, as you did at first?"

"I think very differently about him now than I did then. I tried not to think about him at all . . . but I thought of him constantly." Her heart seemed to expand like a watered plant as she was finally able to tell the truth about her feelings. "I believed there was so much goodness in him. And I was terrified he would see how much I admired him. It was difficult, forcing myself to turn away from him every time he looked at me."

"And trying to make him talk to me and not you?" Magdalen raised her brows. "Turning the conversation to me when he so obviously wanted to talk to you."

"So obviously?"

"Of course. The poor margrave had to turn his attention away from you so you would not look frightened to death that he was talking more to you than to me."

"I was only trying to do as I had been told."

"I know that now." Magdalen's smile faded. "I am sorry."

No one spoke. Magdalen was beginning to look sad.

"He is handsome, except he does have a rather too-large nose."

Magdalen's mouth fell open. "What?"

Avelina laughed. "Very well. He is the most handsome man I've ever seen, even though his nose is rather large." Laughing was better than crying, and she did not want Magdalen to be sad or feel sorry for her because they both knew she could never marry him.

The more she had tried not to think him handsome, the handsomer he became, as she realized his care and concern for the orphans, his easy manner with Jorgen and Odette and friendship with them, his gentle way with the poor addled woman who haunted the west wing—the way he looked at Avelina, so considerate, so intense. She supposed she should have known all along that his interest lay with her, not Magdalen, but something inside her just could not allow her to believe that the margrave could fall in love with a servant—even when that servant was masquerading as an earl's daughter.

She'd never been in love before. She'd tried to save herself this pain, but all her pretending and hiding the truth from herself had not saved her at all. And even though this love was painful, it was worth it to remember how the sight of him and the sound of his voice had made her heart beat faster, that feeling of wanting what was best for someone else, even if it broke her own heart.

By midmorning Avelina could hardly bear to lie in bed another moment. "I think my ankle is much better now, and there must be something we can do to help Lord Thornbeck."

Magdalen frowned at her. "Hegatha will not be pleased if you get up. She and Frau Schwitzer agree, you must stay off your ankle for at least two days."

Avelina sighed, then tried another tact. "What is the worst thing that could happen? It will bleed again." She shrugged. "A little blood loss never hurt anyone."

Magdalen laughed. "Well, you shall have to contend with Hegatha if you get up, that is all I can say."

And as if their speaking of her conjured her, she opened the door.

"What was the gossip in the kitchen?" Magdalen asked.

"Do the servants know what Geitbart is planning?" Avelina added. "Did you find out anything that might help Lord Thornbeck?"

Hegatha gave them both her perpetual frown, then settled it on Magdalen. "Truly, my lady, you should leave Thornbeck as soon as possible, just as soon as the guards arrive. This place is not safe."

"Why? Did something happen?"

"The servants were whispering about someone taking over the castle. They said they heard a rumor that it was the Duke of Geitbart. They asked me if I knew something, but of course I told them nothing. Then, when I was on my way back here, I saw Lady Fronicka speaking with one of the servants. When they saw me coming, they stopped talking and waited for me to walk away."

"Which servant?" Avelina sat up straighter. "Which servant was Lady Fronicka talking to?"

"A rather homely looking woman they call Gerhaws was talking in Lady Fronicka's ear. I would not think such a lady would ever feel a need to speak privately to a servant, especially one with pockmarks all over her face and wild red hair and a red nose. It is well known that this Gerhaws drinks herself into a stupor in the evenings." Hegatha lifted the covers to check Avelina's bandage.

Gerhaws was the servant who introduced Irma to Friedrich. "Gerhaws used to drink with Irma, often getting her drunk. Lady Fronicka and her father must be using Gerhaws as a spy, just as Fronicka used Irma." She tapped her chin with her fingertip. "What if I were to follow Gerhaws? Perhaps I could discover something, could sneak and listen to her conversations with Lady Fronicka."

"No, Avelina." Magdalen was frowning like Hegatha now. "You cannot. Your injuries are not healed and you must not walk on your ankle."

"What does my ankle matter if the castle is attacked and Lord Thornbeck is killed?"

Magdalen stared at her with wide eyes. She had not meant to speak so vehemently. Even Hegatha's mouth went slack, replacing her usual frown.

"Truly," Avelina said quietly, "I cannot lie here doing nothing while Geitbart is plotting how he might kill Lord Thornbeck."

Avelina threw back the covers and stood. "If my ankle begins to bleed too much, I shall come and lie down again. But I must go and see what I can do. It doesn't hurt much anymore." She walked gingerly across the floor. "Do you see? It is not so bad."

When they saw she was determined, Magdalen and Hegatha helped her get dressed.

"I shall go with you," Magdalen said.

"I have an idea to get the servants to trust me. I shall make them think I am being forced to work in the kitchen with all the other servants. Frau Schwitzer will help me."

Magdalen argued with her some more, but Avelina simply smiled and embraced her.

Magdalen frowned. "Please ask for a guard to carry you back up the stairs if your ankle starts to bleed again."

"Very well."

Reinhart sat once again in his library, gazing out the window. How strange to be so idle when his castle might soon be attacked.

After he sent the first guard with a letter to the king, he wrote two more and sent those two couriers in different directions, in case it turned out that the king was away from his home in Prague.

The weather had grown warm enough to melt most of the snow, so he was able to bid farewell to most of his guests the previous day. No doubt they all wanted to be well away before Geitbart did something that would displease the king, like murdering the king's margrave or attacking Thornbeck's guards. The only guests left were Geitbart and Fronicka, Lady Magdalen, whose own guards had only just arrived from Mallin to escort her home, and Avelina.

Reinhart had spent hours strategizing with two of his most trusted knights, who speculated that Sir Klas had been captured by the Duke of Geitbart. They talked of ways they might defeat Geitbart, but Reinhart and his men were outnumbered, and Reinhart was still waiting for Jorgen to get back from his wolf-hunting expedition. He and Odette had taken provisions, prepared to sleep at least two nights away from home to chase the wolves as far away from Thornbeck as possible, if they were not able to kill them.

Reinhart's only two options seemed to be having Geitbart assassinated or running away, and neither of those were honorable. Openly confronting the man would serve no purpose except to alert Geitbart that he knew of his treachery.

Few castles of the Holy Roman Empire had escaped being besieged at one time or another, and it was not so extraordinary that Geitbart would attempt to take Thornbeck. His only hope was that the king would send help, enough soldiers to stop Geitbart and his attackers, or that Reinhart would be able to give himself up in exchange for no harm coming to his people.

He needed to send Avelina away before Geitbart attacked. Fronicka would surely have her killed, and time was running out.

⌒

Avelina found Frau Schwitzer in a storage room. Avelina explained to her what she wished to do, her hands clasped together in front of her chest. "Won't you please help me?"

Frau Schwitzer's kindly face suddenly appeared creased and troubled. "I do not know if it will do any good, but I suppose it can do no harm—except to you. Are you certain you wish to take the risk?"

"Oh yes, of course."

A thought dawned on Frau Schwitzer's face. For a moment it seemed as if she might say something, but she only nodded and nudged Avelina toward the door.

They entered the kitchen and Frau Schwitzer gave two sharp claps. "Everyone, this is Avelina. She will be working in the kitchen today, doing whatever Cook expects of her."

Someone mumbled, "Isn't that Lady Dorothea?"

"She was formerly known as Lady Dorothea," Frau Schwitzer said loudly. "Now she must make up for her deception by working in the kitchen until our lord sends her back to Plimmwald. That is all. You may go back to work."

Everyone quickly resumed their work. Frau Schwitzer went over and whispered in Cook's ear, then she left the room.

A few maidservants glanced furtively in her direction. Would her plan have the opposite effect than the one she'd hoped? Would they resent and dislike her for having played the part of Lady Dorothea, humiliating their lord? Or would they take her under their wing?

Cook was pointing at her with a wooden ladle. "Sit down over there and shell those peas."

Avelina limped to the table and sat on a stool. Already her ankle was throbbing, so she was grateful to be able to do a sitting-down task. And since she was no stranger to shelling peas, she set a fast pace. As soon as she finished all the peas in the basket, another maidservant replaced the empty basket with a full one.

"You're fast," the maidservant said. "I'm Engel." She sat beside her and started shelling the peas into the same bowl with Avelina. "Why were you pretending to be Lady Dorothea?"

"I had no choice. My lord, the Earl of Plimmwald, made me do it."

"Are you sorry you didn't run away? Or was it worth it?"

Avelina shrugged. "It was fun while it lasted, but I'll be punished when I get home. No doubt he has already sent my father and little brother and sister far away and I will never see them again."

Engel was a young woman about Avelina's age, with a stout frame and her brown hair in one braid down her back. She eyed Avelina out of the corner of her eye, when she wasn't looking at the pea pod in her hand.

"But was it worth it to have the margrave fall in love with you?"

Some of the other maidservants turned to look at her, waiting to hear her answer.

Her heart pounded. She must play her part. "He doesn't care for me now that he knows I'm only a maidservant. He would get rid of me if he could."

"Why doesn't he send you away, then?"

More eyes turned to stare.

"He would, but Plimmwald's guards haven't come to fetch me yet, and I injured my ankle. Wolf attack."

"But did Lord Thornbeck not save you from the wolves?"

"He did not know it was me. He heard screams and came to help." She shrugged.

At least they were not looking at her with hatred or resentment.

"Did you like talking to him? To Lord Thornbeck?" a young maidservant who was kneading bread dough asked.

"Anyone would."

"Is he just as handsome close up?"

They were all staring at her now, even Cook.

"He is even more handsome close up."

"Did he kiss you?" This eager question came from another young maidservant.

Avelina shook her head, the heat rising into her cheeks.

"That's enough," Cook said. "Get back to your chores before I send you all home."

They complied, but she noticed a couple of them giving her shy smiles. The plan was working.

When it was time for their midday meal, Avelina was given a place at the table with the other servants, including Gerhaws, who appeared in the kitchen just as the food was being served.

One of the youngest servants brought Avelina a stool so she could prop up her injured foot. "Tell us about the margrave. Was he very chivalrous and romantic?"

So while they ate, Avelina told them stories about her time with the margrave. The things she held closest to her heart—certain things he had said and certain looks—she did not reveal, but she told them endearing stories that illustrated his kindness and bravery—how he gave money to the orphans in the street, and how he had pulled her up as she clung to the broken railing on the balcony. The maidservants hung on her every word.

But it was Gerhaws she needed to get close to. Gerhaws who might know what Geitbart's next move would be.

Finally, after the meal, Cook said, "Gerhaws, you and Avelina go to the dairy and churn the butter. When you've finished, bring it to the kitchen."

So Avelina found herself alone with Gerhaws in the cool of the stone-walled dairy.

As soon as they sat down to the two butter churns, Gerhaws took a small flask out of a pocket in her apron and brought it to her lips. "It's very good strong spirits. I can show you where it's kept if you want some."

"Thank you. Maybe tonight. I only imbibe strong drink after the sun goes down." Avelina started working the wooden staff up and down in the tall churn.

Gerhaws worked with one hand while she held the flask in the other and frequently took a drink. The work was dull and monotonous, and Avelina did her best to get Gerhaws to talk, asking her about her life, how long she had been at Thornbeck Castle, and what she knew about the other inhabitants.

"I've been at Thornbeck Castle two years now. Most people don't know that I came here from a little village in the Geitbart region." She took another drink. "I'm not supposed to tell anyone, but it won't matter soon."

"It won't?" Avelina's heart beat faster. "Why won't it matter?"

Gerhaws chuckled and shook her head, moving the staff up and down in her churn. She took another drink and stared at the floor, as if she had forgotten Avelina's question.

Avelina kept churning. It had been a very long time since she had churned butter, since she was a girl of nine or ten years, so her arms were already getting tired from the unaccustomed motion.

"Lady Fronicka is taking me back to my home," Gerhaws said, her words slow and labored.

"Why is Lady Fronicka taking you back to your home?"

"I don't know why Cook sent you here to work with me. I always work alone."

"Why do you always work alone?" Avelina kept her eyes on her.

"Is it warm in here?" Gerhaws blew out a breath, then touched the back of her hand to her forehead.

"Why is Lady Fronicka taking you back to your home, Gerhaws? Gerhaws, can you hear me?"

"Of course I hear . . . She's taking me back . . ."

The woman's face was flushed. Avelina had seen Lord Plimmwald when he had overindulged in strong drink, and this was how he looked—red nose and cheeks, red-rimmed eyes, and slow movements and speech.

"Why is she taking you back, Gerhaws?" Avelina asked the question again very calmly, as if it was the first and not the third time she'd asked.

"She wanted me to do it one more time, but I told her I . . . I don't want to do it again."

"To do what again, Gerhaws?"

"To . . ." Gerhaws took a deep breath and let it out—and let out a loud belch. Then she leaned forward, holding on to the butter churn as if to keep from falling face forward.

"What does Lady Fronicka want you to do one more time, Gerhaws?"

"I killed the margrave."

Avelina's heart shot to her throat and nearly choked her. "Wha-what?"

Without warning, a tear tracked down Gerhaws's cheek. "I killed the margrave. I killed his lover. I killed them, and she was with child."

Avelina's face tingled as all the blood drained away. She waited for Gerhaws to go on, and after several seconds, her patience was rewarded.

"The duke told me to do it. He told me to. I was just like you." She paused to wipe her large nose on the back of her wrist while she sniffed. "Your lord told you to come here and pretend to be Lady Dorothea. My lord told me to kill the margrave. I had no choice. I had to do it."

"What did you do, Gerhaws?" She asked the question softly.

"I set the fire. I hid in their room, and when they went to sleep, I set their bed curtains on fire." She started sobbing, a deep-throated sound. "I didn't think I would feel guilty about it. I thought if my lord told me to do it, God would not hold me to account for it. It would be on my lord's head and not mine." She rubbed her nose on both wrists now, making a high-pitched mewling sound before going on. "The priest told me it was a sin to disobey my lord, so I did it. I killed the margrave."

Avelina alternately felt pity for the woman, horror at what she had done, and anger that she could be so stupid. But she was right. Avelina had also done something wrong because her lord told her to.

"What was Lady Fronicka saying to you this morning?"

"Lady Fronicka?"

"Yes. She was talking to you. What was she saying?"

More tears ran down Gerhaws's red cheeks, and she wiped her face on her sleeves. She put her flask to her lips and turned it upside down. She held it up and the last drop dripped onto her lip. She licked it off. "She said . . . she was taking me home because I could not do this one last thing for her."

"What else did she say?"

"She said . . . I don't remember." Gerhaws belched again.

Avelina stood. She had to tell Lord Thornbeck the truth about what had happened to his brother. "I have to go to the privy."

Avelina slipped out of the dark room. She made use of the garderobe, and as she was leaving, on a sudden whim, she sneaked behind the screen at the back of the Great Hall. She heard hushed voices nearby, male voices, and peeked around the edge of the wooden screen.

Geitbart was standing with four guards in front of him. "Go apprehend him now. Lady Fronicka saw him enter the library earlier and he should still be there. If he puts up a fight, kill him with the sword. I shall tell the king he attacked you and you were only defending yourselves."

One of the guards asked a question, but Avelina did not wait to hear what was said. She slipped back through the door to the outside, her heart pounding. She ignored the pain in her ankle and ran. She ran past the kitchen and back into the castle through another door. She ran through the servants' passage and into the corridor, past several rooms, and into the library.

"Lord Thornbeck!" she cried in a loud whisper. "They are coming for you! You must hurry!"

24

REINHART STOOD UP from his desk. Avelina ran to him and grabbed his arm, pulling him forward. "Quickly! Please, you must."

Several men's footsteps were coming down the corridor, drawing closer. Avelina gasped. "Hurry!"

If the men found her here, they would likely do to her whatever they intended to do to him.

"Come. This way." Reinhart hurried toward the opposite wall and pulled on the end of one bookcase. The wooden shelves swung out, revealing a hidden space behind it. He pushed Avelina inside and followed her into the darkness. Then he pulled the bookcase back into place.

Avelina held on to his arm with both hands in the complete darkness of the tiny hidden chamber. A voice in the other room said, "Lord Thornbeck, you are requested by the Duke of Geitbart to come with us."

For a moment there was no sound except Avelina's breathing, which was a bit labored, no doubt from running to warn him.

"Search the room," came the command from the other side of the bookcase.

The men stomped across the floor, followed by a loud crash—they must have upended his desk. Footsteps came toward them.

Did they know of their hiding place? They came closer. At any moment they would yank open the bookcase-wall. He tensed, preparing to defend Avelina.

The steps moved away.

More voices, but this time they were too quiet to make out any words. The sounds gradually died out.

He whispered, "You should not have been running on that ankle."

"I did not want them to hurt you." Her voice was strained.

"We are only prolonging the inevitable." He shook his head, but of course, she could not see him in the dark room. Not even her outline was visible.

"What are you saying? Are you going to let Geitbart take you? He wants to kill you."

"Be calm and tell me what you heard."

"I heard the Duke of Geitbart tell four of his guards to come here to the library and take you. He said if—" Her voice hitched and she stopped talking. After a few moments she went on. "If you resisted, they were to kill you."

Her hands tightened around his arm. Did she care so much for him?

"I wish you would leave this place and go to the king."

"A margrave running away from danger? That would not impress the king."

"Your men can fight. They can defeat Geitbart's guards."

"He has a larger force of men nearby. My scouts have seen them. If I had known of his treachery I could have gathered enough men to defeat him. But if my men were to fight now, they would be slaughtered." *And maimed, like me.* And a soldier who could no longer fight would rather have died fighting than to be crippled for the rest of his life.

She said nothing. Her breathing had calmed. He could smell the lavender she used to wash her hair, bringing back the memories of the two times he had held her in his arms. How he longed to hold her again . . .

"You should go back to your chamber." His voice was harsh and more abrupt than he meant.

He placed his hand on the bookcase to push it forward and send her away.

Geitbart's voice barked, "Search the castle. He is here somewhere."

He pulled the bookcase closed, leaving one inch for him to look through.

Footsteps entered the room again. "I want two guards posted here in the library at all times. Search his papers. Bring to me anything that looks important."

"Yes, Your Grace."

Reinhart peered through the crack. A single guard knelt by his overturned desk, picking up the papers scattered on the floor.

Avelina whispered, "I have something else I need to tell you."

He turned. With the crack of light coming in, he could just make out her eyes and mouth. "Sit down," he whispered.

"I will sit, but only if you listen to what I have to say."

He imagined the sparks that were shooting from those pretty blue eyes. "We shall both sit. Put your back against that wall."

She probably could not see where he was pointing, so he touched her shoulder and nudged her until her back was against the shorter wall. He held on to her arm while she slid slowly to the floor, her legs stretched out in front of her. He leaned against the wall and slid down beside her.

The tiny chamber was only about three feet wide and seven feet long, and they were sitting shoulder to shoulder at one end.

"What is this room?" she asked.

"My father used it to store valuables, until some things went missing. My brother and I also played in here. But I don't think anyone has used it for years." He combed a spiderweb out of his hair with his fingers.

"Is there another way out?"

"There is only one way in and out. We shall wait until the guards fall asleep or leave. Now what did you want to tell me?"

She sighed. "It is rather somber news. But I was speaking with a maidservant, Gerhaws, while we were churning butter—"

"What were you doing churning butter? Did someone say you had to work?"

"No. I did it to see if I could find out something about what Geitbart was plotting against you. And I did find out something, as it turned out. But first . . . Gerhaws was very drunk. I don't know where she got such strong drink, but she was crying and saying that Geitbart told her to . . . kill your brother, the margrave."

Reinhart's blood went cold in his veins. "Explain."

"She said she hid in his bedchamber, and when he—when they—went to sleep, she set the bed curtains on fire."

Geitbart. He must have thought it would make it easier to take over Thornbeck. Rage and heat rose to his forehead.

"I am very sorry to tell you."

Reinhart forced himself to take a deep breath. He could think much more clearly if he allowed his emotions to go cold. Someday Geitbart would pay for having his brother killed. The assurance helped the heat to dissipate and him to think calmly.

"You must not tell anyone else what you have just told me. If Geitbart finds out you know, he will kill you. I am surprised he has not killed Gerhaws yet."

"Did you already suspect Geitbart?"

He did not reply immediately. Avelina had already deceived him once. How could he know if he could trust her? But she had come and warned him, had run to him on her injured ankle . . .

"No, I did not suspect Geitbart. I thought it was an accident, a stray spark from the fireplace."

"He must have wanted people to think that you had killed your brother." Avelina sighed. "I cannot comprehend anyone so evil."

"Greed and lust for power will make a man do almost anything."

They sat in silence as he took in this new information. He was sick at the thought of someone deliberately murdering his brother, his brother's lover, and their unborn child. Henrich never had a chance to fight back—or repent of his sins.

Avelina broke the silence. "I don't want him to kill you."

"Thank you for that." He was very aware of her shoulder pressed against his. He should have sat on the other side.

The guard in the next room made enough noise to cover the sound of their voices as he continued shuffling papers and banging around.

"My lord?"

"Yes?"

"Your people need you. I want you to escape and go to Jorgen and Odette's manor house."

Because of her, he had been humiliated in front of powerful people, some of whom were plotting against him and one who murdered his brother and unborn child. Why did she have to sound so good and kind and sweet?

"I have a question to ask you." If he were wise, he would not ask. But if Geitbart was going to kill him, it wouldn't matter anyway. "In the two weeks when I thought you were Lady Dorothea, when you always tried to turn the conversation to Lady Magdalen,

I thought it was because you were timid. But it was not. Why were you so afraid to talk to me?"

"I *was* afraid. I . . . I wanted you to admire Lady Magdalen, not me."

"Ah." He should dwell on that. She did not want him to love her, did not feel anything for him.

"I enjoyed talking to you," she whispered softly. "I wanted to talk to you. But I was afraid if I drew your attention to me, you might . . . that is . . . I knew I could not marry you."

Could he hear regret in her voice? No, he didn't want to hear that, did not want to believe the best about her or to think about her pain.

"I would be punished if you chose me," she went on, "and so would my family."

For whom she had asked for a goose and a side of pork every month. How considerate and compassionate she was . . . and poor.

"Of course. I understand." He tried to sound dispassionate and unconcerned.

There was a long pause. Then she said, "I admired you. Very much. So I tried not to talk to you or look at you. I was afraid you would see how much I admired you."

Her words buoyed him—and twisted the knife in his heart at the same time.

As his eyes had grown accustomed to the low light, he could see her hands were limp in her lap, her head slightly bowed.

"You could have trusted me with the truth about who you were and what Lord Plimmwald had made you do."

"I know that now. But I could not have known that I could trust you not to be angry and tell Lord Plimmwald. I never wanted to hurt you. But you should not have been so angry with me, and you should not treat your servants the way you do. You yell at them, even when they have not done anything wrong. They may be your servants, but you can at least treat them with respect."

For a moment he was speechless. "Did you just rebuke me for not being respectful enough to my servants?"

"Yes, I did. And for being angry with me even after you knew I did not mean to hurt you and never wanted to deceive you." Her voice had lost some of its forceful tartness. Still, she sounded like her old self, when she had boldly proclaimed her opinions about love and marriage and duty and everything else he'd asked her about.

"Perhaps you are right. I should not have sent you to the servants' quarters in anger, with an injured ankle. I regret it."

She was very still, and he imagined his answer had shocked her into silence.

The outline of her shoulders in the dark room showed how small and frail she was. He imagined his arm embracing her, pulling her back against his chest, her head resting against him, her temple against his cheek. How good it would feel to turn her face toward him and kiss her.

A sharp ache stabbed his chest. He must not think such things. She was a servant and he was a margrave.

He could neither love her nor marry her. Besides, she was impertinent and opinionated, two of the very worst traits a woman could have. So why could he not stop thinking that she was the only woman he would ever want?

Avelina was getting cold sitting in the unheated room. The only part of her that was warm was her arm and shoulder, pressed against

Lord Thornbeck. If only she was Lady Dorothea. She would shamelessly tell him she was cold, ask for his embrace, and rest her head against his chest.

Doing such a thing would be an invitation to Lord Thornbeck to make her his mistress, and she would never do that. She might only be a servant, but she deserved respect, even from a margrave, like Lady Magdalen believed. She was a human being, created by God to do good works. So she was not sorry she had rebuked him for being disrespectful to his servants, but she was shocked to hear him agree with her and say he regretted sending her to the servants' quarters out of anger.

He had still been angry with her for deceiving him, so why had he saved her from the wolves?

"Did you know I was the one being attacked by wolves when you came to my rescue? Or did you only hear screams, unaware of who was in danger?"

He spoke slowly, pausing between sentences. "My guards told me they saw you leaving with Irma, so I knew it might be you. We were getting ready to set out to hunt the wolves, and my horse was saddled first. So I was able to reach you first."

Perhaps he did think it was her, screaming for help. At least she had the memory of his taking her back to Thornbeck on his horse, carrying her in his arms despite his bad ankle, until he was able to hand her off to one of his guards. Then he had held her against his chest to stop her shaking. He was so warm. If only he would hold her again.

Lord Thornbeck leaned forward, straining to see through the tiny crack into the library.

"Is the guard still there?"

"Yes." He sat back.

Neither of them spoke for a while, but always Avelina could

feel the tension of his being so near in the tiny, almost completely dark room. If he had not made it clear that he would never have tender feelings for a servant, she might be worried he would try to kiss her . . . and that she would let him.

Avelina leaned forward to look through the crack. "Do you think we will have to stay here all night?"

"My hope is that by morning, he will send these guards elsewhere and we can escape. Or I will cause a distraction so you can get away."

She shook her head. "You are the one who is in danger, who needs to escape."

"If Geitbart finds out you warned me, he will likely kill you, or at least lock you in the dungeon. I cannot allow that."

Why? Why could he not allow that? She wanted to ask him, but whether or not he still cared for her, they both knew that he shouldn't. She should be thinking about how to get to safety, not about how much she longed for a love that could never be.

She couldn't imagine how either of them would escape, truthfully. She should pray. Perhaps God would give them favor and save them from Geitbart. God could keep them from dying as they tried to escape. For those things she could pray. But it seemed too much to ask God for her heart's desire.

Father God, if You cannot save me, then at least save Lord Thornbeck. But perhaps she should not have said "cannot" to God. Forgive me, God. I did not mean to imply that there is anything You cannot do. However, I know that You do not always do everything we ask, so I plead with You to save us. Save us precisely because it is impossible, and because You are God. And make a way for me to marry Lord Thornbeck, unless that is too presumptuous of me.

"Are you in pain?"

She realized she'd been leaning forward, her head almost

between her knees, as she concentrated on her silent prayer. She straightened. "No, I am well."

"Does your ankle hurt?"

"Only a little. I know your accident was a long time ago, but does your ankle pain you all the time or only sometimes?"

"It is worse when the weather changes."

"I am sorry."

"I pray your ankle shall heal better than mine has. I believe it will, if you stay off of it."

He sounded gruff. Avelina leaned forward again to watch the guard. He was still shuffling through papers. Then he stopped to light a candle, as it had grown quite dark outside.

"You said you have a brother and sister. How old are they?"

"Jacob is twelve and Brigitta is six. I miss them." She sighed.

"Are your father and mother still alive?"

"My mother died nearly six years ago and my father worked as the Earl of Plimmwald's stable master. But he was in an accident. One of Lord Plimmwald's stallions kicked my father in the back and in the head. He can no longer walk or feel his legs, and he doesn't think quite so well as he once did."

"Did Plimmwald agree to provide for your father and his family?"

"No. I was already working at the castle as a servant for his daughter. He never even said he was sorry for what happened."

No one spoke for a while. She leaned forward to look through the crack. The guards had stopped looking through the papers on the desk and the floor. They both sat down, one in Lord Thornbeck's chair and the other in Jorgen's. The guards' heads were leaned back against the wall, but they faced the rest of the room and would have a clear view if she and Lord Thornbeck tried to sneak out.

"If the guards fall asleep," Avelina whispered, "is it too dangerous to try to sneak out?"

"We will try it."

What if the guards woke up? Lord Thornbeck had no weapon. She chewed on her lip, then reminded herself to pray for his protection.

They both watched the guards for a while, trying to see if they were falling asleep, until Avelina's cheek brushed against his hair. She had not realized she was so close to him. She moved her head away a few inches.

"I am going to stand," he said.

She drew her knees up to give him more room. He carefully got to his feet, no doubt trying to make sure he did not make any noise. When he was fully upright, he put his eye to the crack.

He stood like that for a long time. A crash sounded, as from something falling to the floor. Lord Thornbeck stepped back. "Not sleeping," he whispered.

Avelina gazed up at him in the dark. He was very tall, with broad shoulders, and her memory filled in what she could not see in the dark—perfect masculine features, dark hair, a shadow of beard on his face, and brown eyes that could melt her heart—or freeze it, depending on his expression.

"Do you wish to stretch your legs?" He seemed to be holding out his hand to her.

She groped for it in the dark, and he pulled her to her feet. Now they were standing only inches apart, her hand still clasped in his. Neither of them moved. She felt his breath on her forehead.

"It is nighttime now. You should get some rest," he said softly. "I'll keep watch." He moved around her, letting go of her hand and touching her shoulder. "I'll sit here and you can lie down, with your head at the other end."

He slid to the floor. Then she sat down at the other end and pillowed her head on her hands, her legs stretched out alongside his. But her body was slow to relax, her muscles still tense. The floor was hard and cold, and her feet were beginning to ache. If she got any colder, she was afraid she would start shivering again.

"Are you cold?" he asked.

"A little. Yes." The pain in her feet reminded her of the frightening experience outside in the snow with the wolves. But she did not want to complain. Besides, what could Lord Thornbeck do about it? There was no blanket in this room and neither of them wore a cloak or outer garment.

"I do not want to make you uncomfortable," he said after a short silence, "but the healer said you should not get too cold this soon. You will have to allow me to warm your feet."

She sat up. "How do you propose to do that?"

"Lie back down. Now put your feet between my knees."

She had no shoes on, only the stockings they had placed on her feet when all her clothing was wet. He held her feet in his hands, then quickly took hold of the stockings and stripped them off. Then he tucked her bare feet between his knees.

The warmth from his legs flooded her cold feet.

Her heart beat fast. She concentrated on staying still, not wanting to make him uncomfortable. Her muscles were cramping and even though her feet were warmer, she was still quite cold. She lay on the stone floor, forcing her eyes to stay closed, commanding herself to fall asleep. But it was no use.

Was Lord Thornbeck asleep? His eyes seemed to be closed, but it was impossible to be sure in the dark little room.

Her shoulder seemed to have turned to ice against the cold floor. She clamped her teeth together to stop them from making noise. A few minutes later they started chattering and she could no longer control them.

Would the guards hear? She put her hand over her mouth.

"Come here," Lord Thornbeck whispered harshly.

"What?" But speaking made her teeth chatter louder.

"Come. Closer."

She sat up and crawled closer, still trying to stop her teeth from slamming together, or at least to keep her lips closed so they weren't so loud.

He scooped her up before she knew what he was doing and placed her in his lap. "Now put your head on my chest. Your chattering teeth will get us killed."

She sat stiffly but had little choice but to lay her head against his chest. His arms were wrapped around her and she was surrounded by his masculine scent and the dried mint and lilac of his clothes. His breath was in her ear, audible through her hair, which hung down unfettered, as she'd lost her ribbons and her braids had come undone when she'd run to find him.

Sitting in his lap like this was very improper, but she was deliciously warm. Of course he was more concerned about alerting the guard than her comfort. But she did not blame him.

She closed her eyes, breathing deeply of his comforting scent. If only she could be held like this every day, to feel loved by this man she had come to care for even more than her own life.

But it was foolish to think such things.

Neither of them spoke or even moved. Finally, warm and comfortable, she felt herself drifting blissfully into sleep.

⌒

It was night. She was in the forest just outside the town of Plimmwald, and she was searching for Lord Thornbeck.

A man, one of Geitbart's guards, was kneeling in front of a fire in the middle of the dark forest. She started to hide, but as soon as she took a step, he looked up and glared at her. He strode toward her. She tried to turn and run but she could not move. Her feet were heavy and would not obey her.

As the guard approached, his head suddenly changed into the head of a wolf. The wolf face snarled and growled, saliva dripping from its fangs. Its horrible yellow eyes held her captive. Finally, she wrenched herself free from the eyes' mesmerizing hold and turned to run, but her feet seemed to be made of iron. She could not move.

The hair on her arms prickled, as if she could feel the breath of the wolf just behind her, even as she could hear it snorting and snapping its jaws. Then, terrible pain tore through her ankle as the wolf sank its teeth into her flesh.

She jerked awake, gasping.

"It was only a dream," Lord Thornbeck whispered in her ear. "You must be quiet."

She clutched handfuls of his shirt, pushing herself off his chest. Had she cried out? Would the guard find them now?

25

Reinhart held her close as her whole body shuddered. She made a strangled sound, as if she was afraid.

"You must be quiet," he whispered in her ear.

She gasped, pushing away from him.

"It was only a dream."

Her eyes finally opened. She stared up at him as if finally understanding where she was.

One of the guards stood and took a few steps in their direction.

"Don't move," he whispered in her ear.

She was clinging to him now, her face pressed against his chest. If the guard found them, Reinhart would give himself up in exchange for her freedom. But the guard would still tell Geitbart that Avelina was there with him.

The guard took another step, then another, staring hard at their little alcove. Could he see the crack behind the bookshelf? The closer he came, the more likely he was to see it, to pull the bookcase forward and find them.

He stood still for several seconds, staring.

Avelina did not move, but Reinhart could hear her breathing fast. He wanted to tell her all would be well, but he did not dare take the risk of speaking, even in a whisper.

Finally, the guard muttered, "Must be rats," and put his sword away. He walked back to his chair and sat down, leaning his head back against the wall.

Her silky hair brushed against his lips as he whispered, "We're safe."

"Are you sure?"

"Yes." He should stop inhaling the intoxicating lavender of her hair. He should not be holding her.

He could have let her be cold. He could have left her where she was on the cold, hard floor. But she had no shoes, her clothing was so much thinner than his, and the healer had said she should not get cold this soon after nearly freezing to death. Besides that, her teeth were making too much noise.

He could control himself. He was not some addle-brained boy of fifteen who would take advantage of any girl who let him. And Avelina probably would not let him anyway.

He had to not think about how good she felt in his arms, how trusting she was, how beautiful, and especially how good she smelled.

"Am I hurting you?" she whispered.

"No. Go back to sleep."

"I'm sorry I made that noise and nearly gave us away."

"Were you having a bad dream?"

"I was dreaming that I was in the forest with one of Geitbart's guards. He was coming after me, and then he turned into a wolf." She pressed her face against his chest, and her breath caressed his neck with every word she spoke. "I know it was only a dream, but it was terrifying. The wolf bit my ankle. It felt just like when they attacked me in the forest."

He resisted the urge to caress her shoulder . . . her hair . . . her back. He closed his eyes, concentrating on not moving, trying not to think.

She was quiet for a few minutes, then said, "How are your arm and shoulder? Are they healing?"

"Only scratches."

"What is our plan, when we get out of here?"

"I will find Jorgen and together we will rally the men from Thornbeck and my guards and expel Geitbart from the castle."

"And I shall help you."

"You shall not. You will go to your bed and rest your ankle."

"I will not argue with you, except to say that I will not be able to stay in my room. I will have to do what I can to help."

She was right. It was no use to argue.

After a short pause, she said, "So why did you choose me?"

"What?" His heart lurched in his chest.

"Why did you choose me instead of Lady Magdalen?"

The last thing he needed to think about was all the things about her that had made him want to marry her.

"Magdalen is a wonderful girl, but she is very young."

"Not much younger than I am."

He grunted.

"Did you not think me very strange, that first day when you asked me those questions?"

"You were . . . not what I thought I wanted." He should leave it at that. He should not say more. For a long time there was silence. Perhaps she would fall asleep again.

"You disagreed with what I said about love?"

He should stay silent . . . "You said people should marry for love, not out of duty, because if there is no love and if you have no romantic thoughts about each other, then you are much more likely to treat each other badly."

"And you liked that?"

"My mother married my father out of duty. They despised

each other. It was painful to see my mother and father treating each other with contempt."

"That does sound painful."

"You also said, 'A woman wishes to be swept up by a man's fervent feelings for her, by love and longing and depth of feeling. She does not wish to be married for her money or her noble birth or because she is a sensible choice. She wants to be wooed, even after she is married, to be cherished and loved for her very self.'"

"You remembered." She sounded breathless. "It is true. It is what I want. To be cherished and loved."

Being with her was what *he* wanted. But it was impossible.

"I wanted to talk to you. I wanted so much to . . . but I am not an earl's daughter."

It must be morning, as more light was finding its way in and he could see her a little better now. Her hair had fallen over her cheek and one eye. He succumbed to his desire and smoothed her hair off her face. As he did so, his fingers caressed her cheek. She made a tiny sound, like her breath catching in her throat. His heart crashed against his chest.

"You passed the tests, and you are the most worthy woman I've ever known."

She sat so still. Would she let him kiss her? Dangerous, tempting thought. So tempting.

Shouts and the sound of footsteps broke through his consciousness. Someone was running down the corridor.

"Fire! Come and help!"

The two guards in the library scrambled to their feet and ran out.

Lord Thornbeck lifted Avelina by her waist, and they were both on their feet in two seconds. He pushed open the bookcase door and they hurried out and across the library and into the corridor.

They were free!

Avelina smelled smoke. Men ran toward the stairs and Lord Thornbeck went after them.

"You stay here," he said over his shoulder at her.

She followed him anyway as he stopped in the first bedchamber he came to and yanked a curtain down off the bed. He rolled it in a ball and tucked it under his arm as he limped toward the stairs.

Avelina followed him, "What if Geitbart set the fire to lure you out in the open?"

"I have to take that chance." He stayed just far enough ahead of her so that she could not attempt to stop him.

At the top of the stairs, he turned to go down the corridor toward the west wing.

The smell of smoke was very strong as it came wafting down the corridor and into their faces. Avelina coughed.

"Come back," Avelina called. Geitbart would surely have him captured.

"Stay there!"

Men were shouting and emerging, coughing from the thick smoke. Lord Thornbeck ignored them and, holding his arm over his mouth and nose, disappeared down the corridor into the thick gray smoke. Avelina followed.

Suddenly the smoke all whooshed in the opposite direction. That was when Avelina saw that the door at the end of the damaged west wing was open, showing the pale light of dawn. As the smoke cleared a bit, she could see that someone was standing in the doorway. Gerhaws.

Gerhaws looked back at Lord Thornbeck, then turned toward the door that led straight down.

Lord Thornbeck called out to her, but she did not look back. She simply stepped forward, disappearing as she fell.

Avelina cried out in horror, but the sound was lost in the roar of the fire farther down.

Just then, another figure emerged as bright-orange flames became visible from a doorway along the corridor.

"Annlin!" called the high-pitched voice. "Annlin!"

Lord Thornbeck went toward Endlein and caught her by the hand, but she pulled away from him, going toward the burning room and disappearing inside it. Lord Thornbeck went after her.

More people were running toward them with buckets of water and blankets, passing by Avelina. She tried to go back toward the burning room and to Lord Thornbeck, but two guards caught her by the arms and pulled her back away from the fire. Soon she could no longer see Lord Thornbeck.

Would he die in a fire just as his brother had, in the very same room where his brother had perished? Would he breathe in so much smoke that he would lose consciousness? If only she could get to him, she could convince him to leave.

She screamed, "Lord Thornbeck!" But no one would let her go to him.

"What is happening?" she called, but as a guard pushed through, he took hold of Avelina's arm.

"You should not be here."

"Where is Lord Thornbeck?"

"He is convincing Endlein to come with him, and the men are putting out the fire. Come." He pulled her away from the smoke-filled, crowded corridor. "This is no place for you."

"No! I will not leave." Lord Thornbeck would die and no one would let her see him.

Finally, the men—Lord Thornbeck's guards and servants—started moving out of the corridor, their faces covered in soot.

"The fire is out," one man said.

They continued to come away from the corridor. Finally, Endlein, the addled old woman, emerged through the smoke, followed by Lord Thornbeck. Both their faces were covered in soot.

Two servants took charge of Endlein, who was muttering questions and obviously confused. They urged her to go with them and spoke soothingly to her.

Avelina rushed forward and grabbed Lord Thornbeck's arm.

"Let us go," she said, eager to get him somewhere Geitbart would not find him.

She hurried him down the corridor, ignoring the people standing around who seemed to want to talk about what had just happened. Two of Geitbart's guards stood straighter as they noticed Lord Thornbeck approaching. They exchanged a look, then took a step toward the margrave.

Three of Lord Thornbeck's guards stood nearby. Avelina got their attention.

"Those men are trying to molest me!" She pointed at the two red-and-black clad guards.

Lord Thornbeck's guards immediately blocked Geitbart's men's way and began a shouting match with them. Avelina and Lord Thornbeck hurried away, rushing down the stairs.

Not sure where else to go, she led him to her own bedchamber.

26

Lord Thornbeck seemed to suddenly notice where they were. He yanked the door open, waved her in, then followed and closed the door.

Avelina went to the water pitcher next to her bed. It was still full. She poured the two goblets full of water and held out a goblet to him while taking a sip. "It's a little stale tasting, but it's water."

He drank the whole goblet without pausing, letting a trickle of water run down his sooty neck. For some reason it reminded her of his fingers caressing her cheek in the tiny room. But that thought, along with his exposed throat and intense eyes, was too distracting and was making her cheeks grow hot.

"Sit down and tell me why you felt you had to put out that fire yourself." Avelina hurried to find a clean cloth and poured some water in a bowl for him to wash his face. "You know you might have had a chance to escape if you had not done that."

He didn't speak for a few moments. "I seemed to go back to the night my brother died. I only knew I wanted to put it out. It was foolish, perhaps." His eyes stayed locked on hers the whole time he was talking.

She handed him the bowl of water and cloth.

"You need this as badly as I do," he said.

Avelina grabbed the small looking glass on her table. She gasped. Her face was covered in soot, almost as much as Lord Thornbeck's, and there were bits of ash in her unkempt hair. "Why did you not tell me I looked like this?"

He stared up at her from the chair where he sat. "I think you look rather becoming."

She quickly found another cloth and dipped it in the water. Turning her back on him and looking in the mirror, she quickly washed her face, cleaning her forehead and cheeks, around her eyes, rinsing her cloth and cleaning her chin and around her mouth. Finally, she turned to face him while she picked the ashes out of her hair.

"Did Gerhaws start the fire?"

"I think Geitbart probably instructed her to, thinking I would try to escape the castle during the tumult." Lord Thornbeck was washing his face and watching her out of the corner of his eye. "She fell to her death. After the fire was out, I went over and looked."

"Horrible."

"Especially since Gerhaws was the only witness to who actually killed my brother."

"The king would not have accepted the word of a servant anyway." Avelina continued cleaning her face and neck. "I was terrified Geitbart would seize you. Why do you think he did not? I don't suppose he expected you to be putting out the fire."

"No, and Geitbart would not risk his life by going anywhere near a fire." Lord Thornbeck rubbed his sooty neck with the cloth. "And only a few of his guards were nearby, while my own guards were there helping to fight the fire. But he will hear that I was there."

"Yes, he will be looking for you. You must escape the castle as quickly as you can."

"May I have some more water?"

Avelina poured him another goblet. He took it and drank it. His stomach immediately growled.

"I'm famished too," she said. "I'll go down to the kitchen and get some food. You can take it with you as you leave."

"Wait. It may not be safe for you to be seen."

"Me? Why not? Do you think someone knows I warned you?"

"They may suspect it since you disappeared the same time I did."

"I don't think so. Frau Schwitzer was aware that I was spying last evening. She would have covered up my disappearance to Geitbart's guards."

He pointed behind her. "Why is your candle still burning?"

The candle was in a candlestick, but it was strange that it had not burned out yet. A piece of paper on the desk caught her eye. "Magdalen must have been here. She left me a note."

"What does it say?"

"'Avelina, my mother's guards have come to escort me back to Mallin. I have no choice but to leave with them early in the morning. If you get this note, please come and say farewell to me.'"

Lord Thornbeck went to the window, opened the shutter, and looked out. "I should have just enough time to write a letter to the Duke of Pomerania to send with Lady Magdalen and her guards."

He sat at the desk, then looked up at her. "You should lie down. Let me see your ankle."

She opened the bed curtains. "But first I should go change my clothes. I think I have rat droppings on this dress." She grabbed a clean cotehardie and went into the little servant's closet and closed the door to undress, which she did quickly.

When she was done and came out, Lord Thornbeck was still sitting at the desk, writing.

She came across the room and he looked up at her. "You don't look at all like someone who spent the night hiding in a tiny storage room."

"Thank you, my lord." She curtsied. "And neither do you." His jaw and chin were covered in dark stubble. Was this how he had looked when he was once a rough knight, fighting in battles and commanding other rough men? But he was too appealing to dwell on.

While he was focused on his letter, she pulled her skirts up just enough to be able to see her bandage. Blood had soaked through in a few places, but it was much less bloody than before. She quickly dropped her skirt to cover it before Lord Thornbeck could see.

He took a stick of rose-colored wax from his pocket and held it over the candle flame, then quickly rubbed the hot end of the wax onto the folded paper. He took off his ring and sealed the letter, pressing the seal into the blob of wax.

Avelina's eyes were gritty and her whole body was heavy with exhaustion, but she could not think about that. "I shall go fetch Lady Magdalen so you can ask her to take your letter."

"Stop."

She halted halfway to the door.

"You should not be running around on that ankle. I'll go get Lady Magdalen." He started toward the door.

"No, you won't." Avelina practically leapt to throw her body in front of the door. "You cannot. If a guard sees you—" She stared up into his eyes. The way he was looking down at her made her heart flutter. "Please. I will go."

He pulled her hand to his chest. She was suddenly flooded by the oh-so-recent memory of lying against his chest, his strong arms around her, the warmth of his breath in her ear as he whispered to her.

"You are already on your ankle, so go."

But he was still holding tightly to her hand. His expression seemed sad. Finally, he let go. She turned and hurried out into the corridor.

Her heart was thumping in a late reaction to wishing she could stand on her tiptoes and kiss him on the lips.

But that would have been foolish indeed.

She knocked on Magdalen's door. Hegatha opened it, but Magdalen ran up behind her. "Are you well?" She reached out to clasp Avelina's hands. "I was so worried."

"I am well. Can you come with me, only for a few minutes?"

She nodded and hurried out, and they went back to Avelina's room. Thankfully the corridor was still empty and no one saw them.

Lord Thornbeck, still standing where she had left him, held out the sealed missive. "Lady Magdalen, I need you to take this letter and have it delivered to the Duke of Pomerania. Would you be willing?"

"Of course. I can get one of the guards to break away and it will only add an extra day to his trip back to Mallin."

"I would be greatly in your debt, Lady Magdalen."

"It would be my honor to help you in such a way, Lord Thornbeck." She took the letter from him. "And I understand that secrecy is of the utmost importance. No one shall know I saw you today or that I have this letter."

"I appreciate that." He gave her a small bow.

Magdalen suddenly turned to Avelina. "Can you come back to my room for a few moments?"

Avelina followed her back. Magdalen took Avelina aside and whispered, "What happened? Where were you all night?"

Avelina told her about going down to the kitchen and having Frau Schwitzer and Cook send her to work with Gerhaws. She told her of Gerhaws's confession.

Magdalen gasped. "I can hardly believe she admitted what she did, and to you, a stranger."

"She was so drunk with wine, or whatever it was she was drinking, I doubt she even remembered telling me."

"Then what happened?"

"I overheard Geitbart telling his guards to capture Lord Thornbeck and to kill him if he resisted. So I ran to the library ahead of the guards to warn him. Lord Thornbeck and I hid in a secret room in the library. We were there all night waiting for the guard to leave."

"Did anything happen?" Magdalen whispered.

"No. He cannot marry me, Magdalen." Tears stung her eyes. "Perhaps he wishes he could, but . . . it's impossible. And anyway, Geitbart is trying to kill him, or at least capture him."

Magdalen looked very grave. "Please be careful. I am so sorry I have to leave you." She put her arms around her.

"It is better that you go. You will be helping Lord Thornbeck by delivering his missive. You should get back home where you'll be safe."

Magdalen said some more about Avelina staying safe and that she would do whatever she could to help. They embraced each other one last time.

Avelina turned and went back to her own bedchamber, a hollow place in her heart as Magdalen closed the door behind her. She pressed her hands over her chest and tears stung her eyes. She might never see her friend again.

But she did not have time to dwell on sad thoughts now. There was much to do in the battle against Geitbart, to keep Lord Thornbeck and everyone else at the castle safe from Fronicka and her greedy, power-hungry father.

When she came back to her chamber, Reinhart was leaning

forward in his chair, his head bowed as if he was praying. Perhaps he was saying a prayer that Magdalen's guard would be able to get his message to his ally.

To keep from disturbing him—or facing his disapproval for going downstairs—Avelina hurried back out and down the barely lit corridors. As she went she made her plan. She would find Frau Schwitzer and see what information she might have. She would also see if the head house servant had any ideas about how to arm the male servants to fight Geitbart.

It was too bad Gerhaws had killed herself. It seemed strange to feel sad about the death of the woman who had murdered Lord Thornbeck's brother, but even though her testimony would not be allowed to convict a nobleman like the Duke of Geitbart, it might have convinced the king at least not to believe the duke's accusations against Lord Thornbeck. Besides, Geitbart was more to blame than the maidservant who carried out his murderous scheme.

When Avelina returned with a tray of food and a fresh pitcher of water, she reported her findings to Lord Thornbeck. "I managed to speak directly to one of your knights, Sir Stefan. He said he would see if he could find a way to arm the male servants with weapons without being noticed or raising suspicion. I shall go back to—"

"No, I do not want you going downstairs anymore. I've already been too thoughtless where you are concerned."

"Very well. But Geitbart's guards are everywhere, roaming the corridors of the castle, stopping people and questioning them. Frau Schwitzer and Sir Stefan are the only ones—besides Lady Magdalen and me—who know where you are."

They ate quickly, with Avelina on the bed with her foot stretched out. When they had finished breaking their long fast,

Lord Thornbeck asked, "Do you have any extra bandages? We have to get this one off you."

She started to get up.

"No. You stay. Just tell me where they are."

"I think there are some on that shelf." She pointed to the cupboard on the other side of the bed.

He brought over a stack of bandages and set them on the bed near her foot. He reached for her ankle.

"Wait." She pulled her feet up and covered them with her skirts.

"I am going to change the bandage on your ankle."

"Only if you let me change the bandage on your arm and shoulder."

He stared back at her. "Very well, but we should hurry. I need to start rounding up my men."

She stretched out her leg and let him unwrap the bloody bandage on her ankle. He looked very stoic about touching her bare foot, but every time his fingers brushed her skin her stomach fluttered.

"It doesn't look as if it is bleeding at the moment," he said.

The gouge marks made by the wolf's teeth were open holes in her skin, but they did seem a bit smaller than before. Perhaps they were closing up.

He picked up the bandages and soon finished wrapping and tying the bandage in place.

"Now it is your turn," she said.

"But I have to look at your arm first."

"I am not even bandaging it." She raised the loose sleeve of her undergown. "See? It is nothing." The scratches on her arm were healing well. She scooted over and patted the bed. "Sit, so I can see your shoulder and arm."

He looked at her askance for a few moments before pulling his outer tunic and shirt over his head, then he sat at the foot of the bed instead of where she had indicated.

She tried to avert her eyes from his bare chest. She *should* avert her eyes and not admire his magnificent, broad, powerful-looking chest, and focus only on his shoulder injury. She swallowed past the dryness in her throat. *Shoulder, Avelina. Injury, Avelina. Breathe, Avelina.*

She unwrapped the bandage, trying not to touch his bare skin any more than necessary. "It is looking well," she said to cover her nervousness.

"Just leave it uncovered. It doesn't need a bandage."

"Are you sure?"

"It's not bleeding, is it?"

"No, but let me look at your arm."

He stretched out his arm to her.

"It seems to be healing quite well," she said unnecessarily as she examined the scabbed-over scratches.

He arose and reached for his clothing on the chair. The muscles across his back bunched and flexed as he pulled his white shirt over his head and put his arms through the sleeves. Even though it had been at least a year since he injured his ankle, he still had the body of a well-trained knight. Lord Plimmwald's knights often trained without their shirts. She'd always thought it was disgusting the way the other maidservants used to watch them. So why was her heart thumping, and why did she not feel disgusted now?

Please don't let him turn suddenly and catch me staring at him.

Soon he was completely covered again and she was breathing more freely. He tied his shirt laces and then pulled on his outer tunic over his shirt.

Suddenly someone knocked on the door. "Go, hurry!" Avelina whispered desperately.

Lord Thornbeck hurried to the little room at the far end of the chamber as Avelina walked to her door. "Who is there?" she asked loudly, checking to make sure Lord Thornbeck was out of sight.

"Guards. Open the door."

Avelina opened and stood in the doorway. "Yes?"

"We are looking for Lord Thornbeck." They wore the colors of Geitbart, red and black.

Avelina shrugged. "I am sorry I cannot help you."

The guard stuck his head in and looked around. "You are to tell one of us if you see him."

"Is the Duke of Geitbart looking for him? Or are Lord Thornbeck's guards looking for him?"

He narrowed his eyes at her. "He is missing. Have you seen him?"

"No, but if I do see him, what should I tell him?"

"Tell him the Duke of Geitbart wishes to speak with him."

"Of course. I will."

She could tell he was trying to decide if he should bow to her or just leave. In the end he simply turned to leave. Three other guards were behind him and they went down the corridor and knocked on Magdalen's door.

Just as Avelina was about to close the door, Geitbart pushed it wide and stepped into the room.

27

"LADY DOROTHEA," HE said. "No, that is not your name, is it? What is your name?"

"Avelina Klein of Plimmwald."

"Avelina. Yes." His face twisted into a wry smile. He seemed to be perpetually leaning forward in an aggressive way that seemed in contrast to his rather short and paunchy body. He had sharp angular cheekbones and bushy black brows that came to a point in the middle above each eye.

"Do you wish to speak to me about something?"

He moved over to the chair and sat down. "I wish to know where Lord Thornbeck is."

"Apparently he is missing. Your guards just informed me."

"I thought you might know where he is." He fingered the goblet on the table beside him that Lord Thornbeck had drunk from earlier.

"Why would I know where he is?" Her hands were starting to shake.

"He chose you at the ball, did he not?"

"Yes, but when he found out I had deceived him, he was very angry with me. He had me sent to the servants' quarters, until

Magdalen demanded that he let me sleep here. He knows I am only a maidservant. He could have no further desire to even talk with me."

"He risked his life to rescue you from the wolves, did he not?"

She shrugged again. "He heard screaming. He would have risked his life to save anyone." A lump rose into her throat at the truth of the words.

The duke's small, sharp gaze roamed the room, seeming to take note of everything. No doubt he took in their discarded bandages. Hopefully he could not tell that one of them belonged to Lord Thornbeck.

"I wonder that he has not sent you away."

"He would have, but he said he would wait until my injury is healed."

"Very compassionate of him."

Avelina despised the mocking tone of his voice and curve of his lips. He was like a small dark rooster who claimed every chicken in the henhouse as his personal property—every chicken, every egg, and even the humans who fed him.

"Since I do not know where Lord Thornbeck is, there is nothing more I can do for you. I suppose you have things to do."

But the duke made no move to get up from the chair. He simply continued to finger the goblet beside him.

"I heard the margrave was very helpful in putting out the fire in the west wing an hour ago."

"It is his castle. I am not surprised he would want to protect it."

"You were also seen near the fire."

"I was curious."

The duke's gaze settled on the basin of water, turned gray from the soot she and Lord Thornbeck had washed from their faces and necks. He inhaled a deep breath before speaking. "Lord

Thornbeck was a knight before he injured his ankle and became Margrave of Thornbeck. Did you know?"

"Of course. Everyone knows."

"I would imagine he knows how to sword fight very well."

"I would imagine that is true." From the muscles she had just seen on his back and arms, she would guess he was very good at it.

"If you see him, tell him I want to challenge him to a sword fight, just him and me."

"I shall be sure to tell him, if I see him."

He rose to his feet and looked directly at her. "If I have need of this chamber, I shall send you word. I suppose you may stay, for now."

Avelina kept her face unreadable, she hoped. She watched him walk to the door.

He looked a bit annoyed when she stayed silent. "Good day, Avelina." He walked out into the corridor without even closing the door behind him.

She closed it and locked it, leaving the large heavy key in the keyhole. She leaned back against the door and closed her eyes. *O God, please don't allow that man to hurt Lord Thornbeck.*

When she opened her eyes, Lord Thornbeck was limping toward her.

⁓

Reinhart ground his teeth together. "That arrogant . . ." He did not want to assault Avelina's ears with the words he was thinking. "He didn't touch you, did he?"

"No." She shook her head.

"I will take him up on his challenge." He could defeat Geitbart in a sword fight even with his lame foot.

"It is only a trick to get you out in the open so he can kill you or throw you in the dungeon. You must not do it. Promise me you will not show yourself to him."

He longed to slam his fist into Geitbart's face.

"I shall help you find your men," Avelina said stoutly. "Your people need you to stay alive. You cannot help them if you are dead, and the duke knows he will need to kill you to take Thornbeck Castle. You cannot trust him. I can tell from his eyes that he is cruel and deceitful."

"You can see that from his eyes?" She was so lovely, it hurt his chest to gaze at her, especially knowing she was courageous and clever too.

"I am a good judge of character. You can see a lot in a person's eyes. There's a certain hardness and coldness in the eyes of a person like Geitbart and his daughter. And even though you had a severe look in your eyes when I first met you, a gentleness was also there, especially when you—" She abruptly stopped and turned away, walking to the water pitcher and pouring herself some.

"Especially when I what?"

She shrugged. "When you look at . . . certain people and say certain . . . things." Her face was turning red. She tapped her fingers on the pitcher and did not meet his eyes.

"I see," he said, even though he was not sure he did. A sudden urge came over him to stride over to her, put his arms around her, and make her tell him exactly what she meant, and then kiss her like it was his last day on earth.

But he could not do that. She was wise not to elaborate on what she meant. She seemed to remember—more often than he did—that they could not be together.

"You need sleep," he told her. "But I shall go and find out what has happened to my guards and enlist Jorgen's help in rounding up a force of men."

"You don't know me if you think I will stay here sleeping while you court danger in the corridors of the castle."

He did know her, and he was not surprised. "Come, then."

⟋⟍

Reinhart used the hood attached to his tunic to shield his face. He took Avelina's hand and led her down the servants' stairs to the kitchen to find his guards and supporters.

"This is insane," Avelina scolded in a whisper. "Anyone could recognize you, even from behind."

"How?"

"Your back is not like anyone else's."

"Is it crooked?"

"Of course not. It's . . . broad and you're taller than most." She pursed her lips. "You have a limp as well. Everyone will know it's you."

"I shall risk it." He brushed past her into the open walkway to the kitchen.

Avelina cried out just behind him.

He spun around. A woman was holding on to Avelina's arm and holding her finger to her lips. It was Odette.

"Come with me," she said quietly.

Reinhart and Avelina followed Odette to a small storage room, which was normally locked, next to the kitchen.

As soon as they were inside, Odette did not waste a moment but began to speak.

"Geitbart has a force of men—we are not sure exactly how many—surrounding the castle and even surrounding the town. We have heard that Geitbart sent a missive to Prague, to the king, accusing you of murdering your brother and of weakening the realm by choosing to marry a maidservant instead of a noble lady."

She gave a sad frown to Avelina. "Forgive me, Avelina. It is what is being said by Geitbart's guards."

"I understand."

"They also have orders to throw you in the dungeon if they find you," she said to Reinhart.

"Where are Jorgen and Sir Klas?"

"Sir Klas has not been seen for the last two days. We suspect he is in the dungeon, which Geitbart's guards are guarding, or possibly killed. Jorgen is being closely watched, but he has not been approached by Geitbart or his guards."

"I had hoped to rally some men to fight the duke."

"That is what Jorgen is doing, but he is having to be very careful. He does not want you to allow yourself to be seen, my lord. Geitbart will throw you in the dungeon, at best, and kill you with very little provocation. They are probably watching me too, so I should go. Give me time to get out of sight."

He thanked her, then Odette left.

Reinhart stared out the window. He needed a plan. Geitbart had already taken over, with his guards everywhere.

He was trapped inside his own castle.

~~~~~~

An angry scowl on his face, Lord Thornbeck was standing by the door of the storage room. She was almost afraid to speak, but he seemed to like hearing her honest thoughts.

"I am very sorry for what Geitbart told the king. I feel to blame."

"To blame? For Geitbart's treachery? Oh, you mean about his saying I wanted to marry a maidservant."

Avelina's stomach twisted at his offhand mention of her as a "maidservant."

"Look at me," he ordered.

She turned and let him capture her with his intense gaze.

"You are not to blame. Geitbart is only grasping for excuses to take Thornbeck. If you had not come, Lord Plimmwald would have sent someone else. But . . . I am glad he sent you. Now let us go. Odette should have had time to get well away."

He was glad she had come?

She would dwell on that and not on the fact that he could never marry her. But . . . *How can I ever be content married to anyone else but him?*

"Foolish, foolish girl." As Irma had scorned her for believing she truly was as noble as a noble-born lady, Avelina had let herself aspire to something that was forever beyond her reach.

They went toward the castle. Two of Geitbart's guards were standing at the back entrance. Would they recognize Lord Thornbeck? They were talking to each other and did not even look at Avelina or Lord Thornbeck as they went inside.

They passed to the servants' stairs and started up.

"I want to get my sword from my room," he said in the deserted stairwell.

"What if the door to your chamber is locked? You don't have the key, do you?"

"No."

"Then come with me first to my chamber, if it's not guarded. I have something that might help us get in."

They reached the floor of Avelina's bedchamber. They both slipped inside. She went to take a small bag out of the trunk against the wall. From inside it she withdrew a metal rod that had a crook at one end. "I may be able to get into the room with this."

He had a confused look on his face, so she said, "I am rather good at getting into locked rooms and locked trunks. It was sometimes necessary, especially when Lady Dorothea wanted something her father did not want her to have."

"I see."

They left and made it nearly to his room when she saw two guards clad in red and black standing near his chamber door.

"Stay here," she whispered to Lord Thornbeck. Before he could protest, she hurried up to the guards. "Oh, please help! My friend was cleaning in the west wing and she fell. She's hanging off the burned-out balcony and I can't pull her up. If you don't hurry, she will lose her grip and fall to her death."

Avelina's high-pitched, panicked voice must have convinced them, because they hurried in the direction of the west wing.

As soon as they were out of sight, she started working at the lock on Lord Thornbeck's door with her little tool. In a matter of moments she had it open.

Lord Thornbeck rushed toward her, his limp barely even noticeable, and entered his room. She closed the door behind them. With God's favor, the guards would not even realize the door had been opened.

Lord Thornbeck stopped short. The room was turned upside down, with furniture overturned, his bedding slashed. When Lord Thornbeck went to find his sword, it was not there.

His face was thunderous and he clenched his fists.

Suddenly they heard a herald's bugle.

Lord Thornbeck went to the window and threw open the shutter, letting in the cold air. Avelina went to stand beside him, and they both peered out.

A man wearing Geitbart's livery blew upon his bugle, loud and long. The Duke of Geitbart was standing beside him. The herald shouted, "Attention all! His Grace, the Duke of Geitbart."

In a booming voice, his head high, reminding her again of

a rooster, the duke said, "Listen to me, residents of Thornbeck Castle! The Margrave of Thornbeck killed his brother, your rightful lord! Find him and bring him to me and no harm will come to you. But if he is not surrendered to me in one hour, I will begin executing his guards, starting with his chancellor, Jorgen Hartman."

Two of Geitbart's guards dragged Jorgen into view in the small courtyard while he kicked and struggled. Something, a cloth, was stuffed in his mouth, preventing him from speaking.

Her heart sank to the pit of her stomach.

Lord Thornbeck stood beside her watching the scene below, his face a mask of stone.

~

Reinhart watched Jorgen being dragged into the courtyard, and his blood changed from a steady boil to cold as ice. "I cannot allow him to slaughter Jorgen and the rest of my men." He turned away from the window and started toward the door.

Avelina grabbed his arm and held on. "Please, let us think. Perhaps there is a way. You have an hour."

He turned his body to face hers and looked into her eyes. "You should leave here as soon as possible. You will be safer in Plimmwald."

The way her eyes caught the light, the desperation in them . . . he wanted to memorize every nuance of her expression, every curve of her beautiful face. While they had been alone together in the tiny room, if it had not been too dark for him to see her, he surely would have kissed her . . . too dark to see how beautiful she was while he was holding her in his arms, while she was lying against his chest and clinging to his tunic, while he whispered in her ear, his lips touching her hair.

He took her face in his hands, caressing her silken skin with his thumbs. She lifted her face to his.

"Please say you forgive me for deceiving you," she whispered. "I could not bear it if you did not forgive me."

"I forgive you." He was so close he could see the depths of her blue eyes, the tear that trembled on her lashes, and feel the breath that escaped her slightly parted lips. "Will you forgive me? For my gruffness and my anger?"

"Yes."

Her eyelids drooped low. He could resist no longer. He bent and pressed his mouth to hers. He kissed her softly at first, making sure she did not want to pull away.

Her hands clung to his shoulders, then entwined around his neck. He kissed her more urgently then, kissed her as if he could erase every cruel memory of life as a maidservant, kissed her as if he was a knight going off to battle.

Kissing her was achingly sweet. But he did not want to hurt her any more than he already had. He forced himself to end the kiss, then held her tight as she buried her face against his neck.

"I must go."

She clung to his shoulders for a moment before letting him go.

He caressed her cheek, then walked out, to his fate at the hands of Geitbart.

~

Avelina followed him into the corridor. He was barely limping as he walked toward the stairs.

He turned around. "Do not draw attention to yourself, or Geitbart may do you harm."

She watched him go but couldn't help following him a little

farther. Her heart was breaking as she stood at the top of the stairs. He made his way slowly down.

The pain in her chest took her breath away as she turned and went back to her bedchamber. She ran to the window. Geitbart still stood there, and she hated him, the way his head was thrown back and his chest puffed out. Finally, Lord Thornbeck emerged and walked boldly toward Geitbart.

The two men faced each other. Avelina strained to hear but could not make out their words. Then Geitbart waved his hand and two guards came forward and captured Lord Thornbeck's hands, holding them behind his back, and led him away.

She touched her fingers to her lips, where she could still feel his kiss. She started to sob but quickly forced away the tears, rubbing them from her cheeks.

She had a plan.

28

THE GUARDS SHOVED Reinhart into the dank cell and slammed the door.

The only light came from a flickering torch in the corridor outside his cell. There was nothing in the cell except a bare wooden bench about a foot high and four feet long. His bed, apparently.

A guard unlocked his cell door. Geitbart walked in.

Reinhart longed to wipe the ugly smile from his face by telling him he knew now exactly what happened to his brother. But he did not want to endanger Avelina, who had discovered the information.

"Come to gloat?" Reinhart asked Geitbart. "Or have you come to kill me?"

The duke shook his head. "I do not need to kill you. I will simply tell the king that you have gone mad after killing your brother to gain the margravate."

"Were you not content with the duchy of Geitbart?"

"Thornbeck Castle belongs to my family." Geitbart pointed to his own chest as he leaned toward Reinhart. "It was taken wrongfully, as you know very well. I intend to have it back. My daughter wanted to marry you, but when you chose a servant over her, I convinced her that we could have the castle for ourselves and we did not need you. We had intended to try to send both you and the servant girl over the side of the balcony, but that failed when you arrived at the wrong time. She hated the little pretender so much, she tried to have the wolves kill her. But she survived—again, thanks to you."

He paced in a half circle around Reinhart. "Avelina. Such a pretty little servant girl. She told me you did not care what happened to her anymore, now that you know she is a servant and not an earl's daughter. Is that true?"

Reinhart made his expression blank as he stared at him with half-closed eyes.

"I don't suppose it matters. It is not as if she can tell her father to send his guards to save you since, as Fronicka learned, her father is only a former servant and a cripple." He shook his head with a chuckle. "No wonder the girl likes you. You are just like her father."

Reinhart would not give him the satisfaction of a reaction. "Why don't you kill me? Why keep me alive?"

"It amuses me to know you are here in the dungeon." He fingered the hilt of his sword strapped to his hip. "And when it no longer amuses me, perhaps I will kill you and end your misery."

Geitbart looked hard at Reinhart, as if waiting for him to reply. But Reinhart refused to speak.

"Or perhaps I will give you someone to keep you company here in your cell—it is the largest one. Are you impressed with my generosity? I could give you . . . *ach, ja!* That servant girl, the one you chose over my daughter and all the other noblemen's daughters. You and your brother seem to have an affinity for servant girls. Must be a family trait. Shall I have my guards escort her here?"

Heat boiled in his veins and roared in his ears. *One blow. Just one.* Reinhart lunged at Geitbart. His fist found its mark as it crunched into Geitbart's nose. The look of surprise on his face made it even more rewarding.

Something slammed into the back of Reinhart's head. He fell to the floor.

"Shall I kill him, Your Grace?" Something sharp pressed against Reinhart's throat. He assumed it was a sword point. His vision was still spinning too much for him to see anything.

Dear Jesus and Lord God, forgive my sins and receive my spirit. It was the quick prayer he had taught himself to pray in case he should be about to die in battle.

"No. I want to show the king how gracious I am to let this murderer live."

The guard removed his sword from Reinhart's throat as his vision started to clear. With both hands Geitbart was wiping his nose, which was dripping blood.

"Shall I break his legs, Your Grace?"

Geitbart took a cloth from his pocket and wiped his hands and nose. "Later. Later we may break both his legs and his arms. But if the king wants us to bring him to Prague to be tried in the royal court . . . We had better wait."

They turned and left the small cell, then slammed and locked the door after them.

Reinhart touched the back of his head. His hand came away red and sticky with blood.

There was no window in the rather large cell. He felt around on the wall, searching for a loose stone, anything he could use as a weapon, but all the stones were tightly mortared and he found nothing. Then he went over to the bars that made up the door of his cell. He shook them. But every bar seemed solid.

What would Geitbart do if Reinhart escaped? He would kill his knights and guards.

He lay down on the wooden bench, remembering what Geitbart had said about Avelina. Would he truly throw her into the dungeon with him? To what purpose? Simply to torture Reinhart with the fact that she was being made to suffer because he had chosen her.

He closed his eyes. *God, don't let Avelina suffer because of me.* Already she had suffered from being chosen by him, becoming the object of Fronicka and her father's wrath, nearly killed twice. None of it was her fault. She had simply done what her lord had told her to do—forced her to do by threatening her.

God, protect her, please. She does not deserve to be punished any more. And if I die and I'm never able to protect her again, take care of her and her family. Don't let her ever be mistreated . . . by anyone. His heart clenched.

What if his brother had never died? What if Reinhart had still been just a knight, a captain of his brother's guard? He could have married Avelina. What would it have been like to love her? He could have fulfilled her dreams of being loved and cherished and valued.

Now that he was possibly about to die—Geitbart could not take the risk of sending him to Prague to be heard by the king—Reinhart couldn't think of very many things he regretted in his life. But he should not have kissed Avelina. It was rather like making a promise that he could not keep. It had been unutterably sweet, but it had made him long for her even more.

His head ached. There seemed nothing left to do, so he kept his eyes closed. Lying on his side on the wooden bench, his head pillowed on his arm, he fell asleep.

~⌐

Avelina stood just outside the back door of the castle on the cobblestone walkway between the castle and kitchen. Two of Geitbart's guards emerged from the kitchen. Avelina ducked her head and walked toward them. They were carrying several loaves of bread in their arms.

Please don't let them notice me. She was wearing the clothing brought to her after the wolf attack, so she looked like all the other servants at the castle.

The guards were talking to each other, their heads close together. They looked at her but passed right by. As soon as they went inside, she turned around and followed them back into the castle and down the stone stairs that led to the dairy-buttery where she and Gerhaws had churned butter. The dungeon, Gerhaws had told her, lay at the bottom of those same stairs.

Avelina crept down the steps behind the guards and ducked into the dairy as they continued down to the next level.

She stood in the doorway. The sound of metal grating on metal rose to her ears, as well as muted voices. Harsh, muttered curses also rose, then a shout of, "Quiet!"

The footsteps were coming back up the stairs. She hid herself in the dark dairy room as the guards passed by her, then quietly followed them back up to the ground level.

Avelina hurried to the chapel to find the priest. She looked all around the beautiful chapel, lighted by the sun shining through the colored glass. Finally, she opened a door to the right of the chancel. Inside was a room with white robes for the choir boys who sang the plainsong hymns every Sunday. There was also a priest's black robe hanging on a hook by the door.

"Just what I need," Avelina said softly, taking the dark robe down off its hook, folding it, and stuffing it under her arm. She quickly left the room.

Avelina hurried down the stairs and out to the kitchen.

Just as she was about to go inside, Odette came around the side of the building. "Avelina." She stopped, then motioned for Avelina to follow her.

She followed Odette to a hidden area between two buildings. No one was around.

"Our scout has told us," she whispered, "that the king is on his way here."

"The king? Coming here?"

"He was visiting the Duke of Pomerania and was on his way back to Prague when a missive from Lord Thornbeck found him somehow."

"God be praised," Avelina whispered.

"Yes, but I fear Geitbart will hear of it and will kill Lord Thornbeck before the king arrives. He will claim it was an accident, or make up some other story, so Lord Thornbeck cannot tell the king what Geitbart has done. We need to get him out of the dungeon and somewhere safe to wait for the king to arrive."

"I don't know if he will be willing to do that. He doesn't want Geitbart to kill his men, and he's willing to sacrifice himself for them. But I do have an idea." Avelina confided her idea to Odette, who went to get the things she would need.

When Odette came back, she had a big, round gourd and a large sack. "Is this too much for you to carry?"

"No." Avelina took the things from Odette.

"And here is a flask of wine, in case they are not giving him anything to drink."

"If my plan works, we may be out in less than an hour. But if things do not go as planned . . ."

"I shall be praying for you." Odette squeezed her arm.

"Thank you." Yes, that was a good reminder. She began to pray as she walked away and reentered the castle.

She went down the stone stairs to the cool, dark room where

all the casks of wine and barrels of supplies were kept. However, this time the door was locked. Avelina pulled out of her pocket the small hooked rod and inserted it into the keyhole. After several moments the lock mechanism turned and the door opened. Avelina slipped inside with her bundles and closed the door most of the way.

Now she waited for the guards to leave their post in the dungeon. Since they'd already fed the prisoners their bread that morning, she was not sure when they would leave again. They might not leave until evening.

She pulled the stool where she had sat to churn butter up to the doorway so she would not miss the guards if they should go by. The room was cold and Avelina used the priest's robe to cover herself.

"God," she whispered, "please forgive me for using this priestly robe for something it was not consecrated for. But life is also sacred, and Lord Thornbeck's life is in danger. And since I know the Holy Writ says You are compassionate, I will believe that You would want me to help him." She paused a moment to get her thoughts together.

"God, if You will help me rescue Lord Thornbeck from the dungeon, I promise I will not ask him to marry me. Even though he kissed me—" She lost her breath at the thought of that kiss, savoring the memory. "I will not expect him to marry me. He is a margrave and it would be humiliating for him to marry a servant like me. But if You will allow him to live, I will be grateful, God, for the rest of my life. Forever and ever." It was on her tongue to say that she loved him. But that seemed an improper thing to say to God. Still, didn't God know all her thoughts?

"God, I love him, which is why I am willing to give him up and not expect anything of him when he gets out of the dungeon.

Let the king realize that Geitbart is the evil one here and that Lord Thornbeck did nothing wrong. Restore the margravate and Thornbeck Castle to Lord Thornbeck.

"Although, if Lord Thornbeck was no longer a margrave he would be free to marry me. Oh God, forgive me for saying that! Such a selfish request. God, I take it back. If he is no longer margrave, my people, my family will be oppressed and possibly killed by Geitbart. Forgive me, God. Give Lord Thornbeck his rightful place. He doesn't deserve to be stripped of his margravate and disgraced." Besides, he might not even want to marry her.

After her prayer Avelina tried to do penance by forcing herself not to dwell on Lord Thornbeck's kiss, but it was near impossible.

As she sat on the stool for hours with nothing to do, she found a churn and some milk that was being stored there and started churning. But the monotonous task did nothing to keep her mind off Lord Thornbeck. Memories of him would not leave her alone. Every interaction she'd had with him seemed to flit unbidden into her thoughts. She tried to tell herself he could never forgive her for deceiving him, but then the memory of his kiss flooded her senses and she had to close her eyes and relive it over again.

No, he definitely forgave her.

A few hours later Avelina's stomach growled. Lord Thornbeck might be hungry, and if they were on the run, they would need food. Why had she not thought of that before?

Should she risk leaving where she was and go back to the kitchen for food? She had been sitting there for hours, and no one had gone in or out of the dungeon.

Avelina stood and peeked out the door. There was no one in either direction. She slipped out and hurried up the stairs to the outside. Quickly she made her way to the kitchen and asked Cook for some food.

Cook looked at her askance, but rather than questioning her, she gathered some fruit pastries and some bread and a small cheese round, wrapped them in a cloth, and tied the ends together.

"Thank you." Impulsively, Avelina gave her a quick hug and smiled at her.

Cook's eyes were wide, but then she smiled.

Avelina took a long drink from the ladle in the bucket of water in the kitchen, then ran out, hurrying back to her post.

Avelina sat on the stool and ate one of the small fruit pastries. She wrapped up the rest of the food and stuck it in her bag, along with the flask of wine Odette had given her.

Footsteps immediately broke through the silence.

Trying to stand perfectly still, Avelina held her breath as the voices and footsteps passed by the doorway. Thankfully, it was the two guards and they were going up.

As soon as she could not hear them anymore, she opened the door and ran down the steps to the dungeon.

At the bottom she whispered, "Lord Thornbeck?"

There were three corridors—one straight ahead, one to the left, and one to the right. She stood in the middle and called a little louder, "Lord Thornbeck? Where are you?"

Was he injured too badly to speak? Was he unconscious? She had to get to him. "Lord Thornbeck?" She started to go straight ahead when she heard a sound.

"What are you doing here?" came his voice.

"Keep talking." She turned to the right and started walking carefully but quickly through the narrow corridor, bad smells assaulting her nose.

"You should not be here. It is too dangerous."

Suddenly his hands wrapped around the bars in the cell at the end. She barely glanced at the men in the other cells as she hurried forward.

Finally, she came to Lord Thornbeck's cell. "Take these." She shoved the priest's robe and the sack of straw through the bars. Then she put the gourd down on the floor and took the small metal tool from her pocket. "I am here to get you out."

Lord Thornbeck leaned into the bars. "You must get out of here now. Geitbart was threatening to throw you in here with me. You must go, Avelina." His tone was harsh and angry.

"No." She was frantically trying to open the lock, but it was proving quite stubborn. What if the lock mechanism was too heavy and she could not turn it with her small tool? She kept trying.

"The king is coming," she whispered. "Odette wants you to go somewhere safe, because when Geitbart finds out, they fear he will kill you to keep you from telling the truth."

"The king? Coming here?"

"He had been visiting the Duke of Pomerania. The letter you sent him through Lady Magdalen must have reached the king as he was on his way back to Prague."

"Avelina, you must go. They will find you here and you will be in danger. I forbid you to be here." He growled. "I want you to go now."

His forceful tone made her hands start to shake. "My lord, I am sorry. I cannot leave without you." But the lock did not want to open. She tried over and over, catching the mechanism with her hook, but each time it slipped off.

She shoved the hook in a bit to the left this time, jerking it downward, and the mechanism clicked and slid open.

"Thank You, God," Avelina breathed, opening the door.

Just then, the voices and footsteps were coming back down the stairs.

Lord Thornbeck grabbed her shoulders and pulled her inside and closed the door, making a clanging sound.

"What was that?" one of the voices said.

Avelina scrambled to stuff the things she brought with her under the wooden bench, the only thing in the room. Lord Thornbeck pulled her up.

"Go stand in the corner," he whispered. "And don't move or make a sound."

She hurried to the back corner of the cell and flattened herself against the wall, as there was no more room under the bench and nowhere else to hide.

The footsteps stomped closer. Lord Thornbeck leaned against the bars of the door, probably trying to block the guards' view of her.

"Who's making that noise? Is it you, Thornbeck?"

He shook the bars with his powerful arms, making a loud metallic sound that reverberated off the stone walls.

Avelina tried not to move as the guards stood in front of Lord Thornbeck. Her heart thumped and she tried to slow her breathing, which was making her chest rise and fall. Could they hear her breathing? They would surely see her if they looked her way. *God, make me invisible.*

"Who is there?" one of the guards said sharply. "Is someone in your cell with you?"

"There is someone," the other guard said.

"Of course there is," Lord Thornbeck said. "Geitbart said he would capture Avelina and throw her in here with me, as you heard yourselves. They brought her in while you were gone, getting the bread." He nodded at the loaves in their hands.

"No one told us," one guard grumbled.

"Since you're so in love with each other, you can share." The second, slightly larger guard shoved the small loaf through the bars. He turned to leave.

The first guard lingered, staring at Avelina, who stared back at him, her heart still pounding in her ears. Finally, he grunted and turned to follow his fellow guard.

"That was quick thinking." She moved toward him.

"You should not be here. If Geitbart finds you, he will do harm to you."

"Did they hurt you? Someone told me you broke the duke's nose."

He shook his head but winced and stopped, as if the motion hurt.

"They did. Let me see."

"It is nothing, only a blow to the head."

"Is it bleeding? Show me."

"It's stopped."

She reached up and touched the back of his head, feeling the stickiness of blood.

He flinched and drew in a breath through his teeth.

Her stomach clenched at his pain. "You should sit down. Are you sure the bleeding has stopped?"

"Yes. I am well. But how is your ankle? Is it bleeding again?"

"No." She lifted her foot and showed the bandage.

"Good." His brows drew together, as he seemed to be thinking. "As long as they don't realize you broke in, we can simply wait until they go for bread again, then you will have to escape."

"You mean, *we* will have to escape."

"No. I cannot go anywhere or Geitbart will execute my men."

"But did you not hear what I said? Odette says the king is on his way here. You need to escape before Geitbart discovers—"

"No."

"I won't leave here without you."

"Lower your voice."

"No. You must listen to me. I—"

He reached out and touched her cheek with the back of his fingers. "I cannot bear it if something happens to you, especially if it's because of me." His voice was so deep and tender.

Her breath came faster at his touch and the look on his face, just visible in the light of the torches in the corridor. She leaned forward to kiss his cheek, but he turned his head at the last moment and captured her lips in an intense but brief kiss.

Oh, his kisses were so wonderful, but she had no right, no right at all to enjoy them. She buried her face in his chest so she would not be tempted to let him kiss her again. She had to think. She had to be clearheaded.

An idea suddenly came to her.

"What if all your men were able to escape? Sir Klas and Jorgen and all the others? Then would you leave?"

"Yes, but—"

"As soon as the guards leave, I can unlock your cell and then you can go get the guards' keys—hopefully they will leave them here—and we can both unlock all the cells and escape before they return."

"Or at least I and my men who have been able to escape can overpower the guards and take their weapons."

"Yes! It will work. I know it will."

"You are wonderful, Avelina." His brown eyes bored into hers, a strange look in them she couldn't quite define. Suddenly he said, "You wanted me to marry Lady Magdalen."

"What?"

"Do you still want me to marry Magdalen?" He seemed to be searching her thoughts, reading her face with those mesmerizing eyes.

Her mind seemed blank as her heart thumped wildly and she breathed in shallow gasps.

"It's a simple question. Do you still want me to marry Lady Magdalen?"

What she wanted was for him to kiss her again. But they should not be kissing at all!

"I could not marry you. You are a margrave and I was . . . I thought . . . No, I don't want you to marry Magdalen." Her voice cracked and tears suddenly swam in her eyes. "I want you to marry *me*."

She gasped and covered her mouth with her hand. "I should never have said that. I promised God."

"You promised God what?"

"That I would not expect you to marry me, that I would not ask—Oh!" She turned her head, trying to hide her face from him. He pulled her in closer, and she buried her face in his shoulder.

29

REINHART PULLED HER close, his hand against the back of her head, holding her to his chest. His heart pounded against his ribs. "Shh," he whispered against her ear. "Do not cry. My *Liebling* . . . my sweet. Don't cry."

He caressed her shoulder and her back and kissed her hair. His heart pounded in his chest at hearing her say she wanted him to marry her.

"If we get out of here, we will marry."

"No, please, you mustn't say that." Her voice was still laden with tears and she kept her head down. "You must not . . . The king. He would never allow it."

"What do I care about the king?"

"No, you must not talk like that. I should not have said what I did. I shouldn't have said it."

He rubbed his cheek against her soft hair, her intoxicating smell filling his senses.

She leaned away from him, wiping her face with her hands. He fought back the urge to lift her chin and kiss her again.

"I should unlock the door so we will be ready to escape when the guards leave again." Her voice trembled.

Reinhart squeezed her hand as he allowed her to leave his

arms. He leaned against the bars to look down the corridor and try to see if the guards were in sight, while Avelina took out the small instrument and stuck her hand through the bars. Her face was intent as she concentrated on her task. Reinhart kept watch.

After a few moments he heard a click. Avelina opened the door a crack and looked at him with a smile. Then she pocketed her tool.

"What are these things for?" He pointed under the bench.

"I planned to make up a form using the sack of straw and the priest's cloak, and using the gourd for a head, so that when we leave, it looks like you are in here. The guards would not realize you had escaped. However, now that they have seen me in here, the plan doesn't seem as likely to work."

"It's still a good plan."

All he could think about was that kiss they had shared a few minutes before. And how much he wanted to kiss her again.

                                        ⁓

Avelina's insides melted at the memory of their kiss. Her lips still tingled.

She moved to the bench and sat, trying to sort out her thoughts, which was impossible with him so near. She put her face in her hands, her eyes closed and head bowed, to shut out everything, especially Lord Thornbeck.

She should be thinking about what to do. What had she said? That she wanted him to marry her. Oh, foolish girl that she was. And what had he said? That they would marry.

It was impossible. She should not be telling him that she wanted him to marry her. Her stomach wrenched at the memory— especially since it was so true.

"Can you hear the guards? Are they still here?" She lifted her head. They needed to focus on escaping.

"I can hear them talking. In a few hours I will sneak down the corridor and watch for them to leave."

There was nothing to do but wait. For hours. Alone with Lord Thornbeck. She was actually glad they were in a cold, smelly, dark, dank, dirty dungeon.

Reinhart tortured himself with all the terrible things that could happen to Avelina if she did not escape. Hours had passed since she had gotten herself trapped in his cell with him.

"I'm going to see what the guards are doing."

Avelina turned from where she had been pacing back and forth. She did not say anything, only stared after him. It was as if she had reverted back to her old behavior when he thought she was Lady Dorothea, when she looked afraid to talk to or look at him too long. It must be because he had kissed her again and told her they would marry. He probably shouldn't have, but he could not bring himself to regret it. She must feel guilty because of the promise she made to God. But she had not promised God she would not marry him, only that she would not *expect him* to marry her.

He pushed the door open just enough to slip through. It creaked. He waited, but the guards did not come. He slipped out and walked slowly and quietly down the corridor.

As he was passing the first cell, he saw Jorgen inside. Their eyes met and his chancellor gave him a nod. Reinhart nodded in return and kept going. At the second cell, one of his guards was pacing the floor and also acknowledged Reinhart with a silent nod. The same thing at the third and fourth cells.

When he reached the place where the three corridors inter-sected, he stopped and listened, his back against the wall.

Geitbart's guards were hardly saying anything. They seemed to be playing a game, possibly backgammon. He could hear them rolling some dice and occasionally discussing their moves. It should be almost time for them to leave for the prisoners' evening ration of bread and water.

He slipped back into the cell where Avelina was still pacing. She stepped closer when he began to whisper, "Can you unlock the other cells on this corridor?"

She nodded, pulling out her little tool. She moved quickly and quietly into the corridor and to the first cell. She worked at the lock for only a few moments before they heard the telltale click. The door opened with a tiny squeak.

They all froze, waiting for the guards to investigate. But noth-ing happened.

Avelina moved to the next cell door. Her hands weren't even shaking as she worked at the lock. It took her a little longer this time, but the lock finally clicked. Reinhart stood by her and held the door so it would not swing open. The prisoner, one of his knights, took over holding the door as they moved on to the next door.

Just as Avelina inserted the little metal rod into the lock, a noise like a shout, then another and another, erupted outside. He and Avelina jumped and spun around. The guards must have had a similar reaction, because they both said together, "What? Who is that—?" Then there was a clatter, and he pictured them dropping their backgammon game pieces all over the floor.

Their footsteps scrambled up and away even as more shouts came and then a long trumpet blast. Was it all-out war going on above?

Avelina was back to frantically trying to unlock the door of the last cell on the corridor. His other three men were out of their cells.

Reinhart peered around to where the guards had been sitting. They were gone. No one was there.

Avelina opened the last door and hurried into the next corridor and continued her task.

"Sir Klas? Are you here?"

"I am here, the last cell. Lord Thornbeck?"

"*Ja.* We are coming."

Shouts continued above, but Reinhart could make out nothing that was happening.

"Here are the keys!" one of his knights cried. "They were hidden in the tinderbox." He immediately started opening the doors in the third corridor.

Soon, all his knights and guards had been freed, a total of fourteen, and they surrounded Avelina and him.

"If you go above ground"—Reinhart met their gazes—"you could all be killed. Geitbart's guards outnumber us, and we do not know what has become of the rest of our guards."

"Then we shall die defending our lord and his castle." Sir Klas raised his fist.

The men rushed toward the stairs, and Avelina appeared to be going with them. He caught her arm and pulled her back.

"I can help." She gave him a defiant stare.

Reinhart stared at her, trying to think how he might keep her safe.

"We shall dedicate this battle to the woman who freed us." Sir Klas turned from halfway up the stairs. "She is the bravest of us all."

"*Ja!*" the other soldiers shouted. "She is our lioness! We shall fight for her!"

They all shouted their war cries as they scaled the stairs. None of them had weapons. Reinhart kept hold of Avelina's arm as they made their way up behind them. "I want you to stay here," he said quietly. "Stay out of the way of the fighting."

"Are you going to go fight?"

"Of course. I am a trained knight, and I am the margrave."

"Then I will fight too."

"But I very well may die. We all may die."

"If you die fighting, I want to die fighting with you." Her eyes were so beautiful, shining up at him.

He knew her well enough to know he could not stop her. "Then stay behind me until I find you a weapon." He would watch out for her and protect her, as would the rest of his men.

She smiled, so beguiling it made his heart stutter. He started up the stairs behind his men.

~~~

Avelina let Lord Thornbeck clasp her hand as he led her up the stairs. Truly, she was prepared to die for this man. All these men were prepared to die. *Lord God, if I must die, take care of my precious brother and sister and my father.*

Her knees trembled a bit, but Lord Thornbeck glanced back at her, concern in his eyes, then faced forward again. She could do this. She could fight for him, and die, if she must.

They emerged to a sudden cessation of shouting. All around, dozens of Geitbart's men were kneeling and bowing toward a mounted figure. Lord Thornbeck's men started dropping to their knees as well.

Lord Thornbeck whispered, "It's the king."

Avelina fell into a deep curtsy while Lord Thornbeck knelt and bowed his head.

All was silent. Avelina peeked up to see many horsemen behind the king. King Karl wore a tunic of hardened leather tiles, and sleeves and leggings of mail were visible underneath it. Something about the way he sat, so straight and tall, made him seem regal, even though he was actually wearing a mail hood instead of a crown.

As his gaze swung her way, she quickly averted her eyes to the ground.

The king said in a booming voice, "I require an audience with the Margrave of Thornbeck and the Duke of Geitbart. Is either of those men here?"

"Your Majesty, I am the Margrave of Thornbeck."

"Very good. When I have quartered my horse in your stable, I shall join you in your Great Hall."

Lord Thornbeck bowed his acquiescence. The king gave him a sharp, narrowed glance—perhaps wondering about his disheveled appearance—before gesturing with his hand. "You may all rise and go."

Lord Thornbeck turned to Sir Klas. "Take Avelina to her room."

He did not look back at her but walked slowly, limping slightly, toward the castle.

Sir Klas gestured for her to precede him, and they walked toward the castle.

In her room Avelina quickly changed her clothes and cleaned herself up. But what was happening with Lord Thornbeck?

A knock came at her door and a wide-eyed maidservant opened it. "His Majesty the king wishes to see you."

Avelina stood, her heart pounding, and followed the servant down to the Great Hall. Several of the king's guards stood surrounding the king, who sat on the raised dais in Lord Thornbeck's large chair. Lord Thornbeck stood in front of the king several feet away. Thornbeck's guards, many who had been locked in the dungeon, stood just behind their lord.

Lord Thornbeck's face was stoic. Was he angry or pleased? She could not tell. But his expression changed when he saw her, and his throat moved as he swallowed.

A few feet from Lord Thornbeck, also facing the king, was the Duke of Geitbart. His jaw was rigid, and his black gaze darted from the king to her and back again.

Avelina fell into a deep curtsy before the king.

"Please rise," the king said.

She did so and stood facing King Karl the Fourth, King of Bohemia, King of Italy, King of Germany, King of the Romans, and Holy Roman Emperor.

She should have been terrified. How could this be possible, that she should be standing before the king? It hardly seemed real. Perhaps that was why she was able to stay upright and conscious in his presence.

"I want to get a good look at the woman of whom I've heard so much."

Was he speaking about her? There didn't appear to be any other women in the room.

The king stroked his short, neatly trimmed, graying beard while he gazed sleepily out at them. His eyelids were so low over his eyes, she could not tell who he was looking at.

Finally, after many moments, he said, "First, I would like to hear your story, Geitbart, about why you had locked Thornbeck, his chancellor, and the captain of his guard in his own dungeon."

Geitbart cleared his throat. "Your Majesty, I had just cause for my actions. Everyone knows Lord Thornbeck murdered his brother so he could take his place as margrave. And when—"

The king raised his hand, palm out, silencing the duke.

"Everyone knows?" The king's words were slow and deliberate. "Who is this everyone? And why should I care what everyone knows unless they show me proof? Lord Thornbeck is my margrave, and I do not allow unfounded accusations to be spoken against my noblemen. So what is your proof?"

Air rushed back into Avelina's lungs. She wanted to glance back at Lord Thornbeck but resisted. Thankfully, she had a good view of the duke's face, which was turning red.

Geitbart's jaw twitched as he stared straight ahead at the king. He finally licked his lips and said, "I do not have any proof, Your Majesty."

"And for what reason did you put your peer in the dungeon?" The king suddenly leaned forward in the chair, toward Geitbart.

"Your Majesty, I was trying to save and protect this region from a madman. He very likely murdered his brother, then allowed a woman poacher to unlawfully kill nearly all of the king's deer from Thornbeck Forest. Then he made that poaching woman's husband the chancellor and even has given that woman a place in his household, assisting in his bride-selection scheme. And in this selection, with several ladies here who were daughters of dukes and earls and barons, he actually selected a servant girl instead of one of them."

Avelina's insides trembled. No one spoke for several moments. Finally, the king leaned back against the chair.

"You are not telling me anything I didn't know. None of it explains why you locked a margrave in his own dungeon."

"Your Majesty, I would never want to do anything you would disapprove of. I simply was trying to make sure your interests were served in Thornbeck."

"No. You were making sure your *own* interests were served. Had you planned on taking over Thornbeck Castle all along? Or did you only decide to do it after the margrave did not choose your daughter? Guards, take him to the dungeon and lock him up." He turned to the man standing nearest to him. "Send his own men home to Geitbart and tell his captain that for now, he is in charge of keeping order in Geitbart."

The duke's eyes were wide and he actually bared his teeth like an animal, his beard trembling. "I did nothing wrong! Your Majesty, you cannot—you must not do this." When the king did not respond or even look at him, his voice rose. "Your Majesty!"

Avelina had to look away from the sight of someone so prideful being humbled to such an extent, led away by the king's guards. But she could not pity him. He had Lord Thornbeck's brother cruelly killed, along with his unborn child and the child's mother.

"Lord Thornbeck, did you kill your brother?"

"No, Your Majesty."

"And did you allow a woman to poach deer in Thornbeck Forest?"

"No, Your Majesty, I did not *allow* it. When she was discovered poaching, she was punished. She has since turned from her lawlessness and is respectably married to my chancellor."

"And as for Geitbart's final accusation, did you choose to wife a maidservant over several young—and I imagine fair of face and form—ladies of this realm who were of noble birth?"

"Yes, Your Majesty. I did."

Would he not explain that he had thought she was the daughter of the Earl of Plimmwald?

"And now, I should like to hear from this young woman, Avelina of Plimmwald, is it? Lady Magdalen of Mallin seems to think very highly of you."

Lady Magdalen. Of course. How else would the king have heard about her? Lady Magdalen and the king must have crossed paths on their journeys.

"Is it true that you pretended to be the earl's daughter, Lady Dorothea? And that she ran away with a knight in her father's service?"

"Y-yes, Your Majesty." She could hardly lie to the king.

"And did you intend to marry Lord Thornbeck?"

"No, I was simply supposed to strengthen the alliance between Plimmwald and Thornbeck by coming here and pretending to be Lady Dorothea."

"Was Lord Plimmwald so desperate to strengthen his alliance with Lord Thornbeck that he would go to such lengths of deception?"

"He was afraid, Your Majesty, that the Duke of Geitbart was planning to attack and overtake Plimmwald. He said he needed the margrave's help if that should happen." Avelina's breath was leaving her. She must not think about the fact that she was speaking to the king and emperor of the Holy Roman Empire.

"I see. And were you at all afraid that Lord Thornbeck might wish to marry you? Did this possibility not occur to you?"

"Not at first. I . . ." She shrugged. Was it bad form to shrug at the king? Her cheeks burned.

He studied her. "What was to be your reward for deceiving Lord Thornbeck?"

She swallowed. Perhaps she was soon to follow Geitbart to the dungeon. "I was to receive a dowry so I could marry." Should she tell him about the goose and the side of pork she had asked for?

"So you did not want to be a maidservant all your life and wanted to marry." He stroked his beard again. "Lady Magdalen told me that you saved Lord Thornbeck from being captured by Geitbart's men. You ran ahead of his guards and warned him. Is this true?"

"Yes, Your Majesty."

"Why?"

"Why? Because I . . ."

"And how did Lord Thornbeck emerge from the dungeon just as I was arriving? How did he get free?"

"I unlocked the doors."

"And how did she do this clever feat? Lord Thornbeck?"

"She sneaked into the dungeon while the guards were fetching the bread for the prisoners and unlocked the door of my cell with a little instrument."

"You picked the lock." The king was staring at her again.

"Yes, Your Majesty."

He suddenly burst out laughing, then nodded. He leaned forward, staring at Lord Thornbeck. "She passed all your tests, better than the other ladies, did she not?"

"Yes, sire."

"Would you say you found her to be the most noble of all the ladies who were here for your bride selection?"

"I would."

"She is obviously very clever. She is the one you chose, and therefore I give you my blessing to marry her. And after all the clever, courageous things she has done, I shall commission my troubadours to write a song lauding the deeds of Avelina of Plimmwald, the wife of the Margrave of Thornbeck. She is a jewel among the women of the empire, and you could not do better, Thornbeck."

Had he truly said what she thought he had said? She turned to look at Lord Thornbeck. His eyes gleamed and he smiled.

"Thornbeck, I require a bath and a feast. Traveling makes me dirty and famished."

"Of course, Your Majesty." Lord Thornbeck escorted the king from the Great Hall to show him to his room and, no doubt, to order a bath brought to his bedchamber.

Avelina stared after them. The king had blessed her marriage—marriage—to Lord Thornbeck. The king had called her, Avelina, clever and courageous. Could it be true? Was she only dreaming?

"Are you well, my lady?" Sir Klas stood at her side. "Shall I take you back to your chamber?"

"That will not be necessary. I am well, and I know the way." She smiled and nearly laughed. Perhaps the numbness and disbelief were wearing off a bit.

She climbed the stairs, wishing with all her heart that Lady Magdalen were here so she could thank her. Lady Magdalen had "spoken highly" of her and had told the king how Avelina had saved Lord Thornbeck. Lady Magdalen must be the reason he spoke so favorably to her—spoke to her at all—and sanctioned her marriage to Lord Thornbeck.

"May God bless you, Lady Magdalen," she whispered when she was safely in her bedchamber again. She lay across her bed, hugging her pillow. "May He bless you a thousand . . . thousand times over."

30

Feeling dirty after a whole day in the dungeon, Reinhart bathed himself quickly, dunking his head in the washbasin and washing the blood from his hair. He was dressed and ready when he realized he hadn't shaved. Ah well. The king wore a beard, so he could hardly be offended.

He glanced out the window as he rushed out. The sun was already nearly hidden behind the trees, indicating it was later than he might have hoped. He did not have much time before he would need to be in the Great Hall for the evening feast his cooks were preparing for the king and his men.

He hurried down the stairs and through the corridor and knocked on Avelina's door. Every muscle in his body seemed to strain in anticipation of her opening it.

Finally, Avelina stood there, her face brightening when she saw him.

His heart pounded and he took her hands in his. "Avelina of Plimmwald, will you marry me?"

She gasped.

As a knight before his liege lord, he knelt before her, still holding her hands.

"As I have chosen you, will you now choose me? And will you forgive me for ever doubting that we should marry, for treating you unkindly when I learned of your deception?"

She was smiling. "Yes."

He stood and put his arms around her. "If the king had not blessed our marriage, I would have married you anyway."

Avelina shook her head. "No, you cannot say that. It is too easy to say that now that everything has changed."

"It matters not if you believe me. You have agreed to marry me, and I shall not let you out of the agreement."

She was still smiling, but she was staring at his lips. "I have little choice since the king thinks I'm clever and wishes me to marry you, to strengthen the margravate of Thornbeck."

"You are jesting, but I don't care, because now . . . I get what I want." Reinhart bent his head nearer, his mouth hovering over hers, so close their lips were almost touching. Her hands slipped up his chest to his shoulders.

"And what is it you want?" Her breath caressed his lips. Her eyes were nearly closed, and she leaned her body closer to his.

"I want to see you laugh and smile every day. I want to hear you tell me you love me. I want to kiss you . . . every day." He pulled her body against his. "Now tell me you love me."

"You are very impertinent," she said, her voice breathless and her cheeks turning pink, "when the king has given you permission to marry me."

He pulled her even closer, looking deep into her eyes.

"You know I love you. But do you love me?" Again, her gaze focused on his lips.

"Yes. And kissing you." He pressed his lips against hers and kissed her long and thoroughly, not holding anything back. Her hands' grip went weak on his shoulders.

He pulled away. Her body was nearly limp and her eyes were slow to open.

"Are you well?"

Her lips lifted in a slow, languid smile. "I'll be very well, if you kiss me like that every day."

Avelina was dizzy by the time he ended the kiss. The intense smolder in his dark-brown eyes made her breath hitch in her throat.

His dark hair was damp and curling slightly, and the three days' growth of stubble on his face increased his masculinity, if that was possible, and took her breath away. Pressing her cheek against his chest, she would forever remember him as he knelt before her and asked her to marry him.

"It is too much joy," she said, relishing the feel of his arms around her and his heart beating beneath her cheek. "I don't know if I can bear it."

He pulled away slightly and lifted her chin.

"But is it truly possible that I shall marry you and that the king approves of me?"

"If you doubt it, you can ask the king yourself, for we must go to the Great Hall. It would not be good to keep the king waiting."

"Oh. But my dress." She glanced down at the maroon silk cotehardie that had belonged to Lady Dorothea. "Do you think it looks well enough?"

"It is lovely. Fit for a margrave's wife. Now let us go."

She gave him her hand and he started down the corridor, raising her fingers to his lips as he walked.

"You are not using your cane."

For a moment he looked startled. "I forgot."

"Do you not need it?"

"I don't suppose I do."

He was still limping, but only a bit.

When they reached the bottom of the stairs, Lord Thornbeck was still holding her hand. The king called to them from above. "Lord Thornbeck. There you two are."

The priest was standing beside the king.

"Since I am here to witness it, I thought you would like to have the priest speak the marriage rites over your union."

"Now?" Lord Thornbeck's face went slack.

"Of course," the king boomed. "Sooner is always better than later. You can have the banns cried afterward, and in a few weeks you can invite the nobles and have a big wedding at the cathedral in town. Be sure and invite the Earl of Plimmwald. He definitely ought to be there." He winked at Avelina.

Lord Thornbeck and Avelina looked at each other. "Do you have any objection?" he whispered near her ear.

"Are you sure *you* don't have an objection?"

"I have no objection to marrying you, whether now or two months from now—although I had rather thought it would be two months from now."

"What are you saying there?" the king shouted from the top of the staircase. "You can whisper to each other after the wedding and the feast. Come to the chapel."

Avelina's heart skipped a few beats.

Just then, Jorgen approached them from the other side of the room.

"Chancellor," the king called. "Have your wife come and the two of you be witnesses to their marriage."

If Jorgen was surprised, he did not betray it. He bowed to the king and quickly went back the way he had come.

Lord Thornbeck squeezed her hand and they started up the staircase.

In no time, Avelina found herself standing in the chapel of Thornbeck Castle facing the priest as he asked them to state their names. Avelina listened closely as Lord Thornbeck said, "Reinhart Stolten, third Margrave of Thornbeck."

They each stated their parents' names, and then the priest said the marriage rites. They both gave their consent. Then the priest told them, "You may seal the covenant with a kiss, if you wish."

Avelina closed her eyes and Lord Thornbeck—Reinhart—briefly kissed her lips.

She had just married the man she had previously not even dared hope to marry. How had this come about? It was a miracle.

Odette was kissing her cheek in congratulations, smiling and squeezing her shoulder.

While the king and Lord Thornbeck—Reinhart—were talking, Odette said quietly, "You look a bit dazed."

Avelina laughed, a nervous sound. "It was a bit sudden."

Odette smiled sympathetically.

The feast afterward was a blur of listening to the king, who demanded their full attention for the entire long meal.

Finally, King Karl announced he was tired and would go to bed early, then was escorted out of the Great Hall by his guards and up to his bedchamber.

The knights surrounding them—their only guests now besides Jorgen and Odette—drank to their health and wished them wealth, joy, and many children.

Lord Thornbeck excused himself and his new wife, and they went the way the king had gone.

Lord Thornbeck seemed to be hurrying when he suddenly

looked back at her. He pulled her into his arms and held her close. "Don't be afraid."

She hadn't realized she was afraid until he said that. It must have shown on her face.

"I shall be a good husband, I promise."

"I am not afraid, I just . . . I was not expecting to be married tonight."

"Should I have told the king no when he pushed us to get married tonight?"

"One can hardly say no to the king. No, I do not regret it at all."

His eyes softened and he caressed her cheek with his thumb. He leaned down and kissed her lips. "Clever, courageous Avelina."

She ran her fingers over the prickly stubble on his chin. "I was too afraid to even hope to ever marry you, until a few hours ago. But I'm full of joy to be your wife."

He kissed her cheek, then they went up the stairs together.

The king left Thornbeck two days later, much to Reinhart and Avelina's relief. Before he left, he declared that he would take Geitbart back to Prague for a more official judgment, but he planned to divide the region of Geitbart into two parts and make Lord Thornbeck the ruler of half, giving it a new name, and bestowing the other half to the duke's cousin.

Jorgen and Odette went to work organizing a wedding celebration, inviting all the noble ladies who had attended Lord Thornbeck's bridal selection—all except Fronicka, who had left Thornbeck as soon as her father was taken to the dungeon and was probably hiding with relatives—as well as their families. The Earl of Plimmwald was particularly invited, including his daughter, if she had been found and brought back to Plimmwald by now. And in fact, she had returned home, and the earl had even granted his daughter and Sir Dietric permission to marry.

Lord Thornbeck sent for Avelina's family and settled them into a wing of the castle. Thornbeck Castle seemed a much more pleasant place with Jacob and Brigitta there, smiling and excited to have a castle to explore. Even her father seemed more talkative and less morose.

King Karl sent his own musicians and minstrels to entertain at the wedding feast. The first night they sang the song they had written about the epic love between the Margrave of Thornbeck and his clever and courageous wife, Avelina. Some of it was far-fetched and made her laugh, and it extolled Avelina's brave exploits, but the lines about the true love between Avelina and Lord Thornbeck made tears flood her eyes. When the song was over, everyone cheered and applauded for the margrave and his new bride.

When the first few courses of the meal were over, the cooks brought out cherry pastries, cakes, compote, and pies.

"Cherries!" Avelina exclaimed. "How did they know?"

"I remembered you said they were your favorite fruit," Reinhart said. "We had some stored in the buttery and the cooks made all these for you."

"Just what I wanted." She nearly drooled at the cherry tart in front of her. Then she leaned over and kissed her husband's cheek.

He turned to look into her eyes. *He* was just what she wanted all those nights she dreamed of romantic love, of her own true love asking her to marry him. Her heart swelled with tender emotion every time she looked at him. So satisfying was the way he had changed, the cheerful expressions she saw on his face, and the way he actually thanked the servants now and was kind to them. He was also kind to her father and siblings and made them feel welcomed and wanted.

Sometimes she was surprised that she was not more in awe of her husband. After all, he was a margrave and she had been very awestruck by him when she first met him. But she sensed that it would not please him if she considered herself anything less than his equal, and they often teased each other about the king's praise of her and how impressed he had been with her.

People had often warned her, when she was a poor maiden and a servant, that romantic love would be ground under reality's heel, that true love was only something invented by minstrels and poets, that she should not be so naive and fanciful as to believe in romantic love. As it turned out, the reality of her love story with Lord Thornbeck was much more satisfying than any of her romantic stories and imaginings.

She no longer had to dream about love. God had given her a love all her own, one that the troubadours would sing about for years to come.

ACKNOWLEDGMENTS

I WANT TO thank my extremely supportive, hardworking, and wise agent, Natasha Kern, and my fabulously talented, thorough, and otherwise wonderful editors, Becky Monds and Julee Schwarzburg. I am very thankful for everyone at Thomas Nelson who works hard to help make my books as successful as possible.

I also want to express my heartfelt appreciation to all my friends and readers who encourage me with their positive reviews and by spreading the word about my books. I truly couldn't keep writing without you.

This past year has been busy, to put it mildly, but I have loved writing and polishing this story so much. I relate so much to the journey of a poor girl who wonders if she deserves to be respected, the girl who feels blessed and highly favored from a very high place, and eventually accepts that God has made her worthy of love. He lavishes love on us, whether we realize it or not, and though there isn't much about Avelina's spiritual journey in this story, I like to think she grows to realize just how much God loves her, and draws a deep confidence from that love, apart from her own performance or the love of the people in her life. Human love often disappoints us, but God's love is faithful and endures forever.

Discussion Questions

1. What was Lord Thornbeck's greatest fear about getting married? How does the pressure from the king, sending a list of ladies he wishes him to choose from, increase this fear? How does Jorgen's suggestion of the two-week party help?
2. What was Avelina's greatest fear in going to Thornbeck Castle? Did she believe she would be able to accomplish what Lord Plimmwald was asking of her?
3. What did Avelina request from Lord Plimmwald for accomplishing this task, and what did her request tell you about her?
4. What would you ask for if you were Avelina?
5. How did it make Avelina feel, once she arrived at Thornbeck, to have important people ask to hear her opinion?
6. Why did Avelina's strong opinions about love and marriage and a margrave's wife's duties cause Lord Thornbeck to feel attracted to her, especially after he said he didn't want a wife with strong opinions?
7. What did Avelina confess she felt about Dorothea being born a noble while Avelina was born a peasant?
8. What were Avelina's conflicting feelings as she tried to step back and make Lord Thornbeck fall in love with Magdalen?

9. What do you think would have happened if Avelina had simply told Lord Thornbeck the truth from the beginning? How might things have been different?

10. Do you understand how Lord Thornbeck might have been confused as to how Avelina felt about him? And how she might have misunderstood his feelings for her?

11. At the end, the king intervened and, to a great extent, reversed his earlier mandate ordering the margrave to marry a nobleman's daughter. How much of the ending was due to the king's whims, how much to Magdalen's intervention, and how much to Avelina's own initiative and bravery?

12. What do you think Avelina and Reinhart learned about the worth of individuals, no matter their social status? What painful circumstances from their pasts did Avelina and Reinhart have to overcome in order to truly love each other and live happily ever after?

The
GOLDEN BRAID

The one who needs rescuing isn't
always the one in the tower.

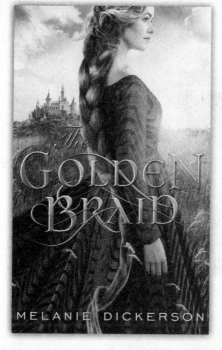

Rapunzel can throw a knife better than any man around. And her
skills as an artist rival those of any artist she's met. But for a woman
in medieval times, the one skill she most desires is the hardest one to
obtain: the ability to read.

Available in print and e-book

About the Author

Jodie Westfall Photography

MELANIE DICKERSON IS a two-time Christy Award finalist and author of *The Healer's Apprentice*, winner of the National Readers' Choice Award for Best First Book in 2010, and *The Merchant's Daughter*, winner of the 2012 Carol Award. She spends her time writing romantic medieval stories at her home near Huntsville, Alabama, where she lives with her husband and two daughters.

Website: www.MelanieDickerson.com
Twitter: @melanieauthor
Facebook: MelanieDickersonBooks